ANNIE HAYNES
THE WITNESS ON THE ROOF

Annie Haynes was born in 1865, the daughter of an ironmonger.

By the first decade of the twentieth century she lived in London and moved in literary and early feminist circles. Her first crime novel, *The Bungalow Mystery*, appeared in 1923, and another nine mysteries were published before her untimely death in 1929.

Who Killed Charmian Karslake? appeared posthumously, and a further partially-finished work, *The Crystal Beads Murder*, was completed with the assistance of an unknown fellow writer, and published in 1930.

Also by Annie Haynes

The Bungalow Mystery
The Abbey Court Murder
The Secret of Greylands
The Blue Diamond
The House in Charlton Crescent
The Crow's Inn Tragedy
The Master of the Priory
The Man with the Dark Beard
The Crime at Tattenham Corner
Who Killed Charmian Karslake?
The Crystal Beads Murder

ANNIE HAYNES

THE WITNESS ON THE ROOF

With an introduction
by Curtis Evans

DEAN STREET PRESS

Published by Dean Street Press 2016

All Rights Reserved

First published in 1925 by The Bodley Head

Cover by DSP

Introduction © Curtis Evans 2016

ISBN 978 1 911095 27 9

www.deanstreetpress.co.uk

The Mystery of The Missing Author
Annie Haynes and Her Golden Age Detective Fiction

The psychological enigma of Agatha Christie's notorious 1926 vanishing has continued to intrigue Golden Age mystery fans to the present day. The Queen of Crime's eleven-day disappearing act is nothing, however, compared to the decades-long disappearance, in terms of public awareness, of between-the-wars mystery writer Annie Haynes (1865-1929), author of a series of detective novels published between 1923 and 1930 by Agatha Christie's original English publisher, The Bodley Head. Haynes's books went out of print in the early Thirties, not long after her death in 1929, and her reputation among classic detective fiction readers, high in her lifetime, did not so much decline as dematerialize. When, in 2013, I first wrote a piece about Annie Haynes' work, I knew of only two other living persons besides myself who had read any of her books. Happily, Dean Street Press once again has come to the rescue of classic mystery fans seeking genre gems from the Golden Age, and is republishing all Haynes' mystery novels. Now that her crime fiction is coming back into print, the question naturally arises: Who Was Annie Haynes? Solving the mystery of this forgotten author's lost life has taken leg work by literary sleuths on two continents (my thanks for their assistance to Carl Woodings and Peter Harris).

Until recent research uncovered new information about Annie Haynes, almost nothing about her was publicly known besides the fact of her authorship of twelve mysteries during the Golden Age of detective fiction. Now we know that she led an altogether intriguing life, too soon cut short by disability and death, which took her from the isolation of the rural English Midlands in the nineteenth century to the cultural high life of Edwardian London. Haynes was born in 1865 in the Leicestershire town of Ashby-de-la-Zouch, the first child of ironmonger Edwin Haynes and Jane (Henderson) Haynes, daughter of Montgomery Henderson, longtime superintendent of the gardens at nearby Coleorton Hall, seat of the Beaumont baronets. After her father left his family, young Annie resided with her grandparents at the gardener's cottage at Coleorton Hall, along with her mother and younger brother. Here Annie doubtlessly obtained an acquaintance with the ways of the country gentry that would serve her well in her career as a genre fiction writer.

We currently know nothing else of Annie Haynes' life in Leicestershire, where she still resided (with her mother) in 1901, but by 1908, when Haynes was in her early forties, she was living in London with Ada Heather-Bigg (1855-1944) at the Heather-Bigg family home, located halfway between Paddington Station and Hyde Park at 14 Radnor Place, London. One of three daughters of Henry Heather-Bigg, a noted pioneer in the development of orthopedics and artificial limbs, Ada Heather-Bigg was a prominent Victorian and Edwardian era feminist and social reformer. In the 1911 British census entry for 14 Radnor Place, Heather-Bigg, a "philanthropist and journalist," is listed as the head of the household and Annie Haynes, a "novelist," as a "visitor," but in fact Haynes would remain there with Ada Heather-Bigg until Haynes' death in 1929.

Haynes' relationship with Ada Heather-Bigg introduced the aspiring author to important social sets in England's great metropolis. Though not a novelist herself, Heather-Bigg was an important figure in the city's intellectual milieu, a well-connected feminist activist of great energy and passion who believed strongly in the idea of women attaining economic independence through remunerative employment. With Ada Heather-Bigg behind her, Annie Haynes's writing career had powerful backing indeed. Although in the 1911 census Heather-Bigg listed Haynes' occupation as "novelist," it appears that Haynes did not publish any novels in book form prior to 1923, the year that saw the appearance of *The Bungalow Mystery*, which Haynes dedicated to Heather-Bigg. However, Haynes was a prolific producer of newspaper serial novels during the second decade of the twentieth century, penning such works as *Lady Carew's Secret*, *Footprints of Fate*, *A Pawn of Chance*, *The Manor Tragedy* and many others.

Haynes' twelve Golden Age mystery novels, which appeared in a tremendous burst of creative endeavor between 1923 and 1930, like the author's serial novels retain, in stripped-down form, the emotionally heady air of the nineteenth-century triple-decker sensation novel, with genteel settings, shocking secrets, stormy passions and eternal love all at the fore, yet they also have the fleetness of Jazz Age detective fiction. Both in their social milieu and narrative pace Annie Haynes' detective novels bear considerable resemblance to contemporary works by Agatha Christie; and it is interesting to note in this regard that Annie Haynes and Agatha Christie were the only female mystery writers published by The Bodley Head, one of the more notable English mystery imprints in the early Golden Age. "A very remarkable feature of recent detective fiction," observed the *Illustrated London News* in 1923, "is the skill displayed by women in this branch of story-telling. Isabel Ostrander, Carolyn Wells, Annie Haynes and last, but very far from least, Agatha Christie, are contesting the laurels of Sherlock Holmes' creator with a great spirit, ingenuity and success." Since Ostrander and Wells were American authors, this left Annie Haynes, in the estimation of the *Illustrated London News*, as the main British female competitor to Agatha Christie. (Dorothy L. Sayers, who, like Haynes, published her debut mystery novel in 1923, goes unmentioned.) Similarly, in 1925 *The Sketch* wryly noted that "[t] ired men, trotting home at the end of an imperfect day, have been known to pop into the library and ask for an Annie Haynes. They have not made a mistake in the street number. It is not a cocktail they are asking for..."

Twenties critical opinion adjudged that Annie Haynes' criminous concoctions held appeal not only for puzzle fiends impressed with the "considerable craftsmanship" of their plots (quoting from the *Sunday Times* review of *The Bungalow Mystery*), but also for more general readers attracted to their purely literary qualities. "Not only a crime story of merit, but also a novel which will interest readers to whom mystery for its own sake has little appeal," avowed

The Nation of Haynes' *The Secret of Greylands*, while the *New Statesman* declared of *The Witness on the Roof* that "Miss Haynes has a sense of character; her people are vivid and not the usual puppets of detective fiction." Similarly, the *Bookman* deemed the characters in Haynes' *The Abbey Court Murder* "much truer to life than is the case in many sensational stories" and *The Spectator* concluded of *The Crime at Tattenham Corner*, "Excellent as a detective tale, the book also is a charming novel."

Sadly, Haynes' triumph as a detective novelist proved short lived. Around 1914, about the time of the outbreak of the Great War, Haynes had been stricken with debilitating rheumatoid arthritis that left her in constant pain and hastened her death from heart failure in 1929, when she was only 63. Haynes wrote several of her detective novels on fine days in Kensington Gardens, where she was wheeled from 14 Radnor Place in a bath chair, but in her last years she was able only to travel from her bedroom to her study. All of this was an especially hard blow for a woman who had once been intensely energetic and quite physically active.

In a foreword to *The Crystal Beads Murder*, the second of Haynes' two posthumously published mysteries, Ada Heather-Bigg noted that Haynes' difficult daily physical struggle "was materially lightened by the warmth of friendships" with other authors and by the "sympathetic and friendly relations between her and her publishers." In this latter instance Haynes' experience rather differed from that of her sister Bodleian, Agatha Christie, who left The Bodley Head on account of what she deemed an iniquitous contract that took unjust advantage of a naive young author. Christie moved, along with her landmark detective novel *The Murder of Roger Ackroyd* (1926), to Collins and never looked back, enjoying ever greater success with the passing years.

At the time Christie crossed over to Collins, Annie Haynes had only a few years of life left. After she died at 14 Radnor Place on 30 March 1929, it was reported in the press that "many people well-known in the literary world" attended the author's funeral at St.

Michaels and All Angels Church, Paddington, where her sermon was delivered by the eloquent vicar, Paul Nichols, brother of the writer Beverley Nichols and dedicatee of Haynes' mystery novel *The Master of the Priory*; yet by the time of her companion Ada Heather-Bigg's death in 1944, Haynes and her once highly-praised mysteries were forgotten. (Contrastingly, Ada Heather-Bigg's name survives today in the University College of London's Ada Heather-Bigg Prize in Economics.) Only three of Haynes' novels were ever published in the United States, and she passed away less than a year before the formation of the Detection Club, missing any chance of being invited to join this august body of distinguished British detective novelists. Fortunately, we have today entered, when it comes to classic mystery, a period of rediscovery and revival, giving a reading audience a chance once again, after over eighty years, to savor the detective fiction fare of Annie Haynes. *Bon appétit!*

Curtis Evans

Chapter One

"Now, POLLY, there you go again! Didn't I promise you the worst thrashing you ever had in your life if you let little Tim out of your arms again? And there he is, crawling in the gutter, and his clean pinny all dirty, and you with one of them nasty, trashy fairy-tale books! I declare you forget everything. I'll give you something to remember!"

The speaker seized the frightened-looking child, who was cowering away from her against the wall and administered a series of shakes, punctuating them with rough blows aimed haphazard on the thin shoulders. Tim, the cause of the commotion, paused in the midst of his happy investigation of the contents of the gutter and set up a loud howl.

A man's shadow darkened the threshold.

"Let be, missis, let be!" a gruff voice said. "What has the child been doing now? Haven't I told you I won't have her thrashed?"

"Doing? Little need to ask that question, John Spencer—look at Tim out there! You are fair silly over the girl—"

But the hand had relaxed its grip; little Polly waited for no more. Experience had taught her that, though her father might take her part at the time, her stepmother was sure to have her own way in the end. She ran out at the back of the house, past the stables, in which she could hear her father's charges, the great Sir Robert Brunton's carriage horses, stirring impatiently. With a passing feeling of wonder that Jim Gregory, her father's underling, should be away from his post, she climbed up a ladder into the loft where the provender for the horses was kept.

High above, almost hidden by the rough straw, there was a small round window. To get to it, holding by the bundles of straw, was an easy matter to Polly. She caught an echo of her stepmother's voice in the yard as she popped through and, clambering by a water-pipe, made a perilous ascent to the roof of the nearest house. There, concealed by a high stack of chimneys, she presently sat down to review the situation.

Mrs. Spencer was the only mother the child had ever known. John Spencer's first wife had died in 1887, leaving him with two daughters—Evie, then just fifteen, and the week-old baby.

It had been a sorry time for the man. Evie adored the baby, but her ideas of managing it, and the house, had been vague, and there had been no one to blame John Spencer when, a couple of years after his wife's death, he had married the buxom cook in the establishment in which he was coachman—no one, that is to say, but Evie, who had resented her father's second marriage passionately. There had been constant skirmishes between her and her stepmother until, when Polly was five years old, Evie had found the situation intolerable and had suddenly disappeared from home.

Polly—whose memory of her sister was now merely a vague recollection of being cradled in tender arms, of loving kisses being pressed upon her cheeks—sometimes had letters and beautiful presents from Evie. The rest of the family had nothing. Her stepmother, loudly opining that the girl had gone to the bad, confiscated the presents; the letters, written very plainly so that the child might read them, Polly kept and conned over and over again until she knew them by heart. It was nice to feel that some one cared for her, even this dimly-remembered elder sister.

She was thinking of that now as she sat hunched up behind the chimneys. She had had a letter from her sister the day before; perhaps that had helped to make her stepmother so cross, she reflected. Young as she was, she realized perfectly that the fact that Evie had so completely emancipated herself from her thraldom was exceedingly galling to Mrs. Spencer—almost as galling perhaps as that other fact which she had heard her father state in one of his rare fits of anger.

"Leave the child alone!" he had growled. "You don't understand her—how should you? Her mother was a lady born."

Polly thought of that now as she looked round with the air of a conqueror exploring some unknown world.

Grove Street Mews ran at the back of Hinton Square, where the town house of her father's employer was situated. At the opposite side, nearer where Polly had emerged, was Grove Street, a precinct which had undoubtedly known better days; fallen as it was, it still retained some remnants of past greatness in the shape of lofty rooms and large windows. It had, however, become the prey of the tenement owner, and each house harboured six or eight different tenants.

It was on the roof of one of these Grove Street houses that Polly now found herself. Above her there arose another story and yet another. Polly ran great danger of being seen as she picked her way carefully along. It was very dirty; soot and grime seemed to have found a final resting-place on the ledges. Looking down at her begrimed frock and pinafore, Polly shrugged her thin shoulders with unchild-like resignation. What did it matter? Her stepmother was sure to be angry anyhow.

At first there was fascination enough in the roof itself—in climbing over the various little projections, skirting the chimneys, or watching the sparrows that sat looking at her with their unwinking black eyes, as if marvelling at this sudden invasion of their territory.

But presently Polly grew more enterprising; she looked up at the long rows of windows. What were the people doing behind the blinds and curtains?

Some of the sills were on a level with her head; raising herself on tiptoe she could just manage to see in. The first was a sitting-room; so much she had contrived to make out when there was a sound of an opening door, and with a little gasp of alarm she drew back.

No sound came from the room, however; evidently she had passed unnoticed; and presently, regaining confidence, she crept along.

At length she was stopped by the wall of the next story. Polly looked up at the overhanging eaves wistfully; it was impossible to think of getting up there, and she was about to turn back hopelessly when a window close at hand caught her attention—it was sufficiently low to be easy of access. Polly found herself unable to resist the temptation. Tiptoeing, she gazed through the lower pane. At first, by contrast with the sunshine outside, everything looked dark, but, becoming used to the dimness, the child saw that the room was a great bare-looking apartment. She was too ignorant to know that the big easel in the middle of the room, the stacks of unfinished canvases against the walls, the untidy litter of paints and tubes and rags on the centre table proclaimed it to be a studio, but something in its aspect attracted her.

A tall man was standing with his back to the window; farther on, nearer the fireplace across the black rug, there lay what Polly thought was a heap of white drapery. But Polly scarcely noticed that; she was altogether absorbed in watching the man's movements. There was something odd about the way he was seizing papers, photographs, books, tearing them, through and casting them hurriedly into the bright, open fire that burned on the hearth.

In the recess, nearest the window by which Polly was standing, was a door; as the child, her big brown eyes wide open, marvelled why the man in the room was recklessly destroying all the pretty pictures she thought so fascinating, a slight movement in the recess caught her eye. She glanced round quickly—the door was being opened. Slowly, very cautiously, it was pushed forward an inch or two; then it remained stationary.

The man went on with his work of destruction; there, was something oddly stealthy about his movements, in spite of his evident haste; scarcely a sound reached Polly's ears, though the window above her was open. Yet there was a certain system about the way he went to work; he would open a book, tear out a few leaves and throw them into the fire, then lay the book down on the table, still in the same furtive, noiseless fashion, and dart to the other end of the table.

As he turned, Polly saw his face plainly.

It was dark, with strongly-marked, rugged features, a mass of rather long, curly hair, a short, neat beard. He was strongly built on massive lines, with big, loose limbs and broad shoulders. Long afterwards other details came back to Polly. She remembered that he was wearing a grey suit, that his linen was clean and white; she recalled the bunch of violets in his buttonhole, the flash of the big red stone on the little finger of his left hand.

Presently he stood for a moment near the easel. Polly could see that he was putting things in his pockets. Was he a thief, she asked herself breathlessly. She had heard her father and stepmother talking of some daring burglaries that had been perpetrated in the neighbourhood. Was it possible that this man, whose whole mode of procedure seemed to her so extraordinary, was a burglar? Would she have to tell the police? Her round eyes grew rounder. But the man by the table had evidently got all he wanted. With a little gesture of repudiation, he pushed from him all the rest of the litter upon the table, then he went farther away from the window, picked up some small object from the floor, and came over to the white heap upon the rug.

The door in the corner moved, opened rather wider. Little Polly's breathing quickened; she stared before her with wide open, dilated eyes, as if fascinated. It was her imagination of course—it was like the ghastly fancies that sometimes, came when she was in bed and the candle was dying down, turning the homely shadows on the walls into things of dread—but it seemed to her, now that she saw things more clearly, there was something terrifying about the aspect of that tangled mass of drapery heaped upon the rug. It was curiously hunched up; at one end a small black object protruded, a stray beam of sunlight caught it, sparkled on something bright.

Polly's little face turned white; she felt frightened! It could not be a buckle on a woman's shoe—it could not be a woman's foot and ankle that were stretched out there, rigid, motionless?

The man was bending down; he was moving the white mass.

Polly, watching, dominated by terror, saw that it was unmistakably a human form that lay there. With the pathetic early experience of the children of the poor, she had looked on the face of death more than once; she needed no words to tell her the reason of that rigid immobility.

With all her heart the child longed to get away; but sheer horror rendered her motionless.

The figure on the floor lay very still, just as the man placed it. Now that he had moved it, Polly could see that there were ugly dark stains on the white, flimsy gown near the shoulder. She could not see the whole face, only the outline of a rounded cheek and a knot of golden hair.

The man lifted one arm, looked at it scrutinizingly, bent it to one particular angle, then put it down carefully and studied the aspect with his head on one side. Polly saw the crimson gleam of his ring against the white of the dead woman's gown. There was something remarkable about the setting: three heavy golden claws seemed to hold the stone.

The man's face was turned to the window now as he stooped over the dead woman, but he did not look up. He was pallid, with an unnatural greenish pallor; even from that distance it was possible to see great beads of perspiration standing on his brow. He paused a moment as if listening for some sound behind. Then he laid the shining object which he had picked up from the polished boards at the other side of the table on the rug close by the girl's hand. Polly knew what that was; she had seen something like it at the shooting booths.

The door near the window moved again; Polly felt a sudden accession of terror. Who was on the other side? Did the man in the room know that some one was there watching him? What would happen when the door, now only slightly ajar, was fully open? She turned away with a frightened sob; in that silent room it had the force of a louder sound. With a quick gesture the man raised his head, his hand sought his pocket; his eyes, wild and haggard, glanced rapidly behind, then met those of the child peering in at the window.

He sprang to his feet; the door at the side moved again; with a cry of terror, Polly fell back on the sooty roof. She heard a sound behind her, and, fearing that the man was coming after her, she ran over the roof back to the hayloft, little sobs escaping from her. She fell rather than dropped into the loft, too terrified to look behind her, and, tumbling into the straw, she crouched down with her head covered, long quivering sobs shaking her body. How long she had lain there she never knew—to her it seemed hours—when there was a noise in the stable below; some one was coming up the ladder to the loft.

Polly sat up and listened, her heart beating fast with terror. She recognized the step in a minute—it was that of Jim Gregory, the groom—and cried out with a deep sigh of relief:

"Oh, Jim, Jim!"

He gazed at her in amazement, his usually florid face paler than its wont.

"Why, what in the world—" he began.

Polly clutched him in an agony; even at that moment a passing wonder as to why he was wearing his best clothes in the daytime struck her.

"I'm frightened, Jim," she moaned, "so frightened."

"Frightened!" The man stooped down and gathered her up in his arms. "Who's frightened you, Polly? Them that tries to hurt you will have to reckon with Jim Gregory!"

"She was lying on the floor all white, and he was there, and the door opened—"

The sentence ended in a little gasp, and the child hid her face on Gregory's shoulder.

Chapter Two

"I won't have the child frightened," said John Spencer obstinately, as he finished lacing his boots. His wife's face was rather redder than usual as she stood opposite, her sleeves rolled up in readiness to begin the week's washing, Tim clinging to her skirts.

"But don't I tell you, John, it's all the talk this morning, and here I've been listening to the child for the past hour, and this is what she's seen—"

Mr. Spencer's face became apoplectic.

"Don't want to know what she's seen! I tell you I won't have the child bothered!"

Mrs. Spencer shrugged her shoulders scornfully.

"If you don't know what she's seen, John Spencer, it strikes me other folk will. Why, the police will be round asking questions! No good you thinking—" She broke off with a little cry.

Her husband had advanced a step or two towards her; his face was very close to hers.

"Let them ask!" he roared. "You will tell them nothing; do you hear that, woman? I'm not going to have the child brought into court and questioned and cross-questioned until the senses are frightened out of her. What is that you say—you don't see why she should be frightened? No, it would be different with you, no doubt, but her mother was a lady born." His voice dropped a little. "It was not fit for the likes of me to touch her gown; and I haven't took the care of her children I ought. You drove Eve from home with your nasty, nagging tongue, and now it is Polly. But I won't have it, missis—I won't have it, so remember!" He banged his great fist on the table as he spoke and glared into the woman's eyes.

Mrs. Spencer shrank back, for once in her life thoroughly cowed.

Her husband was generally of an easy, phlegmatic temperament, but she had always known that he was a man it would be dangerous to rouse—that beneath his apparent placid exterior there slumbered hidden fires. Her common sense came to her aid now. She picked up her basket of dirty clothes and retired to the kitchen.

John Spencer reached down his jar of tobacco from a shelf and sat down in his easy chair, preparatory to enjoying a well-earned rest before he went back to his horses.

He frowned as he filled his pipe. Faulty as he might have been in his dealings with his first wife's children, he was fully conscious that they occupied a place in his heart that the present Mrs Spencer's numerous progeny was never likely to fill. Polly had been talking a lot of nonsense during the night, he said to himself; the child was feverish and overwrought, but he was not going to have mountains made out of molehills. He had been a little touched as well as surprised at the length of the visits his wife had paid to her bedside during the night, but the matter was explained now—women did not mind a bit of trouble if they wanted to satisfy their curiosity.

Just as he reached this point in his reflections there was a knock at the open door.

"Well, what is it?" Spencer called out. Then turning his head and catching sight of the man who stood outside, he got up awkwardly and touched his forehead. "Beg pardon, sir! You were wanting to see me?"

His unexpected visitor glanced at him a moment before he answered. He was a short, dapper man, attired in an immaculate suit; his face, long and rather thin, bore a striking resemblance to a hawk, added to, perhaps, by the gold rimmed pince-nez that was perched high upon the Roman nose; he was clean-shaven save for stubby side-whiskers.

"If you are John Spencer, head coachman to Sir Robert Brunton, I should be glad of a few words with you," he said.

Spencer touched his forehead again.

"That is me, right enough, sir."

The stranger walked inside and deposited his hat on the deal table.

"I must introduce myself, though you and I have met before, Mr. Spencer. But there—time has altered us both. You have not forgotten an interview we had in the offices of Hurst and Pounceby, of Obeston?"

Spencer's face distinctly deepened in hue; he shuffled his feet together awkwardly.

"No, I haven't forgotten sir. But you can't be Mr. Hurst."

The other readjusted his glasses.

"Ah, yes! The progress of years! But I am sure that you will remember that my firm had the honour of representing Mr. Davenant?"

Spencer moved his great foot backwards and forwards along the floor.

"I remember, sir. And he stuck to what you said, then, did Mr. Davenant. Even when my poor wife died he—"

"Ah, well, you must let bygones be bygones!" the lawyer interrupted. "I have brought better news to-day, Mr. Spencer! You heard of the old Squire's death of course?"

"Ay, and Mr. Guy's!"

"And Mr. Guy's son's?" Mr. Hurst added gravely, "You can understand what that means?"

"I don't know as I do," Spencer said slowly. "I don't see as it will make any difference to me or mine, Mr. Hurst, sir. You told me yourself as he vowed—the old Squire did—as never a penny of his should come to anyone as bore my name."

Mr. Hurst coughed.

"Many a man says more than he means when he is angry, Mr. Spencer; the approach of death softens most of us. Mr. Davenant left Davenant Hall to his wife for her life; on her, death it was to descend to his son Guy and his heirs; failing them, he desires her to select one of the children of his late daughter, Mary Evelyn, who shall take the name of Davenant and become the heiress of Davenant Hall. Now, as you know, Guy was killed in the hunting field five years after his father's death; two months ago his son George died of typhoid at his school. Thus you see—" pausing suggestively.

Spencer stood still, his big, red face turned expectantly on the lawyer, only his quickened breathing betraying that his silence betokened no lack of interest.

"So that at Mrs. Davenant's death, under the old Squire's will, the Hall will pass, with all the rest of his possessions, to one of your children, whichever Mrs. Davenant selects," Mr. Hurst went on. "I am here as her representative today. She is naturally anxious—" with a dry cough—"to make the acquaintance of the grandchildren to whom she has been hitherto a stranger."

"I see what you mean, Mr. Hurst, sir," John Spencer' said slowly. "Squire has left it so as she can't help herself, else my children might have died same as their poor mother, without a word from her."

Mr. Hurst took off his glasses and polished them carefully.

"Well, well, Mr. Spencer, as I said before, it seems to me that the time has come to let bygones be bygones. You must remember that there is much to be said on both sides. We have heard that you have formed other ties"—his keen eyes watching the half-open door, behind which Mrs. Spencer was listening eagerly to his words—"you have another family to provide for, for I am instructed by Mrs. Davenant to inform you that she is willing to undertake the maintenance of the children of your first marriage, and to allow you, on condition of their being given up entirely to her, one hundred pounds a year to be paid quarterly."

"Stop!" Mr. Spencer's face became suddenly redder. "I don't sell my own flesh and blood!" he said roughly. "Never a penny of the Davenants' money have I had, and never a penny of it will I take!"

"But my dear sir—" the lawyer was beginning, when there was a sudden interruption.

Mrs. Spencer threw open the door and came forward.

"You would never be such a fool, John Spencer!" she cried energetically. "Begging your pardon, sir"—with a slight curtsey to

Mr. Hurst—"but I could not help hearing what you were saying, and to think of Spencer refusing!"

"I said I should not sell my own flesh and blood!" her husband affirmed stolidly. "No more I shan't!" he went on with dogged determination in his tone, "But it isn't for me to stand in the children's light. Their mother"—with an odd choking sound in his throat—"would have wished it. Mrs. Davenant shall have them, sir—leastways Polly. I don't rightly know where Evie is—she has been away from home for some time, in a place I reckon —but the little one had a letter from her yesterday morning, and she will be coming home fast enough when she hears of this."

"Ay, I dare say she will! But I think I shall have a word to say to this," Mrs. Spencer broke in truculently. "It is one thing to let the child go if it is made worth our while, but if Spencer is going to make a fool of himself it is a different matter. I am not going to put myself out to do without Polly." She looked defiantly at her husband.

Spencer scowled at her and then deliberately turned his back.

"You shall have Polly, sir. It will be for the child's good and it may be as they will let us hear how she goes on sometimes."

"Certainly, certainly!" the lawyer acquiesced blandly. "This decision does you credit, Mr. Spencer. Probably the child herself will be able to thank you in later years. And now—how soon can she be ready? I have business which will keep me in town to-day, but to-morrow I hope to start for Warchester."

John Spencer drew a deep breath.

"Polly shall be ready for you to-morrow, sir."

"Thank you, Mr. Spencer! Thank you!" The lawyer turned to the door. He had seen war in Mrs Spencer's eyes, and he was anxious to avoid a scene. "To-morrow," he repeated, and made his escape.

Mrs. Spencer turned on her husband in a fury.

"Well, of all the fools, John Spencer! But I shall have something to say to this. I'll see if the police can't stop the child from being took away from me as have always been a mother to her. It is my belief if they hear what's she's seen—ah!"

Spencer had gripped her arm.

"Polly is going, and she's seen nothing! You remember that, woman! How should she, a child like her? Don't you be making a fool of yourself! Polly will go back to her mother's folk and be made a lady of, same as her mother before her, and you will look after the young ones yourself, like other people. I ought to ha' seen as you did before; but it's never too late to mend, and you'll bear in mind what I have said. If I hear as you have spoke I'll—" He did not finish the threat, he kept his face near hers for a moment before he released her arm and pushed her from him.

"Well, I never!" Mrs. Spencer was too thoroughly cowed to say more.

She leaned back against the doorpost in silence, while her husband knocked the ash from his pipe, and then, pulling his cap low over his brow, turned to the stables.

It was raining hard the next day when Polly, crying miserably, bade good-bye to her father and stepmother, and set out with Mr. Hurst for her unknown grandmother's house.

It was a long journey to Warchester, and dusk was gathering when the cab Mr. Hurst had hired at the station turned in at the Hall gates.

"We are nearly there now," Mr. Hurst remarked cheerfully to his little companion.

The child made no reply; she shrank a little further from him into her corner. So far, even direct questioning had produced nothing from her but monosyllables, and she had refused to eat a morsel of the refreshment Mr, Hurst had ordered for her.

As the cab stopped a footman came down the steps and opened the door. Mr. Hurst lifted his little charge out.

In the hall the butler, an elderly man whose hair had grown white in the service of the Davenants, was waiting to receive them.

"The mistress is in the morning-room, sir. I am to take you to her at once, and the young lady. So this is Miss Mary's child, sir?"

"Yes, Sturgess, this is Miss Mary's child," Mr. Hurst assented.

He took Polly's cold, thin little hand in his and led her across the hall. Old Sturgess cleared his throat gruffly as he preceded them.

"It seems to bring the old time back, sir," he observed apologetically.

Mr. Hurst made no reply; he was wondering how the coming interview would end. He, knew that the child who was now clinging nervously to him symbolized the bitterest trouble and humiliation of her life to the lonely old woman who was now awaiting them.

Mrs. Davenant had not been a young woman twenty-one years before when that terrible grief had overtaken her, but assuredly from that time she had become old—all her comely middle-age had fled, her hair had grown white, her face lined and marked, her slight frame bowed, Yet there had been many who had blamed her and said that, in her intense love for her son, she had in a measure neglected her daughter —that she had been harsh and imperious with the girl who, as a child, had always been at her father's heels in the garden and round the stables and as a young woman had been in the habit of taking long, lonely rides. The end had come suddenly; a suitor, favoured by Mrs. Davenant, had been refused by her daughter, there had been a period of bickering, and recrimination, useless insistence on the mother's side, obstinate refusal on the daughter's, and then one morning the neighbourhood had been electrified to hear that Miss Mary Davenant had eloped with her groom.

It had been a terrible scandal of course; thenceforward Mary Davenant's name was never uttered in her old home. It was rumoured in the neighbourhood that more than once she had written to her parents, but that her letters had been returned unopened. It was said that the father was harder than the mother. Be that as it might, it was certain that when Squire Davenant was making his will some tender recollection of the pretty, dark-eyed daughter who had been the joy of his life must have obtruded itself, and for once he had dared to disregard his wife's wishes and to add a clause which stated that, failing his son, Guy, and his heirs, the children of his daughter Mary should succeed to the property. That his independent action had been a bitter pill to his widow, none could doubt, but she had given no sign of her mortification.

The door was thrown open. A little old lady occupied the chair in the centre of the room just under the electric light—a pretty, dainty old lady, whose pink-and-white complexion and elaborately-waved white hair gave her the appearance of a Dresden china shepherdess.

Mr. Hurst led Polly to her at once.

"You see I have fulfilled my commission, Mrs. Davenant."

"I see."

The old lady smiled as she looked at the child, who quailed before her gaze. Polly's small, icy fingers instinctively clung to Mr. Hurst's warm hand. Here at least was something tangible, human; anything, she thought vaguely, was better than meeting the gaze of those blue eyes, than being expected to respond to that cold smile.

"So this is my new granddaughter, is it?" Mrs. Davenant said in clear, silvery tones that seemed to hold a ring of her lost youth. "Be good enough to stand aside, Mr. Hurst, and let me look at her!"

Thus adjured, Mr. Hurst had no choice but to obey. He was compelled to disregard the child's mute appeal and release the unwilling fingers.

Polly never forgot her feeling of misery as she stood by herself in the blaze of light, the one incongruous element in the luxuriously furnished room.

So they waited for a moment; the drooping brown eyes raised themselves reluctantly and met the mocking gaze of the blue ones.

The merciless scrutiny included all the child's defects of costume—the shabby, ill-fitting blue cashmere that had been her Sunday best, the big white pinafore peeping out in front from beneath the cloak that had been Mrs. Spencer's and had been cut down for Polly, the child's thin face, the big, frightened eyes, the untidy wisps of hair beneath the sailor-hat, the long thin arms and legs.

Then at last Mrs. Davenant laid her lorgnette down and smiled again.

"So this is the heiress of Davenant Hall! You are a brave man, Mr. Hurst."

Mr. Hurst moved uncomfortably. Long as he had known Mrs. Davenant, he had never learnt to feel at home with her.

"Not of necessity the heiress," he ventured to remind her. "There is another daughter, Evelyn."

"Who has followed her mother's example, and run away from home, I think you told me." Mrs. Davenant shut up her lorgnette with a snap. "I don't think we will trouble about Evelyn, thank you, Mr. Hurst!"

But at the mention of that familiar name some of little Polly's hardly-won composure deserted her.

"Oh, I want Evie!" she cried, with a miserable sob; then, falling on her knees at her grandmother's feet, "Oh, please, please, send for Evie!"

Mrs. Davenant looked at her with cold distaste as she drew her velvet gown out of the child's reach.

"Really, I am afraid that this child is going to be troublesome! May I trouble you to ring the bell, Mr. Hurst? Ah, Mason," as an elderly woman appeared. "Will you take Miss—Miss—Really I have not thought what we are to call the child, Mr. Hurst; Polly is impossible of course, and Mary"—a momentary contraction passing over her delicate features—"I do not care for Mary. Her name is Mary Ursula Joan, I think. Well, Joan was my mother's name, but it will have to serve. Take Miss Joan to her nursery, Mason, and see that she has some bread and milk. Don't let me see her again until she had learnt to control herself."

Mason took the child's hand in hers.

"Come, Miss Joan," she said kindly.

The forlorn child found herself guided across the dreadful space that lay between her and the door; then, when it, had closed behind them she was caught up in the woman's strong arms. "Ay, my child, don't let the mistress frighten you! I'll look after you, my Miss Mary's own child!"

Chapter Three

"THE MARRISTORS and the Stourminsters have accepted, Joan, and this new man, Lord Warchester—you saw him with Reggie the other day. Aunt Ursula will simply have to let you come."

"If you can get Granny to realize the strength of your argument—" Joan Davenant shrugged her shapely shoulders, a slight enigmatical smile curving the corners of her mouth.

The years had changed the neglected child of Grove Street Mews into a remarkably good-looking young woman. Tall and straight, with a certain resemblance to the Davenants in the modelling of her features and the set of her firm chin, she had inherited from a plebeian ancestry on her father's side a strength of constitution, a soundness of mind and limb that made her vigorous youth a joy to look upon. Her eyes were brown, flecked with gold; her hair and the long upcurled lashes were black in the shadow, amber in the sunlight.

Her companion, Cynthia Trewhistle, the wife of Reginald Trewhistle, Mrs. Davenant's nephew, was considerably Joan's senior, a little, delicate-looking woman with fluffy golden hair and big, appealing grey eyes. Her dainty white cloth costume and big black picture hat were curiously in contrast with Joan's shabby blue serge gown and plain straw hat.

The two were walking up the park towards the Hall. The March sunshine which streamed down upon them and made Mrs. Trewhistle loosen her sables, despite the touch of frost in the air, showed up with cruel distinctness the frayed seams of Joan's frock, but found no flaw in the firm whiteness of her skin or the brilliant colour mantling in her cheeks.

Mrs. Trewhistle slipped her arm within the girl's.

"It's a shame the way Aunt Ursula treats you! I was saying so to Reggie before I started. Here are you wasting your youth and beauty cooped up in this dull old place—for you are beautiful you know, Joan," giving her arm an affectionate squeeze. "You have never been to Court, you have never been to a dance, or a picnic even, or any of the delightful things that every girl expects."

"On the other hand I have had a good many things that my father's daughter could not have expected," said Joan quietly.

Mrs. Trewhistle's face clouded.

"Bother your father!" she exclaimed impetuously. "I beg your pardon, Joan—I suppose I ought not to have said that, but you and Aunt Ursula are really too old-fashioned. The idea of worrying about your father nowadays! You are unusually good-looking, you are the greatest heiress in the county, and that is all that matters."

"Is it?" Joan said absently. She stooped and picking three early daffodils tucked them in her belt.

"Yes, of course it is!" Mrs. Trewhistle assured her with decision. "Now, Joan, I am going to see Aunt Ursula. I am frightened to death of her, as you know, but I mean you to come to my dance."

"It will not be any use, Cynthia, but if you like—"

Mrs Trewhistle quickened her steps.

"We will go at once while my courage is screwed up to the sticking-point. Come, Joan!"

The girl looked down affectionately at her companion more than once; her friendship for her cousin's wife was the one bright spot in a life which but for Cynthia would have been dull indeed. Sometimes Joan was tempted to wonder why her grandmother had sent for her to Warchester, why she had troubled herself about her upbringing at all; it was so very evident that old Mrs. Davenant had no love—scarcely even any toleration—for her dead daughter's child.

Joan could look back to her coming to Warchester with a kind of detached pity for the lonely child who had found the new life so difficult and so alarming. She could not recall one sign of sympathy, one word of affection from her grandmother, and but for Mason, her mother's old nurse, her lot would have been lonely indeed. To the best of her powers Mason had mothered her, had rejoiced in her health and strength. It had been through Mason that her few pleasures had been obtained.

For as time went on Mrs. Davenant had developed habits of parsimony. Her own gowns came from Paris; though she never went out she was as elegantly dressed as in her youth; but for Joan it was a different matter. The very plainest of stuff was good enough for her—made up by the village dress-maker. The girl's governesses had found themselves restricted in every way with regard to her education.

Joan had done with governesses now, for the last two years she had been her own mistress, but beyond the actual ceasing of lessons the fact of being grown up scarcely affected her life at all. Her grandmother made her no dress allowance. The only visitors who were ever received at the Hall were the old vicar of the parish and his wife and Reggie and Cynthia Trewhistle. Even with them Joan's intercourse was very much restricted. Cynthia Trewhistle had grumbled to her husband ever since her marriage at the state of seclusion in which Joan was kept; to-day she had come with the express determination of "having it out" with Mrs. Davenant.

Nevertheless, the awe in which she stood of her aunt by marriage was considerable; her knees were quaking as she mounted the steps to the front door.

Joan led the way across the hall to the room to which Mr. Hurst had brought her, a shivering, frightened child, ten years before.

"Here is Cynthia, granny," she said, as she opened the door.

Mrs. Davenant looked up. She was sitting at her writing table, apparently immersed in correspondence. Joan often wondered to whom these lengthy epistles were sent, since comparatively few letters came to the Hall. Time had dealt lightly with Mrs. Davenant; she was scarcely altered since that memorable evening when Joan arrived at the Hall; the lines round her mouth were a little deeper, the tiny network of wrinkles round her eyes had spread a little, but that was all. There was still that resemblance to a Dresden china shepherdess.

"How do you do, Cynthia? You are here betimes," she said slowly.

"I came early because I wanted to ask you something, Aunt Ursula," Mrs. Trewhistle began boldly, taking the bull by the horns, as she afterwards phrased it to her husband.

Mrs. Davenant raised her pencilled eyebrows.

"Indeed! Well, you, know that anything I can do, dear Cynthia—"

"Well, you really can do this quite easily." Mrs. Trewhistle's colour came and went quickly despite her courage. There was something most disconcerting in the gaze of those blue eyes. "You know next week I am having a dance—"

"Ah, yes!" Mrs. Davenant nodded. "I remember you were good enough to send me an invitation. Well, go on, my dear."

"I want you to let Joan come," Cynthia went on desperately. "Oh, I know you never go out, Aunt Ursula, but it is quite a small dance really. We would take every care of Joan, and really she ought to go out sometimes. It is not fair to keep a young girl shut up altogether."

There was a pause; Cynthia did not dare to raise her eyes. Chatter away though she might at other times, she always felt it an effort to speak to her husband's aunt; she was well aware that even this very mild remonstrance would border upon audacity in the old lady's eyes.

"You are really very kind," said Mrs. Davenant at last. "But I thought you understood—I imagined I had fully explained it to Reginald, at any rate—that I think it better that Joan should not go out. Therefore, my dear Cynthia—"

"Oh, yes, I know, and I think, as Reggie thinks, that it is an awful shame!" Mrs. Trewhistle retorted hotly, her sense of Mrs. Davenant's injustice to the girl whom she had learnt to love as a sister overcoming her fear of the old lady. "It is cruel to make her waste her life like this! What good is it to her to be the heiress to Davenant Hall if she never goes anywhere, never sees anybody?"

"'The heiress of Davenant Hall—ah!" said Mrs. Davenant. "And so Joan has been getting you to speak for her; my dear?"

Joan was leaning with one arm against the high oak mantel piece, her fingers gently touching the daffodils in her belt, her head bent; apparently she had been taking no interest in the conversation. She glanced at her grandmother now.

"I did not get Cynthia to speak," she said quietly. "I told her that it would be no use."

"Yes, indeed, she tried to stop me," Cynthia went on impetuously. "It was I who had quite determined to ask you. You will let Joan come, will you not, Aunt Ursula? It is going to be a great success. The new Lord Warchester has accepted—you remember how fond poor Guy was of him when he was Paul Wilton—and—oh, lots of people! It will simply break my heart if Joan is not allowed to come!"

"Oh, really, my dear Cynthia, I do not think hearts are broken quite so easily!" and the old lady laughed amusedly.

Joan looked at her quickly as she heard the sound.

"What does the heiress of Davenant Hall say in the matter?" Mrs. Davenant went on, a little sarcastic inflection in her voice.

"I should like to go, naturally," Joan said composedly. "But you know I never ask favours from you, granny."

"No, no—it is I. Aunt Ursula, do for once!" Cynthia pleaded.

Mrs. Davenant glanced at her anxious face coldly.

"I do not see why it should be any satisfaction to you, but—"

"You will!" Cynthia cried, clasping her hands. "Aunt Ursula, it is perfectly sweet of you!"

"That is settled then!" Mrs. Davenant took up a paper as though to intimate that the interview was ended.

Cynthia turned to Joan.

"Is it not perfectly delightful? About your dress? Of course you have nothing"—with a disparaging glance at the blue serge—"but I dare say, for me, Madame Benoit would get one done in time."

"Ah, that will be my affair!" Mrs. Davenant had caught the whispered words. "Do not trouble Benoit, Cynthia. I may have lived out of the world for some time, but I imagine I am still capable of ordering my granddaughter's dresses."

"Oh, of course, of course! You know I did not mean that, Aunt Ursula!"

Cynthia was glad to get out of the room.

"Horrid old thing!" she whispered to Joan. "How you stand her I cannot imagine. However, you are coming to the ball, that is the great thing. I wish she would have let me order the gown, though; she is sure to get something awful. I would order you one myself, independently of her and make you change, but really there have been so many expenses of late, Reggie has been frightfully extravagant, and I have not been a bit lucky at bridge, so that—"

"As if I should let you! No, Granny must do her best, or her worst, and if I come to your dance like a frump—well, you must just turn me away, that's all."

When Joan waved her last farewell to Mrs. Trewhistle, and that lady's motor was speeding swiftly down the drive she found a footman at her elbow.

"Mrs. Davenant would be glad to see you again, miss." Joan went slowly back to the morning-room, the momentary brightening caused by Cynthia's presence fading from her face.

"You wanted me, granny?" she said on the threshold.

"Yes." Mrs. Davenant took up a fresh sheet of paper and dipped her pen in the ink. "Come in and close the door, Joan. So you are going to have your wish—you are going to Cynthia's dance? And now—now I am thinking how I can best fulfil another request of yours."

"Indeed!" Joan raised her eyebrows slightly as she obeyed the old lady's request. "So much of my own way will surely be bad for me, granny. I shall be getting a swelled head. What is this request of mine that you have in your mind now? I was under the impression that I had carefully abstained from making any."

Mrs. Davenant watched her face keenly.

"Possibly you have forgotten this; you may even have changed your mind; it is years since I heard you mention it. But when you first came—Ah, I see you remember it!" as Joan changed colour—

"you used to ask me to send for Evelyn, to find Evelyn. Well, now," with one of the laughs that Joan hated, "I am going to write to Mr. Hurst, bidding him to set to work to find Evelyn!"

Chapter Four

"You look just the same as usual, Joan."

"That does not sound complimentary," said Joan, an amused look in her eyes. "I am afraid that if you expected a transformation you will be disappointed, Cynthia."

"Oh, you know what I mean! I thought that Aunt Ursula, having allowed you to come, would have given you heaps of new things. Not but what you look very nice, Joan"—with an apologetic kiss— "and as long as the gown for to-night is all right—what is it like?"

Joan shrugged her shoulders.

"White, that is all I can tell you. A young woman came down from town to fit me, but the frock itself I have never seen."

"Joan!" Cynthia interrupted her with a little shriek. You have not seen it? You do not know whether it is a success? Where is it?"

"Granny is going to send it here in time for the ball," Joan said demurely. "I can't help it, Cynthia—she would have her own way about it."

"But this is terrible!" Cynthia clasped her hands in real distress. "It may—nay, it probably will—be something appalling. I wish I had ordered another for you myself. Reggie said this morning I ought to have done so."

"There is nothing to do but to make the best of it," Joan answered.

The conversation took place in Mrs. Trewhistle's bedroom. It was the day of the ball, and at Cynthia's urgent request Joan had been allowed to come over in time for tea and to dress at her cousin's. Now, Cynthia in her pretty chiffon tea-gown was eyeing Joan's severe black frock with obvious disapproval.

"It is too bad," she grumbled. "Just when I particularly wanted you to look nice, and all my things are much too small for you. Celestine"—as her maid came into the room—"see if you can find the Brussels lace I was looking at this morning. I want it for Mademoiselle. Is Aunt Ursula persisting in that absurd idea of hers, Joan?" as the maid departed on her errand. "Insisting on finding that sister of yours? It makes Reggie so angry when he thinks of it."

"Finding Evelyn? Yes I think so," Joan assented. "Don't call it an absurd idea, Cynthia. Evelyn has as good a right to be at Warchester as I have. How I loved her years ago! And how strange it seems to remember that I was that lonely little child in the coachman's house at the back of the mews!"

Cynthia made a little grimace.

"Your sister couldn't have cared for you much, Joan, or she would not have lost sight of you all this time. I should not, I know."

"I am sure she loved me," said Joan with conviction. "Her letters used to be full of the happy time that was coming when we should be together again—her little sister Polly, she used to call me. I have sometimes wondered whether my stepmother kept back her letters after I came to Warchester, for I have never heard from Evie since."

"Perhaps she did," Cynthia replied indifferently. Her private opinion was that if Mrs. Spencer had kept back the letters she had for once done Joan a good turn. "But if Aunt Ursula finds her now and leaves Warchester to her it will be a wicked shame and I shall tell her so!"

Joan smiled, knowing that Cynthia's brave speeches were seldom dangerous.

"I wonder whether she will? Certainly Evelyn has the better right to—to everything. She is the elder."

"What does that matter when you have lived here so many years? But I hope that they will not find her. Ah, Celestine, that is right!" as the maid returned with a scarf of valuable lace. Mrs. Trewhistle draped it about Joan's figure. "There, that is better!" she said, standing back to admire her handiwork. "Now come, Joan!"

Downstairs in the hall, before the big fire of logs, two men were standing. They looked up as soon as the sound of Cynthia's laugh on the stairs reached them. One was Reginald Trewhistle, the master of the house, and the other was a tall, dark, broad-shouldered man, whose clean-shaven face had a look of strength and power, whose abundant dark hair was already thickly streaked with grey. As he glanced upwards at the two women, a gleam of admiration sprang into his deep-set grey eyes.

As she waited a moment at the bend of the stairs and smiled down at Cynthia, Joan made an exquisite picture; against Cynthia's fluffy elegance the long, severe lines of her sombre gown had the grace of absolute simplicity; the dark oak of the wainscoting threw into high relief the small head, with its crown of waving hair, set flowerlike on the long throat.

To the man in the dimness of the hall below she seemed to be bathed in sunlight; he caught the brilliance of her complexion, her arresting, bewildering smile.

"Oh, Lord Warchester, this is kind!" Cynthia hurried down and greeted the stranger effusively. "Joan, dear, this is Lord Warchester—-my cousin, Miss Davenant."

The look in Warchester's eyes as he bent low over Joan's hands did not escape Mrs. Trewhistle. With a little throb of congratulation she told herself that it would be all right, that things would go as she wished.

"You must bid Lord Warchester welcome home, Joan," she said as she moved to the tea-table. "We are all so glad to have him."

Joan gazed intently at the man's dark face. She felt in a curious way that somewhere she and Lord Warchester had met before. Then, as he smiled, she told herself that she was mistaken; she must have seen a chance resemblance to his predecessor, the old Lord Warchester, whom she had met occasionally in the course of her walks and drives.

"I suppose you are very glad to be back," she said simply.

"Very glad to be once more among my old friends," he returned in his deep, pleasant voice. "Among them I used to be fortunate enough to count Mrs. Davenant. I am hoping to be allowed to call upon her soon."

"Upon Granny!" Joan exclaimed in genuine amazement.

He laughed.

"Yes. Why do you look surprised? Your Uncle Guy and I were great friends. I believe that as Paul Wilton I had the honour of being a favourite of Mrs. Covenant's. Of course I understand his death has made a tremendous difference in her mode of life, but I am hoping she will be persuaded to see me."

"Joan! Joan! Come and have your tea! We have so little time to spare!" Cynthia called from her seat near the fireplace. "Lord Warchester, as soon as tea is over we are going to give Joan a dancing lesson—Reggie and I. Positively the poor child has never been taught. You will have to retire to the smoking-room."

"Oh, but why should I be banished?" Warchester protested, his grey eyes smiling as they rested on his hostess's vivacious face. "May I not help with the lesson?"

Cynthia looked at him for an instant with her head on one side as she rose.

"I remember that I danced with you two or three times before I was married, and you were splendid! Yes, you may come if you like, may he not, Joan?

Warchester's dark face was unusually animated as he followed them to the ball-room. It was already prepared for the dance, and Mrs. Trewhistle looked at the shining expanse of floor with satisfaction. She seated herself at the piano and began to play a dreamy waltz.

"Now, Reggie," she commanded, "I have taught Joan the steps, but positively the poor child has never danced with a proper partner in her life."

Reggie Trewhistle came forward obediently. He was a stout, rather vacuous-looking man, already growing bald.

"Now, Joan, allow me—"

"If you please, sir, Mr. Cairns would be glad if you could speak to him for a moment; he desired me to say that his business was very important."

The butler was standing in the doorway regarding them benevolently.

"Oh, bother!" exclaimed Reggie. "I had forgotten Cairns. I must see him for a minute or two. Warchester, take my place till I come back, there's a good fellow!"

"With pleasure!" Warchester stepped forward and laid his hand lightly on Joan's arm. "One, two, three—now!" He swung her round. Joan in her nervousness was inclined to forget all Mrs. Trewhistle's carefully imparted instructions at first, but very soon her feet began to keep time to the music instinctively, the rhythm of the motion grew upon her, and she drew a deep breath of delight as they glided round the room. She was far too inexperienced to realize how much Warchester was helping her on or to appreciate how perfect a partner he was.

"Thank you, Miss Davenant! I shall always owe Cairns a debt of gratitude for coming when he did."

The amber specks in Joan's eyes were very apparent as she glanced at him.

"Cairns, I do not understand."

"I have been your first partner. I shall remember that always," he said, looking at her intently.

"Our pupil does us credit, Lord Warchester," said Cynthia, coming towards him. "Do you know, Joan, it is later than I thought? We shall have to dress immediately." She took the girl's hand. "Hurry, hurry!"

Warchester moved forward quickly and intercepted them at the door.

"How many dances will you give me to-night, Miss Davenant?"

Joan hesitated a second; her colour was heightened by the unwonted exercise, and her breath came quicker through her parted lips.

"How many do you want?"

"Every one you can spare."

"Do you not think you are rather rash?" asked Joan. "I do not expect to be in universal request. Quite possibly you will be the only person who will ask me to dance at all."

"May I take the chance?" Warchester's eyes were very eager as he asked the question.

"We will see later," Joan said mischievously as she followed Cynthia.

"There is plenty of time really," Cynthia confided to her as they went upstairs. "But I felt we must look at your gown. I believe it has just come, and in case Aunt Ursula has sent something perfectly frightful I want Celestine to see what she can do with it. Well, Celestine"—as the maid opened the door—"is it possible? Can Miss Davenant wear it?"

Celestine held up her hands.

"But, madame—possible? It is all that there is of *superbe... magnifique!*"

"What? *Superbe! Magnifique!*" Cynthia hurried across to the couch.

Joan's gown lay there enshrouded in folds of tissue-paper but gleaming lustrously through them.

"Oh, Joan!" she gasped. "Who would have thought it of Aunt Ursula? Celestine, you must do your best for Miss Davenant to-night."

"That will not be difficult, madame," Celestine responded as she loosened Joan's rippling hair.

Joan's thoughts were very far away as she sat silent before the long pier-glass while Celestine's clever fingers were busily at work. The girl would scarcely have been mortal if thoughts of Lord Warchester had not obtruded upon her.

She was trying to recall what she had heard of him from Cynthia. She knew that he had succeeded an uncle with whom he had been at variance for years and that, though he had been a friend of Reggie Trewhistle's in their boyhood, of late they had seen little of one another.

She had heard that the new Lord Warchester had lived much abroad, and that rumour had been busy, as usual, with his past. She had a vague recollection too of having heard that a house called the Marsh, with a certain amount of property around it, had passed on the late Lord Warchester's death to a cousin of the present peer, and wondered disconnectedly whether the cousins were alike—whether the younger one had the same kindly smile, the same, deep-set, haunting eyes as Lord Warchester himself.

"Now, mademoiselle!" The hair was finished, Celestine was waiting to help Joan with the gown, and for the time the latter forgot her speculations in the delight of seeing herself for once really well dressed.

Celestine stood back a few paces to survey her handiwork when all was finished.

"*Mais*, Mademoiselle is perfect—ravishing!"

The flush on Joan's cheeks deepened as she looked at her reflection. Assuredly Mrs. Davenant had known what she was about when she ordered the gown. The ivory-like material, lovely as it was, was merely the background for the most exquisite embroidery of seed pearl and silver that lay like a delicate network of frost over the whole surface. The gown looked at first sight almost severely plain, but it had been designed by an artist to whom Joan's wealth of colouring had been, an inspiration. Nothing could have better become the girl's brilliant complexion, the scarlet of her lips, the warmth of her hair, than the soft ivory-white. The long, beautifully modelled throat rose from a cloud of priceless old lace. Celestine, too, had risen to the occasion. Joan's hair was arranged with seeming carelessness, but with the hand of an artist. A necklace of pearls, which had been an heirloom for generations of Davenants, was clasped round her neck.

Cynthia, with diamonds twinkling in her hair and round her throat, coming into the room in her pale-green chiffon, looked at her cousin almost enviously.

"You are perfectly transformed, Joan! Of course I always knew you could look lovely, properly dressed, but really—that is really magnificent! It looks simple, unpretentious, and yet one sees it is exactly the thing. Beside you, I shall look atrociously overdressed."

"You look perfectly charming!" Joan declared. "I feel very expensive, but it is nice to be properly dressed for once."

"Of course it is!" Cynthia agreed heartily. "I am glad Aunt Ursula has behaved decently at last."

Cynthia was a popular hostess, and dances being few and far between in the neighbourhood, her rooms filled rapidly. Joan, as a cousin of the host, and endowed with unusual good looks and with the reputation of being the greatest heiress in the county, found herself much in request. Warchester was early at her side. He claimed the first dance, and, looking at her programme, Joan felt a little alarmed as she saw how often his name figured. They made a splendid pair with their unusual height, for, though Joan was tall for a woman, her head barely reached to Warchester's shoulder. Many eyes followed them as they circled slowly round the room, and many heads were close together when they passed.

Later in the evening they went into supper together. Warchester secured a table in an alcove a little withdrawn from the others. As she ate her chicken and salad Joan glanced across at her companion.

"How long is it since you were in the neighbourhood, Lord Warchester?"

He looked slightly surprised.

"Fourteen—no, fifteen years. I was twenty-three-the last time I stayed at Warchester. I had no expectation of succeeding to the title then. My cousin Basil, to whom my uncle left the Marsh and most of the unentailed property, was with me."

Joan looked interested.

"He is an invalid, is he not—your cousin?"

"Yes." Warchester's head was downcast; his hand was absently playing with his watch-chain. "Some ten years ago he had an accident, and was frightfully smashed, up, poor chap. He has been more or less an invalid ever since, and his memory has been seriously affected."

"How terribly sad!" Joan exclaimed. "And has he anybody—any sisters or a mother to live with him?"

"His mother died two years after the accident," Warchester said slowly, "I think the shock of it killed her, for she had been so proud of him. But his tone changing to lighter vein—"why are you looking so puzzled, Miss Davenant? What is worrying you?"

"Because I thought—" Joan came to a stop. "But if you have not been here for ten years—"

"I have not been here for nearly fifteen years," he corrected. "As a matter of fact, as you may have heard, my uncle was so seriously annoyed when I refused to fall in with his plans for my future that he vowed that I should not cross the threshold of the Towers in his lifetime, and he kept his word."

"Then of course it must be my fancy, since it is only ten years since I came to the Hall, but I cannot help feeling the whole time that I have seen you before and that in some way you are familiar to me."

Warchester leaned forward.

"I feel as if I had known you all my life. How shall we explain it? Perhaps," with a laugh, "in another incarnation we met—were friends."

"Joan!" It was Reggie Trewhistle's voice. His usually florid, good-tempered-looking face was pale and perturbed. "Aunt Ursula is not well; she—I think you had better go home."

"Granny!" Joan stood up. The sudden revulsion of feeling from the thoughtless enjoyment of the moment before seemed to overwhelm her. She clutched blindly at the curtain behind her. Not for an instant did the apparent carelessness of her cousin's words deceive her. Her grandmother had never been ill since her coming to Warchester, but she knew instinctively that it was no light thing that had overtaken her poor grandmother now.

"What—what is it?" she asked. "Not—"

Warchester was standing behind; over the girl's head his eyes met Reggie's in a glance of perfect comprehension. The next moment he stepped forward and drew Joan's hand within his arm.

"I think, Miss Davenant, we had better find Mrs. Trewhistle:"

Joan made no resistance. It did not seem strange to her that the music in the ball-room had stopped, that already people were leaving, so sure had she been from the first what had happened.

"Oh, Joan, my poor dear!" Cynthia took her from Warchester, drew her into the boudoir, and kissed her cold cheek. "I am so sorry, dear child."

Joan drew herself a little away.

"I don't seem to understand," she said in an odd, tired voice. "Tell me, Cynthia, how it was?"

Cynthia's pretty face was disfigured by tears. She had not cared for Aunt Ursula and had never pretended to do so, but it was dreadful to hear of this.

"It—it was quite sudden," she told Joan, with a little break in her voice. "Bompas had given her milk and brandy as she always did last thing—it was later than usual, for she had been busy writing— and when she had emptied the glass she just slipped down among the pillows with a fluttering breath and was gone. Poor Bompas could not believe it. Now dear Joan, you—"

"I must go back," Joan said calmly. "Poor Granny! She did not care much for me, you know, Cynthia, but I think she would have liked me to be there now."

Chapter Five

"According to the terms of my husband's will, I bequeath Davenant Hall with its appurtenances and revenues to my granddaughter

Evelyn Cecil Mary, elder daughter of John Spencer and Mary Evelyn his wife, and I appoint the said Evelyn Cecil Mary Spencer my residuary legatee. To my younger granddaughter Mary Ursula Joan Davenant, I bequeath the sum of one hundred pounds a year, to be paid quarterly."

Mr. Hurst read out the foregoing sentences in his usual calm voice.

His auditors looked at one another in consternation. They heard little of the legacies to the servants with which the will ended; all their thoughts were for the tall, pale girl in black who sat at Mr. Hurst's right, and who was apparently less affected by what had passed than anyone in the room. The silence that followed the reading of the will was broken by an exclamation from Mrs. Trewhistle.

"Well!"

She and Joan were the only women in the room. The men included Septimus Lockyer, K.C., the dead woman's brother; her nephew, Reginald Trewhistle; two distant cousins and a younger brother of Reggie's; and Sir Edward Fisher, who, like Septimus Lockyer, had been appointed executor.

"That is all," concluded Mr. Hurst, with a dry cough.

"I may add that the documents, with blanks I left for the names, were prepared for Mrs. Davenant three weeks ago; the names were inserted and the will was signed and witnessed on the evening of her death."

"Could it not be upset?" Cynthia inquired eagerly. "She could not have been sane when she did it, you know, Mr. Hurst."

The lawyer shook his head.

"I fear we have no ground for interfering with the will, Mrs. Trewhistle. I assure you that I regret its provisions extremely. I am as much taken by surprise as anyone. In a will made soon after Miss Davenant's arrival here the positions were reversed."

"Could not we act on that?" Cynthia asked hopefully.

Again Mr. Hurst shook his head.

"We are powerless. The will must stand."

"I call it a shame!" Cynthia exclaimed passionately. "Here has Joan been brought up on the understanding she was to inherit Davenant, and now she is thrown on the world penniless—for what is a hundred a year?"

"A good deal to some people," Joan interposed quietly. "No, Cynthia, don't say any more," laying a restraining hand on her cousin's arm. "It—it hurts me rather. I cannot help thinking that it was—it must have been my fault that she never cared for me."

"It was not!" Cynthia cried indignantly. "Aunt Ursula was—"

But her husband was looking at her warningly.

Septimus Lockyer was clearing his throat. He was considerably the dead woman's junior, and no one looking at him would have taken him for her brother. He was a big, burly man, with a wide, florid face and prominent grey eyes. He took off his eyeglasses, rubbed them, and readjusted them at a comfortable angle as he looked at his grandniece.

"There is only one thing to be done now, Joan, my dear," he said kindly, "You must come and keep house for me; I have been thinking of settling down. In fact, I have had my eye for some time on a likely house in Queen's Gate, only I had no one to look after me," giving a regretful sigh as he thought of his luxurious bachelor chambers.

"No, no, Uncle Septimus!" Cynthia spoke quickly, "I can't spare Joan. She will come to us of course."

"There is one point that we are overlooking, as it seems to me," Sir Edward Fisher interposed, leaning forward as Joan was about to speak. "This young lady to whom the estate is left is Miss Davenant's elder sister, I presume. Ought she not to have been here to-day?"

"Undoubtedly!" Mr. Hurst took the answer upon himself. "'But I regret to say that we are in total ignorance of her whereabouts. She left home many years ago in consequence of a disagreement with her stepmother, and, later on, resenting, we imagine, her sister's practical adoption by Mrs. Davenant, ceased to hold any communication with her. A week or two ago Mrs. Davenant began to institute inquiries with a view to discovering what had become of her, but so far with little result."

"Do you mean that you don't know where she is?"

Mr. Hurst bowed.

"That is precisely the situation, Sir Edward."

"And—and, supposing you don't find her—or—or she is dead, or anything?" pursued Sir Edward in a slightly lower tone. "Who comes in to the estate then?"

"Miss Joan Davenant undoubtedly, provided we obtained permission to presume the death," Mr. Hurst answered. "The Squire's will distinctly stated that the estate was to go a child of his daughter's. Only, in the case of there being more than one, was Mrs. Davenant at liberty to choose."

"I see."

"Of course she will turn up now when she hears that she has had money left her—people always do," Cynthia said pettishly. "Come, Joan, there is nothing for us to stay for, it seems to me." She put her arm affectionately round her cousin.

Joan rose slowly. Since the shock of hearing of her grandmother's death she had felt singularly inert and languid. In time her splendid vitality would reassert itself but for the present there was no doubt that she was suffering even more than she realized. Though her grandmother had never been affectionate, never indeed more than tolerant of her, it seemed now to the girl, looking back, that she understood more of that strange, warped nature than any of these people who discussed her testamentary disposition with scarcely a word of regret for the woman who had loved and sorrowed in that great house through many lonely years. She could guess something of the intense humiliation her mother's marriage must have been to that proud nature, and she could be very pitiful to the paltry revenge that had been taken upon her—that dead daughter's child. She had been made to suffer in her mother's default. The will was not so much of a surprise to her as to her relatives; she had always suspected that her succession to the estates was exceedingly precarious, and lately she had seen how her grandmother's mind had reverted to Evelyn.

Mr. Hurst blinked at her over the top of his glasses. He was little changed since the day he brought her to Davenant Hall. He did not see quite as well as in those days perhaps, that was all—all except that now it was he who looked up and Joan-—tall Joan—who looked down.

"I am sure I need not say how grieved I am, Miss Davenant," he began nervously, fumbling with his papers. "If any efforts of mine—"

Joan held out her hand.

"I am sure it was no doing of yours, Mr. Hurst. You have always been most kind to me. Nor must you think, any of you"—raising her head with a new accession of dignity—"that I grudge her good fortune to my sister or blame my grandmother. She has a perfect right to please herself."

"I blame her, though," Cynthia murmured beneath her breath, as, with her hand through her cousin's arm, she drew her through the door. "I should just enjoy telling her what I think of her now," she added when they stood outside in the hall.

"Please don't, Cynthia," protested Joan. "I can't bear to hear you speak like that. It seems so unkind just after we have left her alone in that dreadful vault. I—I am sure it must have been my fault that we were not more intimate."

"Your fault indeed," Cynthia exclaimed resentfully. "When you have been a perfect angel! Joan, you have never grumbled—or—or anything. Why, in your place I should have flown out at her long ago—I know I should!"

Meanwhile in the room they had left the men drew their chairs closer together and looked very uneasy.

Reggie Trewhistle was the first to break the silence.

"Well, this is a pretty kettle of fish!" he ejaculated. "The old lady must have been as mad as a March hare!"

"Mad!" Mr. Lockyer permitted himself a smile. "My sister was as sane and level-headed a woman as I ever knew, I would have you understand, Reggie. Not but what I think she has been wrong over this. But insanity—pouf! There has never been any of that in the Lockyer family. Now, with regard to this other sister, the one that comes into the property now. I am ashamed to say I have never made any inquiries about her. Do I understand that you do not know where she is?"

Mr. Hurst hesitated.

"Personally," he explained, "I have no idea of her whereabouts, but a private detective, whom, against my advice, Mrs. Davenant consulted, discovered that a short time after Miss Evelyn Spencer left her home a family named Molyneux took with them to Montreal a young nursery governess who signed her name in the passengers' book as 'E. Spencer.' Her description leads Hewlett, the detective, to think it is the same girl. That is practically the only clue we have."

The great K.C. looked thoughtful.

"And that may be no clue at all. Spencer is a common enough name. How long ago is this, Mr. Hurst—that the girl left home, I mean?"

The solicitor consulted his notes.

"As far as I can ascertain it will be fifteen years next March, Mr. Lockyer."

"Fifteen years ago! Phew! I had no idea it was so long as that. Why, how old is the girl?"

"I believe Miss Spencer will be thirty-five next month."

"Thirty-five! Good heavens! And you don't know what she has been doing for fifteen years?" The K.C. was startled out of his calm for once. "Why—anything may have happened to her!"

"Precisely!" Sir Edward Fisher agreed. "Mr. Hurst, I am of opinion that it was your duty to have submitted this to Mrs. Davenant."

"Undoubtedly I should have done so had Mrs. Davenant consulted me with regard to her intentions," the lawyer answered.

Septimus Lockyer rose and buttoned his coat.

"Well, she must be found; that is the first thing, Mr. Hurst. Of course you will set the detectives to work at high pressure. Hewlett, you said? Of Hewlett and Cowham's, I suppose—a very good firm! By the way, what is she like? Does she resemble her sister at all? I suppose you have not a photograph?"

The lawyer took out his pocket-book.

"'Miss Joan has supplied us with one her sister sent her, taken a few weeks after she left home. Here it is." He handed a small oval frame to the great lawyer. "It is practically the only clue we have. Miss Joan has been unable to find any of her sister's letters, though she knows that a year or two ago she had one—the last, received only the day before she came to the Hall."

Septimus Lockyer studied the faded photograph the frame contained for a minute or two in silence; then he walked over to the window and turned it about to get the best possible light. The frame was tarnished and dull now, but it had been bright enough once, and little Joan had been proud of it and thought it the purest silver. The photograph was old and faded too. It represented a girl dressed in the fashion of a bygone day, sitting in an affected pose at an open window, beside a table on which stood a great vase of flowers. The attitude was stilted and unnatural. But it was on the face that Septimus Lockyer's gaze was fixed. He could see no resemblance to Joan; nevertheless it did seem to him that he saw a curious likeness to some one he knew in the big eyes set far apart, in the small tip-tilted nose, in the rather wide mouth and the little pointed chin. The elaborately-curled fringe was fair. As far as could be judged from the photograph, Evelyn had been very fair, entirely lacking her sister's colour and vitality.

Mr. Hurst glanced a little curiously at the K.C.

"Do you see a look of Mrs. Davenant, Mr. Lockyer?"

Septimus gave the photograph another scrutiny.

"No," he said slowly, "I don't think so. But the extraordinary thing is that, though she is quite unlike Joan, though I see no resemblance to anyone, this face is perfectly familiar to me."

"What, you know her? You have seen her?" burst, from Mr. Hurst and Reggie Trewhistle simultaneously.

Septimus Lockyer put the frame down on the table, knitting his brows together thoughtfully.

"Certainly I have seen her somewhere—I am convinced of it! She was not dressed like that, but the face is the same. Now where"—staring before him into vacancy—"the deuce could it have been?"

Chapter Six

"WITH LORD Warchester's compliments, madam."

Celestine presented a great bunch of orchids to Cynthia. "His lordships is waiting below."

Mrs. Trewhistle bent over them with a little cry of delight.

"Oh, how perfectly lovely! You must wear some to-night, Joan. These pale mauve cattleya will look lovely against your black gown."

Joan's face had regained all its old colour. She laughed.

"They are sent to you."

"Me—pouf!" Mrs. Trewhistle made a little airy gesture of contempt. "Many kiss the child for the sake of the nursemaid. Make haste and get into your things, Joan. I will go and entertain Warchester till you come down." With a light laugh she left the room.

Joan, who had been out with the dogs for a ramble, and been overtaken by a thunderstorm, looked at her wet skirts with distaste as she slipped them off.

"Let me help you, miss." Celestine came forward and took the wet garments from her, replacing them by a chiffon gown.

For the last two months—ever since Mrs. Davenant's death, in fact—Joan had been staying with the Trewhistles. There had been so far no response to the advertisements for Evelyn which had been inserted in all the principal newspapers. Messrs. Hewlett and Cowham had apparently made small progress with their inquiries, and Cynthia was beginning to exult openly and assume that Joan's inheritance was assured.

Downstairs in the drawing-room Warchester was watching the door with eager eyes, and the momentary shadow that darkened them as Cynthia entered alone did not escape that lady's keen eyes. He had been a very constant visitor since Joan's coming. Cynthia could only guess how often her guest had encountered him in the course of her daily walks and drives.

"What perfectly lovely flowers, Lord Warchester! How good of you to bring them! Joan has just come home soaked. She will be down directly. What is this—a telegram for me, Barstow? She hurriedly tore open the orange-coloured envelope. A clue at last!" she cried. "'Hope to be with you to-morrow morning with particulars—Francis Hurst.'"

She crumpled up the telegram into a ball and threw it with vicious energy into the fire.

"Do you know what that means, Lord Warchester? It means that they think they have found this wretched Evelyn and that Joan will lose her inheritance. I wonder whether Mr. Hurst expects me to be pleased?"

Warchester smiled as he looked down at her crimsoning face.

"I do not know. But I wonder whether I shall incur your lasting displeasure, Mrs. Trewhistle, if I tell you that *I* am pleased?"

"You?" Cynthia looked at him incredulously. "I thought you, liked Joan—that you were her friend?"

"Perhaps it is for that reason that I am glad," Warchester responded. There was an unusual light in his grey eyes as they met Cynthia's. "I think you must have seen how it is with me, Mrs. Trewhistle—how it has been from the first. I—I dare say I am very selfish, but I want to give Joan all the good things of life myself."

There was a pause; then Cynthia caught her breath.

"I—I think Joan is a very lucky girl," she said impulsively, holding put her hand. "You have my good wishes, Lord Warchester."

"Thank you!" he said, as he took the little hand, glittering with rings, in his. "You will stand my friend, Mrs. Trewhistle?"

"Certainly!" Cynthia said heartily. "And, to prove that, I am going to send a return telegram to Mr. Hurst now. Joan will entertain you until I come back," with a mischievous laugh as she rose. "Oh, Lord Warchester," turning back at the door, "is your cousin Basil at the Marsh now? Reggie heard that he came last night, and that he had been ill and had to bring home an attendant with him! I hope it is not true."

Warchester turned abruptly to the window.

"I did not know he had arrived at the Marsh, though I had heard that he was expected shortly. But he had a bad accident—was seriously injured some years ago, and has never wholly recovered."

"I am sorry," Cynthia said regretfully. "He used be so jolly in the old days. And how handsome he was!" Joan came into the room a few minutes later. Her black chiffon gown had been a present from Cynthia; it had been made by that lady's dressmaker, and though of unusually plain cut its severe lines suited her slim figure perfectly. Her hair was dressed very simply, parted in front and waved to the back, where it was gathered in a great coil.

She looked a little surprised to find Warchester alone as he came forward to meet her.

"Mrs. Trewhistle has been called away to answer a telegram," he explained. "I hear you have been caught in the storm, Miss Joan."

As she sank into one of the big easy-chairs he moved to the fireplace, and toyed with one of the ivory ornaments on the shelf.

Some of his obvious unrest seemed to communicate itself to Joan; her colour deepened.

"The storm did not matter," she answered. "I enjoyed it really, and see—I was rewarded by finding these violets—they were beneath the Home Wood hedge." She touched the tiny bunch of violets tucked in the front of her gown.

There was silence. When Warchester spoke again, the intensity of his feeling made his voice sound broken, almost harsh.

"I wonder whether you would think me incredibly greedy if I asked you for the violets?"

"Why, no!" Joan laughed as she held them out. "After the lovely flowers you sent us, Lord Warchester, you are certainly welcome to these."

Warchester caught them and the hand together.

"It is not only the violets—I want this too. Is there any hope for me, Joan? Is it possible you could ever learn to care for me?"

For a moment Join sat motionless; the man before her waited silently. Then she raised her beautiful eyes.

"I think perhaps—" she said, slowly. "Ah, I—I—did you not know—did you not guess?"

Warchester, raising her to her feet, held her before him.

"Know what?" he asked.

Joan's eyes were veiled by their long lashes; the rich, warm colour flooded cheeks and throat and temples.

"I never had anybody to care for me much until—" She paused. "But when you came everything seemed changed. Oh, I know Cynthia and Reggie like me—they have been very good to me—but they have each other! This—this seems—different!"

"Different! I should think it is different!" Warchester's grey eyes were full of triumph as he listened to the halting sentences. "There is all the difference in the world, Joan, my beautiful Joan! Tell me that this is real—that you will give your life to me."

"Oh, yes, it is real!" Joan said with trembling lips. "If—if you want it," she added with a laugh that was half a sob. "But you know, Lord Warchester, that they think they will find Evelyn—that my father—that I may bring a host of undesirable relatives upon you."

"I am not afraid," Warchester declared, the gladness in his eyes growing and strengthening. "Give me yourself, Joan—the rest does not count."

"Does it not?" Joan whispered as for one brief instant she yielded herself to his embrace, his arms closed round her she felt his lips softly touching her bright hair, lingering caressingly on her cheek. Then the sound of a step in the hall made her release herself hurriedly.

"Well, Lord Warchester, you will certainly have to stay to dinner," Cynthia remarked cheerfully. "The storm is coming on worse than ever. Barstow says it is fit for neither man nor beast to be out to-night. I do not know in which category he would place you. O–h!" with an expression of the fullest comprehension as she met his gaze. "You—you don't mean—"

"That Joan has consented to make me the happiest of men," Warchester finished quietly. "Congratulate me, dear Mrs. Trewhistle!"

"I do indeed, most sincerely!" Cynthia cried warmly, while Joan fled from the room. "She is a dear girl," Mrs. Trewhistle went on. "And who should know better than I? I have always been fond of Joan. Reggie will be pleased. And she will always be near us, even if Evelyn does come back."

"You are very good to me, and you will give her to me soon. You will not grudge me my happiness. I have been lonely so long."

As Warchester stood before her, the thought struck Cynthia that happiness was certainly becoming to him. It seemed to her that he looked years younger; the tired lines round his eyes seemed to have vanished as if by magic; there was a buoyancy about his whole bearing that brought back to her very vividly the Paul Wilton she had known before her marriage.

She smiled gaily.

"Ah, that will be for Joan to decide—not me!"

"But you will be on my side?" Warchester asked anxiously.

"Of course I am on your side," she said, "though I shall be the loser. But then I always am unselfish."

"Thank you!" Warchester's eyes wandered past her to a photograph off Joan framed in silver that stood on the table behind Cynthia had placed it there that morning. "Surely that is—Joan? May I have it, Mrs. Trewhistle?"

"Well, as the original is to be yours, l suppose I cannot refuse you," Cynthia said placidly. "But I don't care much for that myself. You will find better ones in the album over there. Choose one while I am away, Lord Warchester. I must go to Joan. But don't be afraid—I will send her, to you presently."

She laughed at his expression as she went into the hall. She found Joan in her own room, ensconced in her favourite chair; she looked up as her cousin entered.

"Oh, Cynthia!"

"Oh, Joan!" Mrs. Trewhistle mocked. "Don't you think you are very cruel to somebody to run away like this? I am so glad, dear," dropping her tone of raillery and kissing the girl affectionately. "Now it does not matter a bit if they do find their tiresome Evelyn. You will be Lady Warchester, and you can snap your fingers at them." She pirouetted round, delightedly. "You will have to go back to Lord Warchester, though, Joan. I promised to send you. He—I think you will find him a masterful lover."

Joan smiled happily. She was confident of her own power over Warchester, and not without reason, but in this matter her own heart was a traitor in the camp, and Cynthia's prognostications were soon verified.

Warchester proved the most, imperious of wooers; all Joan's pretty hesitation went for nothing with him. Day after day he pleaded—insisted on an early marriage, until at length he won the day and gained Joan's consent.

As he truly urged, there was nothing to wait for. Joan's mourning need not interfere with a quiet wedding; the uncertainty as to whether she succeeded to Davenant Hall would matter the less when she was Lady Warchester.

So it came to pass that the neighbourhood, which had by no means got over its first amazement on hearing that Mrs. Davenant had left Davenant Hall to an unknown granddaughter, was astonished to hear that the dispossessed Joan was engaged to the new Lord Warchester, and that the marriage was to take place immediately.

The tidings of Evelyn turned out to be much less definite than Mr. Hurst had expected. The promised clue seemed to lead to nothing tangible, and when Joan and her husband went off for their honeymoon the affair of the Davenant inheritance was as far from settlement as ever.

Chapter Seven

"COME and see what you think of the Dutch garden, Joan."

Warchester was standing at the open window of his wife's morning-room. Joan was sitting at her dainty little escritoire, writing notes. All the vigorous vitality that had been temporarily overshadowed by the shock of Mrs Davenant's death had asserted itself once more, and marriage had increased her comeliness. She looked indeed a wife of whom any man might be proud, as she smiled a welcome across the room, and Warchester's eyes took an added tenderness as he gazed at her. She had discarded her mourning, in so far as she was wearing a white gown with no touch of colour save a bunch of purple heartsease at her throat. Her hair was dressed as Warchester best liked to see it—waved low in front so as to form a frame for the charming oval of her face, and gathered up behind in a mass of curls. She wore no jewellery; the soft transparency of her gown fell away from her rounded arms dimpled at elbows and wrists, and her slender throat rose from a foamy mass of lace.

There had not been time while they were away for the completion of all the improvements at the Towers that Warchester had contemplated. Many of them were scarcely begun. All Joan's rooms, however, were in perfect order; on that point his instructions had been explicit and an army of workmen had been employed.

The morning-room particularly had been his especial care, and he had felt amply repaid when he heard Joan's exclamation of delight.

The walls were painted in the faintest shade of dull grey, with exquisite water-colours let in as panels; the carpet was of the same shade of grey pile, with a tiny pattern of rosebuds forming a border; the furniture was upholstered in white plush; the writing-table of ormolu had once occupied a recess in the Trianon. The bookcase at Joan's elbow held most of the world's classics in éditions de luxe; the great chesterfield near the fireplace was piled with white velvet cushions, painted with palest mauve or glittering with costly Eastern embroidery; and everywhere, on the escritoire, on the Chippendale tables, on the Brackets before the Sèvres mirror, there stood great silver bowls of roses—pink, fragrant La France, big glowing damask Prince of Asturias, tawny, copper-coloured William Allen Richardson.

If Joan, in her heart of hearts, was a little afraid of her beautiful room, and secretly preferred a cosy little den at the end of the corridor where her bedroom lay, she allowed no hint of it to appear.

She rose as her husband spoke.

"Of course I will come! The Dutch garden is going to be a success, Paul."

"I think it is," he acquiesced. "It is just the touch of colour that one needs coming on to the terrace from the gloom of the pinetum, and those stiffly-shaped beds filled with brilliant-hued flowers will look from above like jewels glowing in the grass beneath. It was a capital idea of yours."

"Of mine!" Joan laughed as she stepped out on to the terrace and put her arm within his. "Mine was the merest suggestion; it is you who have carried out everything."

They walked across the lawn together. The sun was beginning to sink below the horizon, and the last rays fell upon Joan, touching her hair with gold.

The terrace lay on the other side of the lawn on the western front of the house. The grass at the Towers was the especial pride of MacDonald the old gardener's heart; soft with the growth of centuries, it was kept as smooth as a carpet. Great beeches shielded this lawn from sight of the avenue, and it was dotted about with big clumps of rhododendrons. From the terrace there was a view of the distant Derbyshire hills; flowering plants, fuchsia, honeysuckle, ampelopsis, sweet-scented hydrangea, climbed the grey old wall; and immediately beneath there lay a level stretch of grass that had been in olden times the bowling-green. It was here that Warchester was planning his Dutch garden. He and Joan lingered on the terrace, while he explained the whole scheme anew. There was to be a fountain in the centre; on either side the oblongs and triangles that were being cut were to be filled with the most gorgeously-coloured flowers—brilliant-hued geraniums, begonias, lobelias, petunias and calceolarias; lower down, beyond the ha-ha which formed the boundary opposite, he was thinking of making a rosery.

Joan listened and approved. It was very sweet to the girl who had been slighted all her life to be first now with one person, to find her every whim gratified, her slightest wish law. Sometimes she would rub her eyes, would tell herself that it must be a dream that she was Lady Warchester, that presently she would awaken to find herself little unconsidered Joan Davenant once more. Her engagement had been so short, Warchester had so hurried the marriage, that it seemed almost impossible that it could be an accomplished reality.

The honeymoon had been comparatively brief. It had been spent on board Warchester's yacht, wandering from port to port, just as fancy led them. Joan had bought all sorts of beautiful things, it seemed to her that she had spent a fortune, while Warchester had only laughed and encouraged her.

It was Joan's first experience of being spoilt, and she found the process very pleasant; nor was her homecoming a disillusionment. The neighbourhood received her with open arms—for was she not young and beautiful, the wife of the principal landowner in the county, and the heiress of the Davenants to boot? It was the general belief that Evelyn would not be found, and that the Davenant possessions would pass to Lady Warchester,

It was a marvellous change for Joan, from being Mrs. Davenant's unloved granddaughter. Unlimited money to spend, a worshipping husband, crowds of admiring friends—no wonder the girl stood in some danger of having her head turned! Warchester was drawing her to the steps that led from the terrace to the garden below when a man came across the lawn towards him.

"Mr. Knight is in the library, my lord."

"Knight!" Warchester frowned. Knight was his farm steward; his business was wont to be of a lengthy nature. "Did he say what he wanted?"

"I understood him to say that he came by your lordship's appointment." The man hesitated.

"My appointment?" Warchester said; then his face cleared. "Of course; I was forgetting. Say I will be with him in a minute, James. I must just speak to Knight, Joan," as the footman departed. "It is about some improvements Warren wants. I will get rid of him as soon as I can. Will you come with me?"

"I don't know a bit about farm improvements, and it is lovely out here. I will wait until you come back. Be as quick as you can, Paul."

"I won't be away from you an unnecessary moment," he promised her.

Left alone, Joan watched, his tall, well-knit figure back to the house, then turned to look at the men at work in the garden below. Truly her lines had fallen in pleasant places, she reflected as she idly plucked a Gloire de Dijon that was nodding at her over the wall, and inhaled its fragrance. Who, knowing her history, would have prophesied that such happiness would fall to her share? Then, as a natural sequence, her thoughts turned to Evelyn, the other child of her mother's disastrous marriage. Her life had been very different, yet for her too there would be a good time now, if she lived to enjoy it.

Joan asked herself afresh what could have become of Evie. There seemed to her something unaccountable in her long silence, in the fact that so far the detectives had utterly failed to trace her. It had been assumed by Messrs. Hewlett and Cowham that Evie had grudged her sister's good fortune, the home that had been offered to her at Davenant Hall but, looking back at the love and care Evie had bestowed upon her, Joan found it difficult to give credence to this hypothesis.

It was quite feasible that Evie had married and gone abroad, where none of Mr. Hurst's advertisements had reached her, that her letters, falling into Mr. Spencer's hands, had been lost. It might even be that she was dead, but Joan found it impossible to believe that she could be jealous of or spiteful towards her little sister. That would not be like Evie.

Joan shrank from the thought of her sister's death. She looked round. Warchester had been away longer than she thought. The gardeners were leaving off work; the horizon was overclouded. She felt suddenly cold in her thin dress.

As she stepped on the broad gravel walk that wound round the house she saw Mr. Knight walking down the avenue. Paul had forgotten his promise to come back to her as soon as possible, she said to herself. She would go and remind him of his broken word and administer a scolding.

The small library, so called, in which Warchester transacted most of his business, opened level with the morning-room, having only the library proper between.

Joan ran lightly along. The windows stood open, and as she came up she saw that, as she had surmised, Warchester was alone. His back was towards her; he was bending over his writing-table, tearing up some papers. As she stood on the threshold he turned, threw the torn papers into the empty fireplace, and then, catching up something from the mantelpiece, tore that up too, and tossed it after the others. Then he stepped quickly back to his table and took up his blotting-book.

Joan watched him, struck anew with the sense of familiarity that had haunted her when they first met. At length he threw the book on the table, and, straightening himself and partly turning so that he stood with his side face towards her, he took up one of her photographs that, framed in silver, stood on the little shelf of the escritoire. The light caught the great ruby in his ring. Then, as she waited, memory rushed over Joan like an overwhelming flood. A curious, bewildering sense of having watched like this before gave way to a fearful certainty the nightmare that had haunted her childhood took shape before her.

She saw herself, a lonely, terrified child, peeping in at a window, held to the spot by fright, watching a man in a grey suit like Paul's, with a bunch of violets in his buttonhole, tearing up photographs, throwing them into the fire, bending over a lifeless form on the rug. She heard herself again give that sob of horror —met for an instant those eyes.

Were they Paul's eyes? Was that why she had always felt that somehow—somewhere she and Paul had looked at one another before?

The horror of the thought drove the colour from her cheeks, threatened to stop the beating of her heart. Her knees felt weak; she swayed uncertainly. It seemed to be growing dark around her. She put up her hands and clutched at the lace at her throat.

Warchester turned to the window.

"Why, Joan, my darling!" he cried in joyful surprise. "Come in! Were you tired of waiting? Knight kept me longer than I expected, and he brought me bad news. Baron has given notice, and he is the oldest tenant on the estate. I was annoyed. Forgive me."

Joan stared at him miserably, her lips parted dumbly. They were the same eyes that had gazed at her across the dead girl—over the window-sill, she told herself—that were looking at her now with love and longing. A low sob came from her lips. She had the old wild instinct of flight to get away anywhere, anyhow from this horror that was possessing her. But the darkness seemed to swallow her up; her feet, numbed by fear, refused to do her bidding.

"Joan, my dear," said Warchester, coming towards her, "what is the matter? You are ill—faint!"

The horror in the girl's eyes deepened as he tried to take her in his arms.

She backed on to the grass behind, putting out her hands, as if to keep him off. But a thick darkness was rising and overwhelming her, blotting out Warchester's face; there was a strange, unaccustomed ringing in her ears; she felt as if a grey mist was closing about her and stifling her; she was conscious only of slipping down, down into dark, formless space.

Chapter Eight

"Would it be possible for me to see some back numbers of the *Daily Reporter*?" Joan inquired timidly.

"Fill up this form, and the attendant will bring them to you. Will you take a seat over there?"

Joan looked round nervously as she took a seat at one of the slanting tables and waited. It seemed to her that she was doing a very extraordinary thing, but the matter-of-fact manner of the clerk at the desk reassured her. He, at any rate, saw nothing uncommon in her wish to read a file of old newspapers.

The attendant brought a pile of papers and laid them before her.

Joan looked at them absently for a moment. This visit to the British Museum was the outcome of a miserably sleepless night.

Throughout its long hours she had lain tossing restlessly racked by an agony of doubt. She had lived over again that terrible indelible experience of her childhood; again and again she had told herself that it was impossible that there could be any real resemblance between Warchester, the husband she loved with every fibre of her being, and the stranger she had seen in that room looking on to the roofs.

And then the dreadful remembrance of that moment when their eyes had met would rush over her, and she would clench her hands together in an agony, remembering how from the first she had felt that vague sense of familiarity.

She sat up in bed, both hands pressed to her forehead, trying to remember the smallest detail, and in a moment a new idea flashed into her mind. If she had made no mistake, if what she had seen had really taken place, there must have been some account of it in the papers—it must have attracted attention. But ten years ago—it

would not be easy to make inquiries now; and then she recalled
some words of Warchester's with regard to some fact he had wished
to ascertain—"I shall have to go to the Museum when I am in town
and look up a file of the *Times*."

Joan had asked questions, had heard that if one wanted to see
back numbers of the papers one must go to the Museum.

It was quite simple really. She determined to go up to town and
ascertain.

Rising early, she caught the first train, despite her maid's
horrified remonstrances.

When Warchester came in to breakfast from his early morning
walk round the home farm he would find her gone; she scarcely
dared to think what he would say.

In the British Museum, however, the affair was more easily
arranged than she had expected.

Her hand trembled as she turned over the papers. She knew the
date of her coming to Davenant —the 12th of May; it was the day
before she had climbed on the roofs, therefore the 12th would be
the date of the paper she wanted.

She unfolded it slowly, "Murder in Grove Street." She could
scarcely believe her eyes were not playing her false now. As she bent
over the paper her heart seemed to stop beating, then to go on in
great suffocating throbs. Presently the mist before her eyes cleared,
the letters ceased to dance up and down, and grouped themselves
into words:

> At eight o'clock last night a terrible discovery was made
> at No. 18 Grove Street. Three rooms on the second floor of
> the house are occupied by an artist named Wingrove. The
> house is divided into flats, each of which incomplete in itself.
> Mr. Wingrove's flat comprised a sitting-room at the front,
> a studio behind at the back of the house, and a bedroom
> parallel with the sitting-room. It was Mr. Wingrove's custom
> when he was at his studio to have supper served at eight

o'clock by the man in charge of the house, who undertook to provide meals for any of the residents who desired it.

This man, John Perks, had not seen Mr. Wingrove in the afternoon, but he took up supper at the usual time. It was eight o'clock precisely when he went up. The door of the studio was slightly ajar, which rather surprised Perks, as it was contrary to Mr. Wingrove's usual habit. He pushed it open and went in. Mr. Wingrove was not there; at first sight Perks thought the room was untenanted, but as he put the tray on the table he saw, as he thought, a young woman asleep on the hearthrug. Glancing at her more closely, he noticed that there were dark stains on her white gown. Horror-struck, he bent over her for a moment, realised that it was unmistakably a corpse at which he was gazing, and rushed from the room, calling for help.

Dr. Harrison, of Upper Cavendish Street, was soon on the scene, and gave it as his opinion that the unfortunate woman had been dead for two hours at least. It was at first thought to be a case of suicide, as the girl had been shot through the heart, and the pistol, since identified as Wingrove's, from which the fatal shot was fired, was lying on the ground close to her right hand; but Mr. Harrison stated that, from the direction the bullet had taken, it was impossible the injury could have been self-inflicted. There is so far no information as to the identity of the victim, who seems to have been a remarkably good-looking young woman of not more than four or five and twenty. She wore a white gown, with no jewellery, but a wedding-ring was found attached to a thin gold chain round her neck beneath her dress. All her garments were unmarked, and evidently home-made. The Caretaker identified her as a lady who had on several occasions come home with Mr. Wingrove to supper, but he had no knowledge of her name or position. Wingrove himself was not in the flat and at the time of going to press no information as to his whereabouts could be obtained.

Joan read the account to the end. She was very pale; there were faint purple shadows beneath her eyes, new lines of pain round her mouth.

As she laid down the pager she sat back in her chair and looked straight before her for a minute. There were few people in the room; all of them were far too intent upon their own business to look at Joan, but later the girl herself could always recall the aspect of the room, the bent white head of the old man by the window, the shabby hat of the woman near her.

So it was true, she said to herself drearily: that scene in the studio into which she could see from the roofs was no figment of a disordered imagination. That motionless form on the rug had been a young girl, only a few years older than Joan herself was now, who had been foully done to death. The man whom Joan had seen moving about the room, burning photographs, placing the pistol in the dead girl's hand, was, there could be no doubt of it, the murderer, trying to conceal his work. But who was he? That was the question that had driven the colour from Joan's cheeks, that had beaten upon her brain with maddening reiteration throughout the long past night. To this the paper, as Joan read it, offered no answer.

Hastily she caught up the next day's edition. Surely there would be something more. Yes, there were two columns devoted to the Grove Street murder—evidently it had loomed somewhat large in the public imagination—but there was little further information. The inquest had been opened, the doctor's evidence, proving incontestably that the victim had not committed suicide, was taken, but no evidence of her identity was forthcoming, and the artist Wingrove did not appear.

Evidence was given as to the state in which the room was found. Many of Wingrove's personal effects were missing; apparently a quantity of papers and a number of photographs had been burned in the grate. It was curious to notice how suspicion centred round the missing man, strange to watch its growth in the terms in which he was mentioned. In the first edition he was spoken of as Mr. Wingrove, the artist; later on he became the missing man. At a further, stage Joan read, "There is still no trace of Wingrove; it is thought that he may have made his way to one of the ports, and thence out of the country." There was a lengthy account of the inquest, which had been adjourned time after time in the hope that there might be some news of Wingrove; but as far as Joan could see there had been nothing to throw any further light upon the tragedy.

At an early stage of the proceedings there seemed to have been some little suspicion of the caretaker. He was subjected to a rigid examination and called upon to account for his movements at the time of the murder, but apparently he cleared himself, for thenceforward the search for Wingrove went on with renewed vigour. There were two curious circumstances that Joan noted—first, that when the girl had been moved, there fell out from her skirts a common tobacco-pouch worked with a circlet of flowers that had once been gaudy, but was now dirty; secondly, a man's malacca cane, silver-mounted, was found in a corner by the door. Neither of these articles, the caretaker testified in the most positive manner, had belonged to Wingrove. Finally, the verdict had been, "Wilful murder against some person or persons unknown." There was a description of Wingrove. Joan read it eagerly: "Above the average height, dark-complexioned, brown beard and moustache, light eyes. When last seen was wearing a dark grey suit and a panama hat."

There was a leading article on the murder after the inquest, deploring the inefficiency of our police system in the usual ponderous style, advocating the use of bloodhounds in every case directly a crime was discovered, pointing out that young women who allowed themselves to be led into a clandestine friendship, to pay clandestine visits to men such as Wingrove, exposed themselves to serious danger.

Then two days later the paper gave prominence to the headline "Sensational discovery in the Grove Street Mystery."

Wingrove's studio coat had been examined, and the pockets had been found to be empty, but later on one of the detectives engaged on the case had felt a piece of paper in the lining. It proved to be a note or part of a note, for it had been torn across and the upper portion was missing. What could be read was: "Be with you not later than four on Monday. Everything is ready. It seems to me that there can be nothing further to wait for. From your own Queenie."

Apparently it was presumed that it was written to Wingrove by the murdered girl, but, beyond establishing the fact that her presence in the studio—if she were indeed the writer—was not an accident, it in no way helped to clear up the various points that were puzzling the detectives. The girl's identity, Wingrove's personality, his present whereabouts, the mystery surrounding them remained as impenetrable as ever.

Joan went on with the examination. The allusions to the Grove Street murder grew less frequent; there were rumours of trouble in the Far East; a General Election was impending. The papers had no more space to waste over the unknown girl who had been done to death in Grove Street.

Joan laid the papers together arid stood up. Her limbs felt cramped and stiff as she moved to the door; she had spent longer than she thought on that hard, uncomfortable chair. She felt giddy. After all, what had she learned? That that horror of her childhood was a ghastly reality certainly, but the question that had tormented her through the long hours of the night remained unanswered.

She left the Museum and walked through the quiet old Bloomsbury streets and squares, asking herself again whether it was possible that she should recognize a man whom she had only seen for a few brief seconds, under such different conditions, ten years ago. She knew that in other circumstances she would not have been inclined to place reliance on such a recognition, but in her own case the whole scene had been so imprinted upon her memory that she fancied she could recall it precisely as it happened, correct in every detail. Even the grey eyes of the man who had looked at her for a moment over the window-sill—were they the same eyes that had met hers last night in the library at the Towers? She shivered as she drew her veil more closely over her face. As she neared the noise and bustle of Oxford Street she paused, regardless of the passers-by. It was ten years since the tragedy occurred; in all those years was it not possible—nay, was it not most probable—that something had been discovered, that the murderer had been arrested even if for the time he had managed to evade justice?

She went; on again, walking with quick, uneven steps, turning along Oxford Street to the right, heedless alike of the tempting display in the shop windows, of the jostling of the passers-by.

At Tottenham Court Road she had perforce to wait while a great stream of traffic passed her. On the other side of the street there was a motor-bus waiting. Seeing her glance the conductor vociferated loudly, "Bond Street, Marble Arch, Queen's Road." The words recalled a thousand memories. Grove Street lay not far from the Marble Arch at the back of Hinton Square. She had a fancy that if she got out at Marble Arch she could find her way to the Grove Street Mews just as she had done in her childish days. Mechanically she threaded her way across the street and seated herself in the omnibus.

Chapter Nine

"MARBLE Arch!" Joan alighted from the omnibus in amazement.

Modern improvements had altered the Marble Arch she remembered almost out of recognition. She made her way across to Edgware Road, and took the turning down Connaught Street that led to the quieter squares that lay behind, parallel with Bayswater Road.

It all looked exactly the same here; she had fancied the squares larger, the streets wider, that was all. In her childish days every step of the way she was taking now had been familiar to her.

Mrs. Spencer, never unduly nervous with regard to the perils of the London Streets, had been wont to send little Polly across to Praed Street or Edgware Road half a dozen times a day on errands.

Joan found her way to the Mews without difficulty. A couple of stablemen stood in the archway; farther down a group of children were playing. It all seemed so familiar that Joan involuntarily rubbed her eyes. Surely the last ten years had been a dream. She would wake to find herself little Polly Spencer again, with fat baby Tim to carry about and look after, and one of these men would probably be Gregory. But both the red faces were strange to her.

"Can you tell me whether John Spencer, Sir Robert Brunton's coachman, lives down here?" she asked. It was an idle question: her father had never kept his situations for any length of time.

One of the men shook his head.

"No, miss, I have never heard the name. There is nobody in Sir Robert Brunton's employ down here now."

"Thank you!"

Joan had no further excuse for lingering. She glanced down the Mews; there was the house that had been her father's—they might have been the self-same boxes of mignonette and scarlet geranium in the windows; behind she caught a glimpse of the loft whence she had climbed on the leads. She turned away with a shiver.

Grove Street itself was unmistakably dingier than she remembered it. Probably the murder at No. 18 had dragged it considerably lower in the social scale.

Almost without realising where her steps were taking her, she went on up the street. No. 18 looked just like its neighbours, neither better nor worse. There were the same drab-coloured curtains in every window. Joan's eyes strayed fearfully to the second floor. Then for the second time that day she acted on an impulse that seemed to come from without, to be altogether independent of her own will. She stepped forward and rang the bell.

It, was answered immediately by a stout woman of middle age, who had the appearance, of a respectable lodging-house-keeper. She looked at Joan with surprise.

""I heard—that is, I thought you might have rooms to let."

"We have one set vacant, miss, but they are at the top of the house. I don't know whether they would suit a young lady."

"Perhaps I might look at them," Joan suggested timidly.

"Oh, certainly, miss! Come this way, please." She preceded Joan up the stairs. "There really ought to be a lift, I always say," she volunteered. "But still when you are used to it, the stairs are not so bad."

Joan glanced towards the room on the second floor, but the door was closed.

The rooms at the top certainly justified the woman's doubts—they were small and dingy. From the windows there was a good view of the neighbouring chimney-pots. With a cursory glance at them Joan turned away and slipped a shilling into the woman's hand.

"They would not do, thank you!"

"No, miss—thank you, miss! I was afraid they would not be suitable. Not but what I should be pleased to do my best to make a young lady like yourself comfortable."

"You are very kind." Joan turned to the stairs. As she reached the second floor she paused. "I wonder whether I might just look inside those rooms? I—I have heard of them."

The woman glanced at her suspiciously.

"We do not show them, madam. They are let to Mr. Cohen."

"I should be very glad if you could manage it." Joan was holding her purse in her hand—there was a chink of money. "I used to live near, and remember hearing—"

She hesitated. The woman glanced covetously at the gleam of gold.

"Well, just for a moment, miss, as Mr. Cohen is out, though I do not know that I ought. But perhaps you have been told something of what happened there."

"Yes—yes—at least I told you I have heard. My people were living near then," Joan said incoherently as the woman opened the door and she stepped forward.

The aspect of the room was entirely altered. All the artistic disorder had given place to an array of books and desks; it had now the appearance of a business man's office.

There was a square of Axminster carpet before the fire-place. Joan's brain quickly conjured up the black, woolly rug, the still form that had lain across it. Her eyes wandered to the window. It was there she had stood, her curly head on a level with the first pane, her eyes just peeping in. There was a door in the recess between the fireplace and the window. With a momentary return of the horrible nausea that had overwhelmed her the previous evening, she remembered how it had opened—she knew that somebody must have been watching the murderer at work. What—who would he have seen if he had looked behind in that other room?

She pointed to the door.

"Where does that lead?"

The woman watched her white face inquisitively; evidently there was more here than met the eye.

"That's the door into Mr. Cohen's bedroom." She walked over and threw it open. "See!"

It was a fairly large, commodious room. Joan noted that a door on the opposite side opened on to the landing, so that anybody might have come in from there, crossed the room softly, and, finding that door into the studio ajar, have pushed it open and watched. Who had that unseen witness been, and why had he or she kept silence?

She walked back and put of the room quickly. Downstairs, in the vestibule, the pallor of her face was noticeable. The woman of the house hesitated a moment. In some curious fashion her face seemed to have caught the pallor of Joan's.

"You look fair tired—worn out, miss," she said tentatively, her eyes watching the girl's face from beneath their down-dropped lids. "If you would care to come in and rest in my room, I could get you a cup of tea or anything; and any of the lodgers would tell you that Mrs. Perks knows how to make them comfortable."

Joan had had nothing to eat since early that morning. So entirely had her supposed recognition of Warchester the previous evening possessed her, that she had lost desire for food; but now her healthy young appetite was reasserting itself, and she became conscious that there was something very attractive in Mrs. Perks' suggestion. Besides, it would give her an opportunity of putting the questions she was longing to ask.

"Thank you very much!" she answered as Mrs. Perks opened the door and disclosed a comfortable-looking sitting-room.

Mrs. Perks pulled forward the one easy-chair the apartment boasted.

"If you will take a seat, miss, I'll soon make a cup of tea, and there's a wing of cold chicken, or I could get you a chop."

"Oh, the chicken, please! You are very good. I believe I really am hungry!" Joan said with a little laugh. "I have been walking about a good deal."

She had thrown off her hat and Mrs. Perks, as she moved backwards and forwards over her preparations for the meal, cast a good many furtive glances at her.

"It is tiring walking about looking for rooms," she said. "But you know this neighbourhood, I think you said, miss?"

"Yes. At one time we lived behind there," Joan answered pointing in the direction of the Mews.

"Yes, those Hinton Square houses are very large!" was Mrs. Perks' comment, and Joan did not think it worthwhile to undeceive her. "Did you say you were there when we had that sad affair here, Miss? You must have been only a child then?"

"I was quite a child," Joan replied as Mrs. Perks poured out a cup of tea and set it before her, still watching her in a suspicious fashion, "but I never forgot it."

"Bless you, no, miss! One does not easy forget a thing like that, child or no child!" Mrs. Perks shuddered as she carved the chicken, and cut some thin slices of bread and butter. "I am sure it is a thing I shall never forget to my dying day myself!"

"Were you here at the time?" Joan asked. Already the warm fragrant tea was bringing a tinge of colour to her pale cheeks.

"There, miss, now, I am sure a bite will do you good!" Mrs. Perks placed the chicken before her. "Yes, indeed I was here at the time! Many is the time I have wished I wasn't, for it was poor Perks that found her, and on account of that they asked all sorts of questions at the inquest that might have done him no end of harm if the owners had not known him and trusted him, having had the best of characters with him."

"You knew Wingrove?" Joan ventured as the woman paused for breath.

"Knew Mr. Wingrove!" Mrs. Perks pursed her lips. "I should think I did, ma'am! He had been here a month when it happened, and though I didn't see so much of the lodgers when poor Perks was alive, still I'd often had a word with Mr. Wingrove."

"Do you know what became of him?" Joan's voice trembled as she asked the question.

Mrs. Perks lifted up her hands.

"We never heard a word of him from that day to this, miss. Nor the police never found any trace, search as they would. Me and Perks often used to say it seemed as if he had vanished from the world."

"But you think it was he who murdered the poor girl?" Joan questioned doubtfully.

Mrs. Perks shook her head. She looked white and scared.

"That isn't for me to say, miss. But she had come to see him two or three times. I had seen her, so had Perks, and the last time she come I know they had words. Who else could it have been? That is what me and Perks always said. Folks always thought the verdict would have been against him at the inquest, only nobody really saw him come here that day at all."

"But how could the girl who was murdered get in if Mr. Wingrove was away?" inquired Joan. "Did he leave the door unfastened?"

"No, miss. But that poor young thing, she had a key that would let her into Mr. Wingrove's rooms. I found it myself in her pocket when the police were there."

"Oh!" Joan drew a long breath. "Was she Mr. Wingrove's wife, do you think, Mrs. Perks?"

"I couldn't say, miss, I'm sure. They seemed to know one another very well. I couldn't say more than that."

There was one question that Joan was longing to put; she felt her heartbeat faster:

"What—what was he like?"

"Well, miss, he was a big tall figure of a man, with a pair of grey eyes that always seemed to have a smile in them, and brown, curly hair and a short, crisp beard, and he always had a laugh and a word for everybody."

"Oh!" Joan paused. The description was certainly that of the man she had seen, as far as outward appearances went; allowing for the passage of time, it seemed to her that it would apply equally well to Warchester. And yet there was a certain reserve about Warchester. The very fact that he did not get on with everybody had been in his favour in Joan's eyes; it had added a touch of subtle flattery to the marked preference he had shown for her society from the first. She could not imagine him with a laugh and a word for every one. Insensibly her heart lightened; her supposed recognition of Warchester must have been imaginary; a chance likeness must have misled her.

Mrs. Perks cast a quick look at her.

"You take quite an interest in Mr. Wingrove, miss. Maybe you have come across him?"

Something in the tone grated on Joan; she drew up her head.

"That is scarcely likely, I think."

"Well, miss, it would not surprise me. Me and Perks always knew Mr. Wingrove was a real gentleman. Once I saw a little crown—a coronet they call it—on one of his handkerchiefs, and I've always had it in my mind that he come of a high family."

"But in that case surely he would have spoken. I—I don't think he would have run away!" Joan said impulsively.

"Well, miss, there is wheels within wheels," Mrs. Perks said oracularly. "Maybe he will come forward again when he can prove as he was not the murderer. My husband told me one day that he made sure he saw Mr. Wingrove driving down Regent Street in a carriage with another gentleman."

"What?" Joan put on her hat with a trembling hand and went over to the little glass in the overmantel to adjust it. "How long ago was this? I think your husband must have been mistaken. Surely he—Mr. Wingrove—would not come to London?"

"That's what I say, miss. But poor Perks, he would have his way. It would be about a month before he was took. 'Twas Mr. Wingrove, sure enough,' he said, 'though he was looking older and his beard was shaved off, but I should know him among a thousand!' Men are always like that if they get a notion in their heads—obstinate isn't the word for them."

"I think he must have been mistaken," Joan said steadily as she laid some silver on the table. "Thank you very much for the lunch, Mrs. Perks; it has done me good."

"I am sure I hope you will soon find something to suit you, thanking you kindly, miss!" Mrs. Perks responded, her eyes wandering restlessly from her young visitor's face to the rings on her hand. "If you don't meet with anything else there is a Mrs. Gower, 28 Ladbroke Crescent, I'm sure would be pleased to give you every satisfaction, and, being a bit farther out, would do it very reasonable."

"Thank you very much; I will think of it!" Joan said eagerly. "Good afternoon, Mrs. Perks! It was very good of you to give me lunch."

"Not at all, miss!"

Mrs. Perks accompanied her to the door. Her face had resumed its ruddy hue now, but her eyes looked troubled. She watched

Joan's departing figure to the end of the street; then she turned back with a deep sigh.

"What does that mean?" she murmured. "It—it can't be that it is going to be opened up again? And did she think I shouldn't notice—shouldn't see—"

Chapter Ten

"WARCHESTER wants to come up, Joan." Mrs. Trewhistle's entrance was always faintly suggestive of a whirlwind.

Joan was sitting before a table which held a number of vases. She always preferred to arrange the flowers in her own room herself.

She did not answer for a moment; her fingers trembled as she selected a particularly fine Marsh marigold.

"Bonham has gathered me all these king-cups, Cynthia. I believe I like them better than anything, though they are only wild flowers."

Cynthia ran to her side.

"Well, of all the exasperating people! Didn't you hear me say that Warchester was waiting?"

Joan's head bowed lower over the flowers.

"Please tell him that I don't feel well enough to see him to-day."

"Rubbish!" Cynthia said calmly. "What do you mean by behaving like this, Joan?"

"Mean?" Joan repeated weakly. She was picking up her flowers now and placing them in the vases with scant regard to their artistic arrangement.

"Mean!" Mrs. Trewhistle exclaimed in a high, exasperated tone. "What do you mean? This absurd nonsense of not being able to see Warchester, when, after that bad fainting fit of yours on Monday, you felt able to tear up to town on Tuesday—Heaven knows what for! Warchester is very patient—more patient than most men would be in his place, but he is getting restive now, and you can't wonder at it."

"No," Joan assented slowly. "No, I suppose one can't." She leaned back in her chair as though her strength had suddenly given way. "I suppose I must see him sometime, I know, but I can't this afternoon. I—really I don't feel well, Cynthia."

Seen thus, the light from the northern window falling full on her face, the ravages of two sleepless nights were very apparent. A shadow seemed to have fallen across her fresh young beauty; the great brown eyes were dim; the cheeks were pale; the lips that had seemed made for laughter had taken a pathetic downward curve.

Cynthia's voice became very gentle.

"What is troubling you, Joan? Tell me! It is not surely that you do not trust Warchester—that—"

Joan put out her hand.

"No, no, you must give me a little time, Cynthia! Perhaps to-morrow."

Cynthia's feeling of sympathy passed.

"I will tell him that, then. But, mind, you will have to keep to it, Joan! I shall not aid and abet you in refusing any longer. You—I suppose you will not change your mind?" pausing at the door. "He will be terribly disappointed, Joan."

"No, no! I can't!"

Mrs. Trewhistle departed reluctantly on her errand.

Joan sank back in her chair. It was on Monday night that she had looked in at the library window that she had fancied that she had recognized Warchester as the man whom she had seen in the studio at Grove Street.

It was Wednesday now, and, in spite of her hurried journey to London, Joan had continued to plead illness as an excuse for refusing to see her husband. She was wise enough, however, to recognize that this state of things could not continue, and, though she had been weak enough to delay the interview, she knew that to-morrow it was inevitable.

How she shrank from a private talk with Warchester even Joan herself had not realized until now.

The files of the newspaper; the interview with Mrs. Perks—these had not in any way helped to solve the problem that was eternally present to Joan. Her mind swayed backwards and forwards. Had she really recognized Warchester—had she been misled by a chance resemblance? In the daytime she would incline to the latter belief, but at night the thought would reassert itself that the man she had seen in the Grove Street studio was none other than her husband. Her thoughts would revert to that terrible scene of the past, conjuring up the minutest details, recalling the turn of the murderer's head as he caught up the papers from the table, the jerk of his hand as he threw them into the fire. It was always Warchester's eyes that she saw, though the lower part of the face was hidden by the dark beard.

What had Mrs. Perks said? Her husband had been positive that he had recognized Wingrove in Regent Street, though he was clean-shaven now. Joan trembled at the thought suggested.

Mrs. Trewhistle came back presently.

"I have persuaded Warchester to go and look after the improvements. He is dreadfully anxious. You are very hard-hearted, Joan."

"Am I?" Joan spoke listlessly, "I will see him tomorrow. To-day I don't want to talk of it, Cynthia."

"As you like." Mrs. Trewhistle's answer was spoken in decidedly displeased accents. She moved over to the window and stood drumming with her fingers on the panes and reflecting that Joan was very strange. She had never guessed in old Mrs. Davenant's days how intractable the girl would prove.

Outside in the park the hawthorns were in full blossom of pink and white, the bushes looking like gigantic roses dotted about, the soft green of the spring grass; nearer at hand by the side of the house the laburnums made a golden glory, and the sweet scent of the lilacs was fresh upon the air; in the drive the horse-chestnut spikes gleamed pink and white. Cynthia looked at them absently. Presently her expression altered; she leaned forward.

"There is some one coming to the door. I wonder who it is, Joan. A tall woman in black, with such a hat! Who can she be?"

Joan did not betray much interest in the question; she sat up, occupying herself with the flowers until a footman appeared in the doorway.

"Miss Davenant has called, my lady. She would be glad if you would see her for a few minutes."

"Miss Davenant!" Joan looked at him in bewilderment. "What is it you say, Joseph? Miss Davenant? I don't understand."

"The lady s-said Miss Davenant, m-my lady!" the footman stammered. In common with the rest of the household, he had heard of Mrs. Davenant's will, and of the search for the missing heiress. He and his fellows had freely canvassed Joan's chances downstairs. Joseph had even gone so far as to make a bet with Roger, the head-groom, on the subject. "I have shown Miss Davenant into the drawing-room, my lady," he added. "I thought—"

"That will do, Joseph! Say we shall be there in a minute."

Joan rose swiftly and caught her cousin's hands in hers.

"Do you understand, Cynthia? It is Evelyn. Come, we must welcome her!" The girl's cheeks were very pale now, but her brown eyes were shining like stars. "We must not let her think that I regret—that I am not pleased."

"Evelyn!" Mrs. Trewhistle's small fair face grew crimson. "But I am not pleased. What does she mean by coming here? I think it is a great impertinence! I shall let her see plainly that I am on your side—that it is a monstrous injustice."

Joan laid her cheek for a moment against her cousin's soft hair.

"Cynthia, there are no sides about this—Evelyn is only coming to her own, and it is only natural that she should come here—to her sister's house. Come, Cynthia, for my sake!"

"Umph!" Mrs. Trewhistle's ejaculation scarcely betokened assent, but as she looked at Joan her expression changed. After all, the girl must not be left to herself; there was no knowing what mad, quixotic thing she might do. "Still—well, if you will see her, I suppose I must come too."

"That is right!" Joan said heartily. She took her cousin's arm as they crossed the hall.

When the drawing-room door was opened the tall woman in black, who was sitting on a sofa in the middle of the room, looked up eagerly and rose.

"Is it Polly?" she said, stretching out her hands. "Surely it is Polly!"

Joan went forward quickly. The sound of the once familiar name seemed to bring back the old time vividly. Her heart warmed to this unknown sister. Cynthia, standing in the background, watched the meeting with cold, critical, eyes. She noticed the airy, casual manner in which the elder sister just touched Joan's cheek; she saw how the light, prominent eyes wandered perfunctorily from Joan's face to her own. Joan looked at the new-comer earnestly.

"So you are Evelyn! How often I have thought of you, and wondered whether we should ever meet again! I can scarcely believe it really is you."

Miss Davenant laughed.

"I guess it really is," she said in an affected, mincing voice, with just a suspicion of a nasal twang. "As for meeting you again—-well, you would not have been to blame if you had hoped we shouldn't. But"—glancing at Cynthia—"won't you introduce me? I guess this is your cousin, isn't it?"

"Yes, this is Cynthia."

"How do you do?" 'Mrs. Trewhistle said coldly.

She was by no means prepared to welcome the relationship Miss Davenant appeared to be eager to claim. Her partial eyes saw no resemblance between the sisters. Evelyn was tall, though an inch or two short of her sister's height; she was very fair, with large blue eyes, already engirded with a network of tiny lines, and a profusion of golden hair, in which Cynthia's quick eyes noted more than a suspicion of dye. Mrs. Trewhistle drew in her lips. The new-comer's appearance gave an impression of bad taste, Cynthia said to herself.

"How is it that you have come upon us in this way, without any warning?" she asked. "I think Mr. Hurst should have written."

"Guess he did not get much chance!" Miss Davenant said. Her outstretched hand dropped by her side; it was evident that Mrs. Trewhistle had no intention of taking it. "It was only last night that I succeeded in convincing Mr. Hurst that I really am Evelyn Spencer, and this morning I made up my mind to come over here straight away. I was anxious to see Polly—Joan, you call her now, don't you? It seemed as if I couldn't wait any longer."

"Yet I believe it is ten years since you took the trouble even to write a letter to her," Cynthia commented dryly,

"I—I couldn't!" Miss Davenant hesitated a moment; then she turned to Joan. "I have had a hard life of it all these years. I have tried my hand at most things—teaching first; then I went on the stage, and it isn't easy to get a living there unless you make a hit, and I never did. It has been living from hand to mouth and hard work all the time for me. Do you remember how I used to write to you and scrape up my earnings to send you little presents as long as you were at home, Polly? But when I heard you were going to be made a lady of and have everything you wanted, why, there didn't seem to be any more use for me in your life—I just dropped out. Still, when I heard luck had turned for me at last, I couldn't help coming to claim it. You don't blame me, Polly?"

"Of course I don't!" Joan threw her arms around her sister impulsively. "I am glad, Evie. You have had a hard time, and it is only fair you should have your share of the good things now."

It seemed to Mrs. Trewhistle that Joan's display of affection was rather embarrassing to Evelyn.

"You shan't lose your share either, Polly," she observed magnanimously. "It always used to be share and share alike in the old days, and I will see that you don't go short now."

Mrs. Trewhistle laughed a little.

"Joan will not need your help now, I think, Miss Davenant. She is a very great lady indeed. Lord Warchester is one of the richest men in the county."

"Oh, I dare say! But a woman is never the worse for being independent of her husband, and it is my place to see that Polly—" Evelyn broke off with a shrill laugh. Her eyes had strayed to the window. If there isn't that dry-as-dust old lawyer! I guess he thinks I am not to be trusted to come here by myself."

"Mr. Hurst! Oh, I am so glad!" Cynthia threw open the door just as the lawyer was admitted. "Do come in! You know—"

"My dear Mrs. Trewhistle, I come, I fear—" Mr. Hurst's expression altered, stiffened, as he looked beyond. "Miss Davenant—I am amazed—"

"Thought you would be!" the visitor interrupted equably. "But you men of business are so uncommonly slow, and I wanted to see my sister, so I just got into the train and came down. While you and Sir Edward Fisher put your heads together wondering how the thing was to be accomplished—hey, presto, it was done!"

"So I see!" Mr. Hurst responded coldly. "But I presume you scarcely imagined you could take possession of Davenant Hall in that fashion, my dear madam. You would not be admitted unless you presented certain credentials from me."

"Shouldn't I?" Miss Davenant laughed again, the same shrill, hard sound. "I guess I should make it unpleasant for them later if I wasn't. But now I see you have a cab at the door I guess we will just drive up, you and me and Polly, and you will put all that straight for me. Come, Polly! Put your hat on and come with us." She pointedly ignored Cynthia.

But that lady was not accustomed to be ignored,

"It is impossible for Joan to go with you," she said calmly. "She has not been well lately, and Lord Warchester is out."

Joan went over to her and kissed her.

"I feel much better now, Cynthia, and I think I ought to go. The old servants are fond of me; and if Evie goes alone they may not understand; they may be just a little—difficult."

"I dare say. I should not blame them!" Evidently Mrs. Trewhistle was not to be easily placated. "But if you do go, Joan, I shall insist on one thing—you are to come back as soon as possible. You are not to stay. Am I not right, Mr. Hurst?"

"Certainly, Mrs. Trewhistle. I am sure Miss Davenant will understand that."

Miss Davenant looked sulky.

"It must be as Joan pleases, but I shall expect to see a good deal of her later on."

"Of course I shall come back directly!" Joan promised, clinging to her cousin for a moment. "You—you must excuse me, Cynthia. I feel I must go with Evie. I will not be a minute. Evie, come with me while I put my hat on."

When the door had closed behind the two, Cynthia glanced at Mr. Hurst.

"Well, this is a pretty thing you have done!"

He spread out his hands as if disclaiming all responsibility.

"My dear lady! Could I help myself? And she seems genuinely attached to her sister. Things might have been much worse."

"They couldn't!" Cynthia said succinctly.

"My dear Mrs. Trewhistle—"

"I say things couldn't be worse!" Cynthia insisted with a stamp of her foot. "Did you see how she looked at Joan just when she was pretending to be most affectionate? She reminds me of a cat or a toad! Joan's sister! Ugh!"

Chapter Eleven

"JOAN!"

Joan was standing by the fireplace, one hand resting on the mantelpiece; her simple black gown fell around her in long straight folds. The last rays of the setting sun streaming through the window touched her hair with gold.

To Warchester she had never looked fairer, more desirable. There was ardent longing in his eyes as he came swiftly across to her with outstretched hands.

"Joan, Joan, I have been mad with anxiety! You have been ill, and you refused to see me. Why have you been so cruel?"

With old memories thronging quickly upon her, Joan shrank from him against the old tapestry on the wall at her side; then, as she slowly raised her eyes to his dark face, transfigured by love, a great rush of tenderness swept over her; the resemblance she had seen to the murderer in Grove Street had vanished. She told herself that she had unconsciously exaggerated some chance likeness, that she had been foolishly, culpably credulous. How could she, ever have imagined that the grey eyes, now full of love, that smiled down upon her were the same that had met hers that dreaded day ten years ago?

She laid her hands in Warchester's with a sigh of content.

"I wasn't well," she said softly. "And I was nervous, and—and frightened and foolish, but—I have wanted you too."

A look of joy illumined the man's anxious face. He drew the girl towards him; then as she let her head rest on his shoulder with a sigh of relief he held her closely to him, and, stooping, laid his cheek caressingly against her bright hair.

"What was the matter, Joan? I can't have you frightened."

"Oh, it was nothing! It was only that I was silly."

His clasp of her tightened, but he had noticed the tense look in her eyes as he entered the room, and as he felt her tremble he told himself that her nerves were strained, that it behoved him to be careful. He led her to a settee and carefully arranged the cushions so that she could lean back.

"Now you are to rest," he said quietly. "Lay your head back so, I am going to sit here and you shall talk or not just as you feel inclined."

The mingled tenderness and authority of his tone were just what Joan needed. She leaned back on the settee and let her hand rest in his. For the present at any rate; the black cloud of suspicion had rolled away; she resolutely thrust even the remembrance of it aside, while Warchester talked quietly to her of the Dutch garden, which was rapidly nearing completion, of changes that were likely to take place among his tenantry.

For a time Joan was content to listen silently, but at length when he paused she looked up.

"You know that Evelyn has come back, Paul?"

"Oh, yes! I have had a long interview with Mr. Hurst," he answered. "He seemed to think she was coming here to-day, but I have seen nothing of her; and I thought it might be better not to call until we could go together."

Joan made no rejoinder; her fingers moved softly, half caressingly over his hand.

After a pause Warchester spoke in a lighter tone.

"Well, about the new sister, Joan—what is she like? Does she accord with your recollection of her?"

The girl's face clouded.

"I—I don't know," she said dreamily. "She is very kind, but I think we have grown apart all these years. Paul, I can't feel to her as a sister should, I am afraid."

"I suppose that cannot be helped in the circumstances. It is not your fault, I am sure," Warchester assured her. "Cynthia says you behaved like an angel."

Joan smiled and shook her head.

"I am afraid Cynthia is partial. There is no generosity in not grudging Evelyn her inheritance, which never was mine. I always thought it was very likely Granny would leave it to her. But now—

perhaps for your sake—I am inclined to wish it had been different."
She looked wistfully at Warchester.

"I am not!" he contradicted heartily. "I want my wife to myself—
you, Joan, and not the heiress of Davenant. We shall have plenty
to do at the Towers, sweetheart. Your sister is heartily welcome to
Davenant, as far as I am concerned."

Joan was silent. She could not explain that she had not been
speaking wholly of her sister's inheritance, and yet she could
not help feeling that in Evelyn she would give Warchester an
exceedingly undesirable sister-in-law. Even in the little time she
had spent with Evelyn she had found that not all her recollections of
her sister's kindness to her in the old days, not all her real sympathy
with the hard life the girl had led, could blind her to Evelyn's many
deficiencies—deficiencies which were not merely of manner, but of
heart and mind.

Despite the effusively expressed affection for herself, Joan had
seen plainly how little interest apart from their monetary value
her new possessions had in Evelyn's eyes. She had known that
the years that had passed; the different lives they had led, must of
necessity have made a gap between them, but this was even deeper
and wider than she had expected. Evelyn had been curiously silent
about her own experiences; she had given certain particulars to Mr.
Hurst when she had presented her credentials in town, but, beyond
telling Joan that she had been on the stage, she carefully avoided
any reference to her past life. She had taken with her to Mr. Hurst
all the necessary proofs of her identity—little personal trifles that
had come to her from her mother, her birth certificate, a couple of
Joan's childish letters.

What the lawyer had learned beyond this Joan did not know.
She could scarcely help surmising from his manner that it did not
redound to her sister's credit. Evelyn was almost openly anxious
that Joan should invite her to stay at the Towers, but to this idea
Cynthia and Mr. Hurst were emphatically opposed, and Joan

herself, though feeling it might be her duty to acquiesce, could not help shrinking from the suggestion.

Warchester was emphatic in his condemnation of it when Joan consulted him.

"No, no!" he said determinedly. "Spend as much of the daytime as you like with your sister, but don't ask her to stay here for a while until we know more of her. Later on we must think of having people to stay with us, but for the present you will be content with me, won't you?"

The shadow on Joan's face deepened as he waited for his answer; she fancied that she caught a far-off look of that baleful glance that had haunted her childhood. She turned away from him.

"Oh, Paul, Paul, don't!"

The gesture no less than the words chilled and pained him. He was not a man who had frittered away his affections, but he had never found it difficult to gain a woman's liking, and he had been confident of Joan's love. He felt convinced that there was more than met the eye in his wife's fainting fit on Monday night, in the aversion with which she had turned from him. He could allow to the full for overtaxed nerves, but there were both pain and shrinking in the brown eyes as he bent nearer, and a quick, involuntary movement that was almost a shudder did not escape him. He had not understood her refusal to see him; the journey to London was difficult to explain as merely a whim. It was evident there was some mystery here that must be fathomed.

"What do you mean, Joan?" he asked quietly. "Aren't you happy with me?"

Joan's piteous glance round the room made him wince.

"Yes—yes—I am happy—of course I am happy!" she answered unsteadily. "But, Paul—"

"Yes. But"—Warchester's dark face was set in stern lines of pain—"Joan, does this mean that you have mistaken your own heart—that you do not care for me?"

Joan sat silent, her slender hands lying motionless on her lap; her long lashes flickered for a moment, then, drooping, veiled her eyes.

To Warchester it appeared that her silence could mean only one thing.

"Joan," he said sharply, his tone quickened by fear, "is it so? Has it all been a mistake? Was I too old for you, dear? Why don't you speak? Joan—have you ceased to—love me?"

Joan raised her eyes slowly and looked steadily at him.

"No, you know it is not that." The words were spoken with a manifest effort.

Warchester caught his breath. He held out his hands.

"Thank Heaven it is not that! Anything else we can bear together. Trust me, and tell me what troubles you."

Joan's eyes still scrutinised his face. Was the resemblance as strong as she had fancied? Was not Warchester taller, broader than the man she had seen in the studio in Grove Street?

"Come, Joan!" Warchester's tone was more masterful.

"I—I can't tell you!" Joan said in a low tone.

How could she, she was asking herself—how could she tell him, who was in her eyes a veritable king among men, that she had found in him a likeness to an undiscovered murderer, and that the horror of it was driving sleep from her at night, and haunting her by day? No, no! At all hazards the secret must be kept—he must never know.

"It is only that I am nervous, fanciful." She put out her hands with a little sob, "Bear with me, Paul!"

Warchester took her hands; his eyes were puzzled and unsatisfied.

"Can't you trust me, Joan?"

Joan's throat was hot and dry; she longed for the relief of tears, but she must not give way now.

"It is nothing. One has strange fancies sometimes—most people, have, I think, haven't they?" with a piteous, wan smile. "But if one talks of them they seem worse, and I—I want to forget them, Paul."

The appeal stirred Warchester's manhood; he bent down and touched her fingers with his lips.

"It shall be as you wish, Joan. Some day perhaps you will know me well enough to trust me with even these vagrant dreams of yours. Till then I will wait."

The door opened, and Cynthia was ushered in.

"Now don't tell me that I have come at an inopportune moment!" she exclaimed gaily, as she kissed Joan and gave her hand to Warchester. "This letter came for you by the last post, Joan, directed to our house by mistake, and as it is marked 'Immediate' I thought perhaps you had better have it, though I don't suppose it is anything important."

"For me?" Joan looked at the envelope listlessly. "I don't know the writing."

Cynthia turned back to Warchester.

"After all, I believe I only made the letter an excuse for obtaining a little rational companionship. Reggie —you know what Reggie is after he has been about the farms listening to the tenants' grievances all day. I simply can't keep him awake, whatever I do! And I must relieve my mind about that dreadful Evelyn. She actually came over to see me this afternoon and they were silly enough to admit her. I have told them that I shall never be at home to her again. She is impossible, simply impossible!"

"Cynthia! Paul! I shall have to go to him. My father is ill—he is asking for me!"

Joan struggled to her feet and stood facing them, catching at the table beside her for support,

Cynthia stored at her blankly.

"What do you say? Who is ill? I don't understand."

"My father." Joan glanced at the letter in her hand. "This is from Amy, the eldest of the children—my stepsister. She says, 'Father is very ill; the doctor says it is pneumonia, and he is not likely to get over it. Part of the time he is not himself, but sometimes he is conscious, and then he asks for you. Mother says it won't be any use, you are much too fine a lady to come here, but anyhow I promised Dad, so I am writing. From your affectionate sister, Amy.' You see, I must go," Joan concluded, looking appealingly at her cousin.

Mrs. Trewhistle frowned and shook her head.

"I don't see the necessity at all. You haven't seen your father for years; he has never been a father to you in anything but name. I do not think there is the least need for you to go. Probably he would not know you when you got there. You see the girl says he is delirious most of the time, and it would harrow your feelings for nothing. Don't you agree with me, Lord Warchester?"

"I can't say I do," he answered, going over to Joan's side and putting his arm about her. "I think Joan must go, Mrs. Trewhistle. I do not see how she can refuse. The only thing for us to do, it seems to me, is to help her to get there as soon as possible. Where is it, by the way? Let me see, Joan." He took the letter. "Bell Hotel, Willersfield. Willersfield—ah, that is in Shropshire, is it not?"

Cynthia was too much amazed at his unexpected behaviour to reply. Joan gave him a grateful glance.

"I must go at once!" she said quickly. "To-night! When is there a train, Paul?"

Warchester looked at his watch.

"It is too late to-night. You could not get there. There is the express to Birmingham at 7.30. We can get that by driving to the junction, and Willersfield is only an hour's run from Birmingham. I shall take you of course."

"You are very good," Joan said wistfully. "But indeed I would so much rather you did not, Paul. I don't think I could bear that. No"—resolutely—"I would rather go alone or with Evelyn. Naturally Evelyn will want to go. I must send to her. I was forgetting Evelyn."

Chapter Twelve

JUNE though it was, the morning was cold. An east wind whistled round the station, working havoc among the flowers that bordered the line, blowing little scuds of rain in Joan's face as she stood waiting for the express. The girl shivered in her long coat, telling herself that when the sun came out she would be hot. At present she was feeling miserably cold and depressed. Treherne, her maid, who was standing near, did not look particularly amiable. She was evidently inclined to resent this hurried journey.

Warchester was at the bookstall buying papers for the journey. A groom from Davenant came up to Joan, touching his hat.

"Miss Davenant desires me to say, my lady, that she is very sorry, but she is too ill to come out this morning. She fainted while she was dressing. She sends her love and hopes she may be able to come by a later train."

"What is it, Joan?" Warchester asked as he sauntered over to her. He looked very big and handsome in his big motoring coat with his cap pushed back from his brows. "Your sister ill? In that case you cannot go by yourself. I shall come with you."

"No, please, Paul!" Joan put out her hand. "I shall be all right. I may be foolish, but I do not want you there—just when I first see them all again. Please, please, don't come, Paul!"

"Well, I suppose Treherne will look after you," Warchester said gloomily. "And, mind, if you do not come back at the earliest moment I shall fetch you."

The noise of the approaching train drowned the end of his sentence. He busied himself in looking out a comfortable corner seat in the carriage, and laid a big box of chocolates and a pile of illustrated papers beside Joan, and then stepped back as the train began to move.

"Remember what I said! I hope you will find your father better," he cried, keeping pace with the train for a moment while Joan smiled at him from the window.

When at last he was out of sight and the girl turned back with a sigh, she found Treherne regarding her with dissatisfaction.

"We ought to have had a thicker rug, my lady, if it is going to be as cold as this."

"I dare say it will be warmer by and by," Joan remarked indifferently as she took up one of the periodicals and settled herself in her corner.

She had plenty of food for thought as the express thundered along through the pleasant Midlands, and it was only natural this morning that her mind should revert to her childish days.

In his rough way her father had been good to her, and had always interposed between her and Mrs. Spencer's violence. Since Mr. Hurst had brought her to Davenant she had not heard her father's name mentioned, but her memory had a certain tenacity—she had never forgotten him. Always when she had speculated on the possibility of becoming her grandmother's heiress she had made up her mind that in that case he should share to some extent in her good fortune. Now he was ill—probably dying. None of her schemes could benefit him. She fell to wondering how the passing of the years that had changed her from a child to a woman had affected him. She remembered him distinctly—his red, clean-shaven face, his, broad back, the crook of his knees when he walked. Then her thoughts strayed further to the mother she had never known, the strange girl, Mrs. Davenant's daughter, who had thrown the traditions of her caste to the winds and left her home to marry the man of her choice. That she had lived to rue it Joan had faintly guessed even in that far-off time of her childhood. Yet, though the bare outlines of the story were familiar to her, of the real mother, the girl who had lived at Davenant, the woman who had been John Spencer's wife, Joan knew almost nothing. She had never even seen a portrait of her, since every likeness of the rebellious daughter had been banished from sight at Davenant, save that as a child Joan had a faint recollection of being lifted up by Evie to kiss their mother's photograph.

Evelyn had taken the photograph away with her, and Joan had no real remembrance of the pictured face, but she knew that the photograph was among the papers Evelyn had placed in Mr. Hurst's hands, and she was looking forward to seeing it again. Next she thought of Evelyn herself. As she had said to Warchester only yesterday, Joan was realizing how impossible it was that they two, who had been parted for so many years, should feel the ordinary sisterly affection for one another. It seemed to her that if Evelyn had been with her now, if they had been able to compare their recollections as they went along, if they had gone together to their father's house, some remembrance of old association would have been revived.

It was a bitter disappointment that Evelyn was unable to come. She had appeared genuinely distressed at hearing of Joan's news the preceding evening, and had written at once to say that she would go up with her the next morning.

The journey to Birmingham ended before Joan expected. From there to Willersfield was but a matter of half an hour, and very soon the train was slowing down again. The girl looked out of the window anxiously. The environs had been picturesque, but the town itself looked grim and smoky, dominated by the tall chimneys of the ironworks. The streets were narrow and crooked and none too clean. There was no cab to be had at the station, so they were obliged to walk to the small hotel where Warchester had telephoned for rooms for them. Then Joan left Treherne while she set out to find the Bell Inn. It was only ten minutes' walk away, she was told, on the outskirts of the poorer part of the town.

She found that her father was the landlord of the Bell. The chamber-maid informed her that he was very ill—not expected to live the day out, she added, and was surprised to see the sudden pallor that overspread the visitor's face.

Joan walked quickly across the old market-place, paved with cobble-stones, and turned down one of the poorer streets to the right, getting a glimpse of the Wrekin between the gabled roofs of the houses before her.

The Bell Inn was easily found. A tiny child came out from the next door and ran along the pavement. Joan had an odd feeling that surely it must be Tim, but when the mother ran after him and picked him up she smiled at her own folly. Tim would be a big boy now.

The door of the inn stood open. Joan knocked at it timidly, but there was no response. She went into the wide-bricked passage; at one end there was the bar, but there was no one there; everything looked deserted. Joan was about to turn back, when a sharp, hard-featured woman came bustling in from the back regions. Joan knew her at once; this was the tyrant of her childhood. In imagination she could feel again the hard blows, hear the angry scolding that had made her life in her father's house one long misery.

Evidently the recognition was not mutual. Mrs. Spencer looked at her in some surprise.

"Did you wish to speak to me, ma'am?"

"Yes, yes!" Joan said hurriedly. "At least I want to see him—my father. How is he?"

"Your father!" The woman stared at her. "Do you mean to say—why, you can't be—no, it isn't Evie!"

"No, no! Not Evelyn—Joan! How is my father, Mrs. Spencer?"

Mrs. Spencer took no notice of the question.

"What—Polly! Well, I couldn't have believed it! You have growed into a fine-looking young woman. You favour my Amy a bit, though—I see that now—the one that wrote to you. But come in."

She threw back the flap of the counter and marshalled Joan into the little parlour behind.

"We got the telegram first thing this morning saying you were coming to-day, but I didn't think you could be here so soon, nor did I reckon on seeing you tall and grand-like—though I might ha' knowed. Married—and to a lord too! Your father has been asking for you terrible often. He has fair wore the life out of me with his 'Polly —Polly—bring Polly here!'"

"I hope he is better," Joan said as her stepmother paused.

Mrs. Spencer shook her head.

"There will never be any better for him in this world. The doctor said to me an hour ago, 'He may last the day out, Mrs. Spencer, or he may not; I can't promise you.' It—it will be terrible hard on me. What will become of me and the children I don't know!" putting the comer of her apron to her eyes.

But there were no real tears, as Joan was quick to see. She remembered how this woman had tyrannized over her father in the old days, how she had driven Evelyn from home and rendered her own childhood miserable, and she felt in no mood to sympathize with her now. She refused the proffered chair decidedly.

"I should like to see my father as soon as possible, Mrs. Spencer."

Mrs. Spencer was in no wise abashed.

"And so you shall, my dear. I will just run up first and see how he is. But here is somebody that will like to see you. Jim Gregory—you'll remember Gregory, don't you, Polly?—my lady, I mean I should say!"

Joan put out her hand with a pleasant smile to the big, awkward-looking man.

"Of course I remember Gregory. You used to be very good to me. Don't say you have forgotten me."

Gregory took her hand awkwardly.

Joan decided, as she glanced at his coarse, reddened features and small, roving eyes, that the years had certainly not improved him.

"No, I haven't forgotten you. How should I?" he said slowly. "But I shouldn't have known you. You—you mind me a little of your mother, though," he added in a lower tone.

Mrs. Spencer had hurried up the narrow stairs; they were alone. Joan turned to him eagerly.

"Oh, did you know my mother? I never thought—"

Gregory gave a short laugh.

"Ay, I mind her well when I was a lad! I was stable boy first, and then third groom when your father was coachman to Sir Robert Brunton. 'Twas there your mother died, and he married her," with a jerk of his head towards the stairs.

"And you think I am like her?" Joan said with interest.

"Yes. You have a look of her," Gregory pronounced slowly. "You are taller than she was, and her hair was yellower, but there is a look."

"Shorter and fairer," Joan said thoughtfully. "That sounds more like Evelyn. I do wish she had been able to come with me to-day."

"Evie—ah!" It was almost a groan that broke from Gregory.

Glancing at him in surprise, Joan saw that his rubicund countenance was several degrees paler.

"Yes, Evelyn," she repeated. "She was ill this morning or she would have been with me. Is there anything the matter with you, Gregory? You don't look well."

"That is nothing," he said testily. "An old pain in my side—never take any notice of it. What is that you were saying? Who was it that would ha' come with you? Not—not—"

"I said Evie, my sister Evelyn, Miss Davenant."

"Evie?" Gregory echoed, gaping at her. "Evie would have come with you—"

"Why, of course she would!" Joan said a trifle impatiently. "Naturally she too is anxious to see our father again."

Gregory's eyes were still fixed on her; his expression did not alter. "Where is Evie?"

"You have not heard! How stupid of me!" Joan said with a faint smile. "My grandmother left the property to her—not to me. She is at Davenant Hall now."

Gregory looked half dazed, she thought. He fingered his neckerchief with trembling fingers.

"Evie, at Davenant Hall?" he muttered slowly. "I don't understand. If you would say it again—"

"Certainly she is at Davenant Hall," Joan said impatiently.

"Will you come upstairs, now, my dear?" Mrs. Spencer called from the stair head. "Your father is awake. You'll find the way quite easy, and these stairs do try my breath, and he is calling out for you."

It was somewhat of a relief to get away from Gregory. Joan ran upstairs lightly.

"It is one more flight and then you are up," Mrs. Spencer said encouragingly. "Gregory would be rare and pleased to see you, I know."

"Yes, I suppose so," Joan assented doubtfully. "He—he seems rather peculiar. I could not help wondering if he had been drinking."

"Oh, no!" Mrs. Spencer shook her head. "He may be the worse for drink sometimes in an evening, but never at this time of day; unless"—as an afterthought—"he had a glass or two when he heard you were coming. Here's your father. Amy, you can go away now. Your sister has come."

Amy, a thin, lanky girl of sixteen or seventeen, got up from the bedside.

"You will remember to give him his draught, mother?"

Joan went forward softly. Was this indeed the father she remembered—this gaunt, haggard man lying in the middle of the four-poster, fighting painfully for every breath? The big face was pale now; in the features sharpened by illness Joan saw a shadow of the good looks that had won Mary Davenant's heart.

He was watching the door anxiously.

"Polly—I want Polly! Who"—as the girl came up to the bed and took his wasted hand in hers—"is this? Not—not—Miss Mary."

They were alone now. Mrs. Spencer had retreated with her daughter. Joan bent forward and touched the wrinkled forehead with her lips.

"I am Polly—your little Polly, father, don't you know me?"

"You are Polly?" The failing eyes sought hers pitifully. "Ah, well, it was right you should be made a lady of, as your mother was! You were safe enough. I knew the old lady, Mrs. Davenant, would see to that. It—it is Evie as I am worrying about. I ought to have found out where Evie was long afore this. When that lawyer-fellow come down asking questions about her a month ago, I see how I'd been to blame and I made up my mind to look for her. Now—now I'm going to die and that is all at an end, but you—you must find Evie, Polly."

Joan's eyes were dim with tears as she stooped over him.

"Evie is found, father dear. She is at Davenant Hall. She wanted to come with me to-day, but she is ill."

He looked up at her with lack-lustre eyes.

"Evie has come home? No, no! She hasn't! You haven't done your duty by Evie, Miss Mary said—she comes to me in the nights, Miss Mary does."

It was strange to Joan to hear him talk of her mother as he had thought of her no doubt when he was the groom at Warchester and she was his young mistress. It was not as his wife that he recalled her now, but as pretty, dark-eyed Miss Mary Davenant.

He moved his head about restlessly.

"Polly is all right, Miss Mary says. But where is Evie? You ought to have thought of Evie before this. I—I'm going soon, Polly. I shall see her there—Miss Mary. What am I to say to her about Evie?"

"Tell her that Evie is at Davenant Hall—in her old, home—that everything is going to be very well with both her children in the future."

One of the restless hands began to pluck at the bedclothes.

"Ay, ay! Polly is married to a lord—I see it in the paper. It is Evie—Evie that I am thinking about. You will find her, Polly? Promise—for Miss Mary's sake!"

It was no use trying to make him understand. Joan held his clammy hand in her warm young fingers.

"I—I promise, father. I will take care of Evie. You must not worry about her any more."

A shade of content crept into the dying eyes.

"She was a bit high-spirited, was Evie, and she did not get on with the missus, but she was rare and good to the little 'un. She allus put little Polly afore herself. You'll remember you have promised to find Evie?"

"I will remember," Joan answered clearly.

Chapter Thirteen

"EARTH to earth, ashes to ashes, dust to dust." Joan shivered as the solemn words of the Burial Service sounded in her ears. She looked fixedly at the clergyman standing at the head of the grave, at Mrs. Spencer, heavily veiled in black, clinging to her son Robert's arm and sobbing convulsively. Tim stood at Joan's right, changed by the passage of years from a solemn, podgy-faced baby into a fat, rosy-cheeked urchin of twelve. With the exception of Evelyn, all John Spencer's children had gathered round his grave.

To Joan it had a curious feeling of unreality; she felt as if she were taking part in a play. Life had flowed on quietly during the ten years at Davenant. Now everything seemed changing.

Her father had died on the day of her arrival; his last thought apparently had been for Evelyn, for the daughter he had not seen for fifteen years: Joan had remained at Willersfield for the funeral, in spite of Warchester's remonstrances.

As the clergyman read the last Collects, with their ring of triumphant faith, she was thinking very pitifully of her father, of his pathetic fear that Miss Mary would reproach him for neglecting her children. Joan wondered if that early headstrong marriage of theirs had brought happiness to him any more than to her mother.

She moved forwards with the rest of the mourners for one last look at the coffin. The sun streamed down on the plate. She could read the words "John Spencer, aged fifty-five." An arm was put within hers, she was drawn gently away; looking up, she met Warchester's eyes.

"Paul!"

"Yes?" He led her away across the grass to where several coaches were awaiting them, for, as Mrs. Spencer phrased it, it had been a very comfortable funeral. "Did you not know that I should come to fetch you home? I have obeyed you long enough by staying at the Towers; but to-day I could not let you be alone, I was grieved that I was not in time to start with you, but we had to wait half an hour outside Birmingham—there had been a collision and the line was blocked. But now I am going to take you back by the next train, and we shall be home in time for dinner."

"Yes," Joan acquiesced slowly, "there is nothing more for me to do here, and I shall be glad to be at home."

Warchester's face lighted up; it was joy enough for him that she should let him care for her, that she should be glad to come back to him. A carriage waited behind the mourning-coaches; he guided her to it.

"We will drive to the station at once."

"One moment!" Joan stopped to say good-bye to Mrs. Spencer.

"You—you are not going now, my dear?" inquired that lady amid her sobs. "Why, we have not said half I meant to, and I wanted to ask you—"

Warchester frowned.

"If you have anything more to communicate to Lady Warchester it must be written," he said brusquely. "She is not well, and all this has been too much for her. I am taking her home at once."

"Oh, yes! I am sure, sir, I mean, my lord"—Mrs. Spencer fumbled with her handkerchief—"it isn't me nor her poor father that would have wished to keep her against her will. I take it as very kind her coming down like this, but—but there was one little thing I wanted to mention—"

"Write to-night, then," said Warchester impatiently.

He saw that the scene was telling upon Joan and was anxious to put a stop to it. "Lady Warchester will attend to it, as soon as possible."

Mrs. Spencer cast a vindictive glance at him as he walked away. To a woman of her nature the sight of Joan, high in the world's esteem, with rank, wealth and an adoring husband, must always be an aggravation.

Joan leaned out of the carriage for a few seconds.

"Good-bye, Amy!"

The tall, thin girl, approached rather timidly; it was from her that Joan had learned all the details of her father's illness; she knew that Amy mourned him sincerely.

"Good-bye, Lady—my lady," the girl stammered confusedly.

Joan stooped down and kissed the thin young cheek impulsively.

"Don't call me that Amy. Remember I am Joan—your sister, Joan. Good-bye, dear!"

Warchester watched his wife closely as they drove to the station. He had been seriously anxious about her of late. Her prolonged fainting fit the previous week, her manner, fitful and variable, had filled him with alarm.

At the station he had engaged a special carriage for her. He would not let her speak until he had seen her ensconced in a corner amid a multiplicity of cushions and wraps. Then as he caught her glance fixed upon him wistfully he came towards her.

"Well, Joan, what is it?"

"Evelyn," Joan questioned—"I want to hear about her. Is she very ill? How do you like her, Paul?"

Warchester sat down beside her, and, taking her hand, pressed it gently.

"I haven't seen her; I have called twice, but she has remained in bed. Dr. Wilkins says it is nothing serious—more nerves than anything else, I fancy."

Joan moved restlessly.

"I wish she had been able to come. Poor Father—he was so anxious about her! He did not seem able to believe that she was safe and sound at Davenant. It was pitiable to hear him saying that my mother would say that he hadn't taken care of Evie. I do think she ought to have made an effort to come, don't you?"

Warchester frowned; he was strongly of opinion now that it would have been better if Joan had stayed away. With regard to Evelyn, he knew little and cared less.

"She had not seen him for fifteen years, you know," he said. "I don't suppose her interest in him was very acute. As for the rest—

well, he had not been much of a father to either of you as far as I can make out. It was likely enough he would feel that at the last."

Joan sighed.

"He—I think he wanted to do the best for us," she said loyally. "There was not much in his power, remember, Paul. Amy, the eldest of Mr. Spencer's children, is a nice girl. Did you notice her? She is nearly seventeen, and there is not much of a life before her. I should like to do something for Amy."

"So you shall! You are always thinking of other people, Joan. Just for the present I want you to let me look after you."

Joan smiled at him; her hand touched his face softly.

"You are very good to me, Paul, my dear!"

Warchester had arranged that their carriage should be attached to the Warchester train so, that there was no change at Birmingham. Their luncheon was brought to them there, and Warchester poured out a glass of champagne and insisted on Joan drinking it, smiling as he saw the colour coming back to her cheeks, the light to her eyes. Then he made her rest quietly, and watched beside her until he saw her eyelids droop and her low regular breathing told him that she was asleep.

When they reached the station before Warchester he roused her.

"Only ten minutes before we get out, dear!"

With an effort Joan opened her eyes and sat up.

"Oh, how could you let me sleep so long, Paul? What a dull journey it has been for you, and you have not even smoked! Do you know when I was lying half-awake I could not help thinking how all this must have worried you and how good it was of you not to reproach me with giving you such a very undesirable family of brothers and sisters-in-law?"

Warchester looked at her with eloquent eyes.

"I am proud to share everything connected with you," he said quietly.

Joan laughed a little unsteadily.

"Even Mrs. Spencer? Oh, Paul!"

"Mrs. Spencer has nothing to do with you," he replied. "You are in no way responsible for your father's choice of a second wife. I hate to think you were ever in that woman's power, Joan. To-day I went to the inn first, you know, hoping to be in time to start with you. I was picturing you there—a little frightened child tyrannized over by your stepmother, but growing up like some fragile tender lily untouched by the gloom and grime of the inn."

"That is a very pretty simile," Joan observed, her smile deepening in spite of herself, "but, unfortunately for its truth, I never lived at the inn—I never was in Willersfield at all until Friday."

Warchester was watching her as she put on her hat and adjusted her veil.

"You never lived at the inn?" he cried. "You never were in Willersfield till Friday? And I—I have been looking at everything with interest to-day, thinking to myself 'perhaps as a child Joan played here!'"

"But how strange that you should not have known!" Joan remarked with evident amusement. "A great part of the time we were in the country, at Merton Park, you know. And yet, looking back, it always seems to me that most of my childish days were spent in London in that little house at the back of Grove Street."

"I hope the car is here all right." Warchester put his head out of the window as the train steamed into the station. "I told them we should probably come by this train, but Bonham is a careless beggar! Grove Street, did you say, Joan? What Grove Street?" His voice was unaltered.

Joan had spoken in the first place without any ulterior thought, but now she could not help remembering; she looked quickly at him. He was standing up, reaching his cane from the rack; as he met her glance he smiled at her.

With a sense of profound relief, Joan smiled back.

"Oh, Grove Street at the back of Hinton Square! Do you know it?"

As he sat down he laid one hand on the door-handle. Insensibly, it tightened its clasp, the knuckles showing white through the tense brown skin.

"I used to know Hinton Square very well," he replied, but the appearance of a porter at the carriage-door terminated their conversation.

To-day there was no occasion for blaming Bonham; the car was waiting in the little station-yard, as well as the omnibus for Treherne and the luggage.

Joan settled herself in her corner with an exclamation of pleasure as they started.

"How nice it seems to be back! And how fresh everything looks after the smoky town of Willersfield!" she exclaimed, glancing about her with appreciative eyes.

The dog-roses and the honeysuckle that wreathed the hedges were shedding their blossoms, but tall up-standing meadow-sweet and big ragged-robins still fringed the ditches; in the fields the green and gold of summer were beginning to give place to the russet tints of autumn. Over the top of the trees they could catch a glimpse of the chimneys of Davenant Hall.

Suddenly Joan turned to her husband.

"I wonder whether you would mind, Paul? We still have an hour before dinner, and it would not be far out of our way. I should like to ask how Evelyn is."

"I sent up this morning," answered Warchester. He wanted his wife to himself this evening; he did not want to share her with anyone, least of all with this unknown elder sister; but when he saw the disappointed look on her face his tone altered. "Of course we will go! As you say, it is not far out of our way, and naturally there will be much you will want to talk over with your sister."

Joan's grateful smile was his reward.

The Hall was looking much as usual as they turned in at the gates. Joan was glad to see the windows unshuttered, the blinds drawn up once more. Half-way up the drive they met Mr. Hurst in his dog-cart. He pulled up.

"I should be glad if I might have a word with you, Lord Warchester?"

"Of course!" Warchester opened the door and jumped out. "You will excuse me, Joan? Drive on to the house, and I will come to you in a minute or two." As the car went on he turned to the lawyer. "Well?"

Mr. Hurst climbed down slowly. His limbs were getting stiff; age was telling on him.

"Dr. Graves came to see me this morning," he said slowly. "He wished to speak to me about Mr. Wilton. It appears to me that he has been much worse lately; the journey down to the Marsh tired him terribly. Besides, the servants are talking. His eccentricities are increasing, and—and before long Dr. Graves says some more definite steps will have to be taken. It is probable, Graves thinks, that a splinter is pressing on the brain, and if that could be removed—"

"I dare say; but I haven't any faith in these operations," replied Warchester. "As for this particular one, from all I can hear the recoveries are only about five per cent. Graves spoke to me about it some time ago, and I told him plainly it was out of the question."

"I know! I know!" The old lawyer nodded. "He told me as much. But, if you will excuse me, I do not think you quite realize how the matter stands. Graves says that if the operation is not performed the terrible paroxysms of rage to which poor Mr. Wilton is subject will increase, and — and, in short, there can only be one ending—absolute insanity."

"Yes—I see." Warchester muttered. The lawyer glanced at him curiously, and saw that his face was white and drawn. But that may be better than—"

"I think you are wrong," Mr. Hurst said gravely. "I feel sure Mr. Wilton would prefer death itself to such an existence. And Dr. Graves says that there is a distinct chance of perfect recovery."

Warchester did not answer; his lips were set in a rigid, obstinate line.

"Graves was particularly anxious I should speak to you as soon as possible," the lawyer resumed after a perceptible pause. "He thinks that if you would consult Mr. Wilton's sister, Mrs. Mannering—"

"How on earth can I consult her when she is in New Zealand?" Warchester inquired savagely. "You can't explain this sort of thing in a letter."

Mr. Hurst coughed.

"I should have thought that difficulty might have been arranged," he suggested mildly. "But it will not be an obstacle in the future, Mrs. Mannering telegraphed from Marseilles last night that she expects to land at Southampton tomorrow."

"Ah!" Warchester caught his breath sharply. There was a curious light in his eyes as he glanced quickly away from the lawyer; then his tone altered to one of absolute indifference, "Well, it seems to me that you and I need not concern ourselves further, Hurst. The question will become one for Mrs. Mannering to decide."

Chapter Fourteen

IT SEEMED strange to Joan to drive under the old familiar portico, to hear her footman inquire for Miss Davenant. In a minute she came back. Miss Davenant was better; she would be glad to see her ladyship.

In the hall, Sturgess, the old butler who had been in the service of the Davenants when Joan's mother was a child, was waiting to receive her. He looked whiter—older, Joan thought as she greeted him pleasantly. Mrs. Davenant's death and the changes that had come since had tried him sorely.

Evelyn was in the boudoir. The furniture was precisely as it had been in Mrs. Davenant's time, but the new mistress had contrived, even in this short time, to infuse an atmosphere of subtle change. The wide couch that had always stood in the recess between the windows had been pulled before the fire and piled with cushions brought in from the drawing-room; great pots of flowering plants stood everywhere; some exquisite old china that had been the pride of Mrs. Davenant's heart was standing on the writing-table. The air was heavy with the scent of hothouse flowers mingling with the perfume Evelyn affected and the stale smell of her endless cigarettes.

To Joan, coming in from the fresh air outside, it felt oppressively hot and stuffy. But possibly Evelyn herself presented the most incongruous element, in her tumbled white muslin peignoir, with her untidy golden—too golden—hair, her crudely tinted cheeks. She sprang to meet her sister, throwing a cheap edition of a popular novel on the ground.

"So you are back! Well, I call this good of you to come in to see me first thing."

Joan submitted to be kissed, blaming herself for the inward distaste she always felt for Evelyn's caresses.

"Yes, I wanted to know how you were, and I thought you would be anxious to hear all about Father and everything. He was terribly anxious about you, Evelyn. I wish you had been able to come with me."

Evelyn resumed her lounge on the couch as Joan took a seat nearer the window.

"I was sorry I couldn't in a way, but I think on the whole it is just as well. After all, he hadn't troubled about either of us much, and I don't mean to be bothered with Mrs. Spencer and her second family, I shall let her see that plainly if she makes any appeal to me; and if you are wise you will do the same, Joan, or we may have them sponging on us for ever."

There was a certain justice in the remark, as Joan could not help feeling, but Evelyn's careless manner and hardness of tone grated on her.

"Mrs. Spencer was unkind to us, to you especially," she said slowly. But she did not do us any real harm, Evie; and I thought perhaps we might do something for the children. The eldest, Amy, is such a nice girl."

Miss Davenant contemplated the big buckles on her shoes.

"Well, anyhow, I couldn't go," she remarked with an air of dismissing the subject. "I was downright bad, Joan. I had your doctor from the village. Wilkins his name is, isn't it? He seemed a bit of a muff, I thought, but, anyhow, he was quite clear that it wouldn't do for me to go to the funeral. Besides—well, I hadn't seen the poor old Dad for fifteen years, and funerals give me the hump."

"If you feel like that perhaps it was better that you should stay away," Joan said coldly.

"Yes, perhaps it was," Evelyn mimicked. She got up suddenly from her seat and crossed over to Joan. "Have a cigarette?" holding out her case. "What—you don't smoke! Why, I don't know how I should live without it! But, phew—how hot these rooms do get! Do you mind if I open the other window?"

"I should be delighted," Joan said heartily. "Let me do it."

"No, no!" Evelyn put her aside determinedly. She opened the French window and then paused and looked out. "There is somebody coming up the drive—a man. Who —who can he be? In some surprise Joan joined her.

"It is Paul, my husband! I left him in the drive with Mr. Hurst. Now he is coming on to fetch me."

"What?" Evelyn turned and stared at her with wide-open eyes. "I —you don't understand, Joan. I am talking of the man who is in the drive now, not of Lord Warchester. Quick, look—tell me who it is!" She gripped Joan's arm, and almost pushed her through the window. Who is it, I say?"

Half frightened, Joan looked again, but there was no one that she could see to account for Evelyn's agitation—no one at all in sight but Warchester, who was now glancing across at the window.

"'Yes—of course, as I told you, it is Paul. Why do you look at me so strangely, Evelyn? And, do you know you are pinching my arm? I believe I shall be black and blue to-morrow."

"Oh, I forgot!" Evelyn's hand dropped. She laughed harshly. "I—I was a little surprised. I—I hadn't thought Lord Warchester was like that. He—he reminds me of some one I used to know long ago."

"Does he?" Joan questioned coldly. She stepped outside on to the grass. "Ah, he has seen me—he is coming across! You don't mind, do you, Evelyn?"

A strange light gleamed for an instant in the elder sister's eyes as she stood behind and waited.

"Ask him to come here."

Joan waved her hand and Warchester came towards her quickly.

"Are you ready, Joan? How is your sister?"

"Here she is to answer for herself." Joan stood aside. "This is Paul, Evelyn."

To Warchester in the sunshine the interior of the boudoir looked almost dark. He could only distinguish a tall figure standing behind Joan. He bowed.

"Surely Lord Warchester and I have met before?"

He started as he heard the voice and looked round incredulously.

But Evelyn was coming forward now with outstretched hand. Beside Joan, in her severe black coat and skirt and simple toque, Evelyn's crumpled garments, her tousled hair, her artificially darkened eyebrows, looked very tawdry.

But Warchester's eyes noticed nothing of this; they sought her face eagerly, apprehensively. The expression that had flashed into them when he heard her voice deepened. Was it one of fear or one of recognition?

He made no movement to take the hand Evelyn had extended. With a shrug of her shoulders she let it fall by her side again.

"I remember Miss De Lavelle perfectly well," he said in a cold, hard tone. "But surely this is not your sister, Joan?"

"Of course it is!" Evelyn said with a laugh that somehow sounded strained. "When I went on the boards, I didn't think Spencer a very taking name, Lord Warchester, I changed it to De Lavelle. Sounded better, somehow, I thought. But, say, is it not strange we should meet again like this—you a lord, and I your wife's sister?"

"It is strange," Warchester assented moodily.

Joan watched them with startled eyes, resenting with a bitterness of which she was scarcely conscious this unaccountable previous acquaintance with her sister. She saw that Warchester's face had grown white, that the lines round his tense mouth were curiously sharpened.

What had been the tie between these two in the past? Joan asked herself miserably. That this was no meeting of mere chance acquaintance she saw plainly enough.

Evelyn was leaning nonchalantly against the woodwork, smoking a cigarette. As she spoke she raised her eyes; they flashed a quick warning to Warchester.

"Come inside, Lord Warchester; there is an iced drink I learned to make in the States. I have been teaching it to my man here; he has got the hang of it pretty well, and a glass will do you all the good in the world after your journey."

Warchester obeyed her imperative gesture. Inside he waited, apparently oblivious of even Joan's presence, watching Evelyn's every movement as she rang the bell and gave the order. Then when the man had brought in the tray, he drank eagerly the contents of the glass Evelyn poured out for him.

Evelyn turned to her sister.

"Can't I persuade you, Joan? It isn't bad, really, is it, Lord Warchester?"

But Joan shook her head.

"Not now, thanks! And I think if we do not make haste we shall be late for dinner. So, if you are ready, Paul, we will go now," She moved to the door; Warchester followed.

Evelyn accompanied them.

"I feel ever so much better now!" she cried in a loud voice that was a continual offence to Joan's ear. "It does one good to see people, and it is nice to meet an old friend."

Outside in the hall Mason was coming out of the study. Joan guessed that the old woman had heard of her arrival and had planned to speak to her as she went out. She held out her hand pleasantly.

"How are you to-day, Mason?"

Tears came in the woman's eyes as she took it and made a curtsey.

"I am not very well, thank you, my lady. I was wanting to tell your ladyship that the other day I found a work-box you had when you were a little child. There were two or three little things in it. I thought perhaps my lady, if I brought it over to the Towers one day you would maybe give me two or three minutes."

"Why, of course, I should be only too pleased! I must ask my sister to spare you to me for the day."

"Oh, I shall be spared easily enough, Miss Joan!" The old woman spoke bitterly, reverting to her young mistress's maiden name in her excitement. "I am not wanted here," glancing round to see that Evelyn was out of ear-shot. "Miss Davenant as good as told me I was too old to be of any use to her yesterday when she gave me notice."

"Gave you notice? Oh Mason, I am sorry!"

To Joan, Mason had always seemed inseparable from the Hall.

"I will speak to Miss Davenant," she added. "She could not really have meant—"

"I beg your pardon, my lady!" Mason drew herself up with dignity. "But I would rather Miss Davenant was not asked to change her mind. It is most likely that I should not have stayed here much longer anyway. I am over-old to learn the ways of new mistresses. But if I might speak to your ladyship to-morrow or the next day—"

"Why, of course," Joan said heartily. "Come over before lunch, Mason, and we will have a long afternoon together. I dare say I shall have thought of some fresh plan—"

"Oh, my lady—" Mason could not voice her thanks.

Evelyn and Warchester had walked to the door. On the threshold Evelyn paused and looked up into Warchester's face with mocking blue eyes.

"It is strange that Lord Warchester should turn out to be an old acquaintance, is it not? When I heard of my new brother-in-law I little thought that in him I should recognize my friend, Paul Wilton. Do the good stick-in-the-mud folks down here know of Lord Warchester's multiplicity of names? Why, this is the third I have heard —Wilton first, Warchester now, and once—"

"Hush!" Warchester interrupted her sternly with a glance at the two footmen who, it seemed to him, might be within hearing. "Do not mention that name! Heavens, don't you realize—"

Evelyn laughed recklessly.

"Guess I realize enough to know it might be awkward if I called you by it in the market-place!" Her eyes gleamed strangely. "Good thing I didn't meet you there, wasn't it? Now we are both prepared—"

Warchester's face had become very pale.

"For what?" he questioned beneath his breath. Involuntarily his eyes strayed to Joan, looking so fair and dainty in spite of her fatigue, then wandered from her to the painted face of the woman beside him. How was he to have guessed, he asked himself passionately—how should it have ever entered his mind that these two out of all the world should be sisters?

Evelyn shook her head.

"I do not know—how should I?" Her eyes narrowed as she watched him closely, as she saw how he flinched beneath her gaze. "Perhaps"—with another of the hard laughs that Warchester was learning to hate—"you would come in and talk it over, say, to-morrow morning. You know you must be careful for Joan's sake."

Warchester controlled himself with an effort.

"We will leave Lady Warchester's name out of the question, if you please," he said sternly. "If you wish it I will come over to-morrow, though I fail to see what purpose it will serve."

"To-morrow then, I shall expect you," Evelyn responded, waving her much beringed hand at him as she turned back. "Ta-ta!

It is rather cold out here now the sun has gone down. I hope you have plenty of wraps, Joan?"

"I don't think I shall need them. I like the touch of chill in the air," Joan responded absently. "Good-bye, Evelyn," kissing her sister's cheek. "I am glad you are better. You must come over and see me at the Towers soon."

"Of course!" Evelyn smiled and glanced at the tall dark man standing by the car. It was a pleasure to her to think that, in spite of his apparent calm, these seemingly innocent words of hers were making him wince. "Naturally, I want to see my sister's new home, and also that of my old friend, Lord Warchester."

As they drove down the avenue Warchester glanced more than once at Joan. She was sitting upright in her corner, her head bent forward, two little perpendicular lines between her level brows telling their own story of mental perturbation. She did not speak until they turned out of the lodge gates and were bowling swiftly along the road to the Towers. Then, still without looking at him, she said slowly:

"It is very strange that you should have known Evie. When we were trying to find her did you never guess—"

"Guess! How should I guess?" Warchester questioned roughly. "I had known her as Cécile De Lavelle. What should make me think—what faintest likeness between you is there that I should dream it was possible that she could be your sister? Even now—now that I have seen you together, that I have heard you call her sister, that I have seen you kiss her—I cannot bring myself to believe that this monstrous, this inconceivable thing is true, that you and that woman are sisters."

Something in his tone brought a ray of comfort to Joan's heart. She glanced at him timidly. She ventured to slip her hand in his beneath the rug.

"You didn't like her in the old times, did you, Paul? Not as you like me?"

"Like her as I like you!" Paul replied. "Joan, haven't you realized that you are the only woman in the world for me? Oh, my dear, have I failed so utterly to make you understand?"

Chapter Fifteen

"MR. LOCKYER and another gentleman are in the library, my lord."

"Mr. Lockyer!" Warchester was lounging on the divan, his thoughts, to judge from his expression, none of the pleasantest. He sprang up. "I will come to them at once. Tell her ladyship Mr. Lockyer is here."

"Yes, my lord."

The footman withdrew and Warchester hurried to the library. He had taken a great fancy to Septimus Lockyer, though so far he had seen little of him. He had heard that he was expected at the Trewhistles' however, and had sent a pressing invitation to him to spend a few days at the Towers.

As he opened the door he was wondering whether the keen-faced, kindly lawyer would be of any help to him now. Then with a sigh he shook his head. His affairs were of too tangled a nature even to be set straight by Septimus Lockyer.

Mr. Lockyer was standing by the fireplace, talking in a low, earnest tone to his companion.

"Ah, my dear Warchester; this is kind!" he said as his host entered the room. "I hope I have not disturbed you. I ventured to bring Mr. Hewlett with me. Mr. Hewlett—Lord Warchester. Mr. Hewlett has been actively engaged in the search for my missing niece, and, hearing last night that you had recognized an old friend in Miss Evelyn Davenant, he thought it would be interesting to hear where you had met her."

"Certainly! Won't you sit down, Uncle Septimus?" Warchester's change of countenance did not escape the eyes of either of the two men watching him. "I really knew very little of Miss Davenant—that is to say, I only met her in a casual way one does meet such people.

She was only known to me under her stage name of De Lavelle. I need not say I had not the very remotest idea she was identical with the missing Evelyn Spencer."

"Quite so, quite so!" Septimus Lockyer assented.

He had settled himself comfortably in one of the morocco-covered easy-chairs by the fireplace. Warchester took the opposite one facing the window; Hewlett, the detective, sat farther back in the shadow of the curtains. He was totally unlike the popular idea of a detective—short and thick-set in figure, with a florid complexion, a big fair moustache, fair hair retreating from his temple, and mild blue eyes, in one of which was screwed a monocle.

"We—that is to say Mr. Hewlett—had already discovered that she had gone on the stage under the name of De Lavelle before, in reply to the advertisement, Evelyn appeared on the scene," Mr. Lockyer went on. "I say the stage, but I believe, as a matter of fact, it would be more correct to say—er—the music-halls."

He looked inquiringly at Warchester, who nodded his assent. What in the world did these two men want? he was asking himself. By what concatenation of unlucky events had they come to hear of his early acquaintance with Evelyn Spencer?

"Would you just tell me what you knew of her, when you were introduced and all that?" Septimus Lockyer went on persuasively. "There were two Miss De Lavelles, I believe?"

"At one time," Warchester acquiesced, "they were called the Sisters De Lavelle, but it was perfectly well-known that they were not related, though there was a certain vague likeness between them. They used to sing and dance together, had turns at two or three halls every evening, for at one time they were very popular. But in spite of the undoubted resemblance between them, in spite of the fact that they were dressed alike, it was their very contrast that made them so piquante. We used to call them the Saint and the Demon."

"I remember." Septimus Lockyer nodded. "I have heard of them. I saw them once—that was why I fancied the photograph was familiar. And my niece, Evelyn, was—"

Warchester laughed.

"Your niece and my sister-in-law, my dear Uncle Septimus, was the Demon! I fear we have to face that fact both of us."

"Is that so?" Mr. Lockyer looked amused. "Ah, well, what's in a name, and what became of the Saint?"

"Ah, there I can't help you!" Warchester was brushing a speck of cigar-ash from his waistcoat. My acquaintance with the Sisters De Lavelle ended before their partnership was dissolved. I have no further knowledge of their movements."

"And the Dem—I mean my niece, Evelyn—was Marie," Septimus Lockyer remarked.

"Evelyn was Cécile," Warchester contradicted curtly.

"Oh, Evelyn was Cécile, was she?" Septimus Lockyer said slowly. "Oh, ah, of course—Evelyn Cecil Mary! Took her second name instead of her first, didn't she? Quite so, quite so!"

There was a pause. Warchester sat silent apparently contemplating the immaculate polish of his boots with interest. Mr. Lockyer was tapping his fingers thoughtfully on the leather-covered arm of his chair; the detective was gazing out of the window absently.

The door opened suddenly and Joan entered with a rush.

"Oh, Uncle Septimus, is it not funny that just as I heard you were here I should have found—I beg your pardon," as her glance fell on the detective. "I fancied you and Paul were alone."

"Dear, dear, did you? And what does that matter?" The great K.C. was smiling at the pretty, blushing face as he imprinted a paternal kiss on her forehead. "This is Mr. Hewlett, who has been spending a good deal of time looking for your sister, Evelyn, lately. And now what is it you have found just as you heard I was here? And why is it funny?"

"Well, it is funny, because you have wanted it so much, and have looked for it so often," Joan answered. "But I don't suppose you will care about it now—it is too late."

Mr. Lockyer's smile deepened.

"Something that I have wanted very much and you have looked for very long? You are exciting my curiosity, Joan. What is this wonderful discovery, and why is it too late?"

"Why, because Evelyn is here now!" Joan replied, answering his last question first. "It is her last letter, Uncle Septimus—don't you remember how vexed Mr. Hurst was when I couldn't find it? Well, Mason was clearing up the Hall the other day, attending to some alterations Evelyn wanted made, and she found this little work-box of mine," holding it up. "I used it for a year or two after I came to Davenant, and then it was thrown aside and I think I forgot all about it. But, see, Evelyn's last letter is in it. When I heard you were here I could not help running down to tell you, but it is just too late after all. It will not interest you now. I got it the day before I came to Davenant, and I never heard of my sister again until she came here the other day. She wrote several times, she says, but the letters never reached me. I suspect Mrs. Spencer did not forward them."

"I dare say she did not," Mr. Lockyer assented. "Yes, your discovery comes a little late, my dear; however, better late than never! I should like to look at the letter, if you will allow me."

"Of course; I am sure Evelyn would not mind."

Joan searched in her work-box, produced the missing letter, and handed it to him. It was directed in a weak, straggling handwriting to "Miss Polly Spencer, No. 10A Grove Street Mews, Hinton Square, W."

Mr. Lockyer opened it. A small object dropped out and rolled on the floor. Joan darted after it, but the detective was before her.

"Allow me, madame!" He pursued it into a corner and captured it.

"Is this madame—the half of a sixpence?" he inquired as he laid it on the table. "I can't see anything else, but—"

"Yes, that is it, thank you, Mr. Hewlett!" Joan said gratefully. "My sister sent it to me as a keepsake."

"Ah, she mentions it here!" Mr. Lockyer remarked. "And I see she writes from 15 Suffolk Lane, Highgate. Lovely part that; I have stayed there myself when I was a junior. May I read this aloud, Joan?"

The girl hesitated a moment.

"Oh, certainly, if you like! But it will sound rather silly, I think, now that we have found Evelyn."

"I don't think it sounds silly at all," Mr. Lockyer contradicted. "It shows that your sister was very fond of you, Joan."

"My darling little Polly"—he read aloud—"This is just to tell you that I am often thinking of you and of the time when I shall be able to have you with me again. I hope it will not be long before I can now, for I am doing pretty well. You must not be frightened if you do not hear from me now for a little time; for I may be going where letters will take some time to reach you, but you may be sure of one thing—I shall never forget my little sister Polly. I send you a sovereign with this; you are to give it to Dad and ask him to see that you have a new dress. A little bird who saw you the other night when you did not see her, my little Polly, told me that you were very shabby and wanted a new dress—oh, so badly! Mind you get a pretty one. Yesterday I had a bright new sixpence given me. I thought of my little sister, and I broke it in two. I send you the one half, the other I shall wear round my neck always. I have bored a little hole in your half, and you are to put a piece of cord through and tie it round your neck to remind you always of your loving sister Evie.

P.S. My love to Dad. Send me a line soon to let me know how you are."

"Quite a nice letter, I call it," Septimus Lockyer remarked as he laid it down.

"And I suppose you never answered it?"

"Of course I did! I wrote and told her I was coming to Davenant Hall. I used to wonder whether she resented my good fortune. But it seems she did not have the letter."

"Would you allow me to glance at the letter, madame?" Hewlett was fixing his glass more securely in his eye as he leaned forward.

Joan looked a little surprised.

"Oh, certainly! I don't suppose there is any reason why you should not, more particularly"—with a smile—"as you know what is in it already."

Mr. Lockyer handed it to him.

"I have never studied handwriting myself, but I believe it is one of your hobbies, isn't it?"

"To some extent, yes," the detective replied as he scrutinized the paper. It was a fancy blue, poor in quality, and the writing ran across it in straggling, uneven lines. In some curious fashion it seemed to interest Mr. Detective Hewlett intensely. He turned it upside-down, looked at it that way and this, and finally held it up to the light as if trying to see through it. As he gave it back to Mr. Lockyer he gave an almost imperceptible sign.

Mr. Lockyer looked at Joan.

"Well, now, my dear, I must wish you good-bye. I have promised to drive Mr. Hewlett to the station."

"Oh, Uncle Septimus, at least you will stay to lunch!" Joan exclaimed in dismay.

Warchester laid one hand lightly on her shoulder.

"We must make your uncle promise to come to us for a few days when he leaves the Trewhistles, Joan."

"Well, well, you are very good. We will see about that later. But now I must be off. I am due to pick Reggie up at the Home Farm in half an hour. Ready, Hewlett!"

Mr. Lockyer picked up the letter and the half of the sixpence from the table.

"I suppose you don't mind my taking these, Joan? I may want to look at them later."

"Oh, of course, if you like," Joan said uncertainly.

Mr. Lockyer apparently did not notice her hesitation. He carefully put both in his pocket-book, and held out his hand.

"I must say good-bye, for this morning, Joan. Later on perhaps I might come up and have a smoke with your husband."

"By all means, pray do!" Warchester responded politely.

But the lawyer noticed that the note of cordiality was absent.

Outside, when the motor-car was fairly started, Lockyer looked at the detective.

"Well, I did your bidding, but for the life of me I can't see what you want with that letter!"

"No? I had a fancy—" the detective began slowly, when there was a diversion. A carriage and pair had dashed in at the lodge gates, and the horses, coming suddenly upon the motor, began to shy. The coachman had them well in hand, however, and when the commotion had somewhat subsided Septimus Lockyer looked at his companion.

"The Davenant liveries. Now, Hewlett, you will have a chance of being introduced to my new niece. Come along!"

He drew the car to the side of the road; recognizing him, the coachman pulled up. The carriage had only one occupant, as the lawyer had surmised—the new mistress of Davenant Hall.

Evelyn was resplendent to-day; she had declined to wear full mourning, having had it modified to some extent by white. Her gown was of a black filmy material, the yoke and sleeves being exquisite lace; a lace scarf, which had been one of Mrs. Davenant's most treasured possessions was floating round her shoulders. Her yellow hair was elaborately curled and waved beneath her enormous hat. Altogether she had the appearance of being entirely satisfied with herself and with the world.

She greeted Mr. Lockyer with an expansive smile.

"You are out early this morning, Uncle Septimus! Been up to see Joan? How is she? I thought she seemed pretty dicky yesterday."

The lawyer looked amused.

"I think Joan is very well. Perhaps by contrast with you, my dear Evelyn. But may I introduce a gentleman who has been most anxiously looking forward to see you for some time—one to whom, I may say, you have given a great deal of trouble? Mr. Hewlett—Miss Davenant."

"I have given trouble, Uncle Septimus?" Evelyn said, bowing graciously as the detective raised his hat. "To this gentleman, do you say? I reckon you are beyond me. I don't know what you mean."

"Well, I think he can corroborate my statement." The lawyer laughed. "You found Miss Davenant a difficult person to trace, didn't you, Hewlett?"

"We did indeed, sir." The detective had been glancing with apparent admiration at Evelyn's face, dwelling on the big, coarsely moulded throat already threatening to emerge into a double chin, then straying to the blue eyes, set rather near together, to the forehead sloping slightly backward from the arched artificial eyebrows.

"Mr. Hewlett is the head of the firm of Hewlett and Cowham, which is probably the best-known private detective agency in London," Mr. Lockyer went on. "We confided the search for you to Mr. Hewlett, Evelyn, and I think I may say you have proved a great disappointment to him, eh, Hewlett?"

"Miss Davenant could not disappoint anyone," the detective declared gallantly. "It was our own stupidity in failing to ascertain her whereabouts that disappointed us."

"Oh, really! A detective!" Evelyn remarked nonchalantly, her manner altering perceptibly. It was evident, Mr. Lockyer remarked with some internal mirth, that the new mistress of Davenant Hall was inclined to resent as a liberty the introduction of a detective. She drew back in her corner. "Ah, well, you see, you didn't look in the right place, Mr.—er—Hewlett! I was out in South Africa when I saw the advertisements."

"So I heard." Mr. Hewlett spoke politely. "Well, I suppose nobody can be successful always. We must put you down as one of our failures, Miss Davenant."

Mr. Lockyer laid his hand on the carriage door.

"The most extraordinary thing to me is that you should have known Warchester. We were talking of it just now."

"Yes, wasn't it?" Evelyn agreed. "He was called Wilton then, you know, Uncle Septimus, and his cousin was Basil Wilton. I never knew that people changed their names when they became lords."

Septimus Lockyer smiled.

"Wilton is the family name; Warchester's children, if he has any, will be Wiltons too. But I remember seeing you once at the Apollo myself. What became of your sister? Funny thing the two of you should be so much alike! Have you any idea where she is now?"

Miss Davenant moved her parasol to one side.

"Bless you, no!" with a flicker of her white eyelids. "We did our turns together as long as it paid us, and then we just went our separate ways. I have never had a word from her since we parted and don't suppose I ever shall. Well, Uncle Septimus, this coachman of mine hates to keep the horses standing, so I must be off. Come up and see me at the Hall and have a chat as soon as ever you can. So long for the present!"

She nodded condescendingly to Hewlett as the carriage rolled on.

Septimus Lockyer and Hewlett walked back to the motor-car. When they were fairly seated the lawyer turned to his companion.

"Well, your wish has been gratified; you have seen the new owner of Davenant Hall. Not much like Lady Warchester, is she? "

Hewlett did not answer for a moment; his eyes had an absent, far-away expression.

"No, I can't say I see much resemblance," he said at last.

Mr. Lockyer glanced at him curiously, half doubtfully.

"You had not finished telling me why you wanted the letter and that broken sixpence, when we saw the carriage, Hewlett."

It was only a few minutes' run to the station; already they were in sight of it. The detective was gazing with interest at the flying landscape.

"Well?" Septimus Lockyer said impatiently.

Hewlett looked round.

"Well, sir, I once saw a letter that one reminded me of, and the other half of a broken sixpence. It was just a stupid fancy, I make no doubt, but I took a good deal of interest in the case the other one was mixed up in. It was when I was at Scotland Yard, before I started on my own, and I think I may say that first and last it has been the one affair that has baffled me more than any other I have ever been engaged upon."

"What case was that?" asked Mr. Lockyer. "And what connection can there possibly be with this letter?"

"I don't see the connection clearly myself," the detective acknowledged. "As for the case—well, least said soonest mended, if you don't mind, sir. I won't say any more until—until—"

"Yes, until—" Septimus Lockyer prompted curiously as they entered the station yard.

The detective hesitated and looked round.

"Until I have seen whether the halves of the sixpence fit," he answered cautiously.

Chapter Sixteen

"I am going to walk over to Davenant Hall, Paul."

"What—to-day again?" Warchester looked disappointed. "I wanted to take you out for a long spin in the car. Can't you put your sister off until to-morrow?"

"I don't think I ought. I promised to go over this afternoon. People may be calling now, and I fancy Evelyn is a little nervous. She was most anxious I should be with her."

They were on the veranda outside the smoking-room. Warchester was glancing at the newspaper. Joan had just appeared dressed for walking; she laid her hand on his arm.

"Come with me, Paul; it is a lovely walk if we take the short cut through the Home Wood."

Warchester shook his head.

"I would ask nothing better. But I must go over to Market Burnham on business, and I ought to call at the Marsh to see whether anything has been decided about Basil's operation. Tell you what—I will drop you at the Hall if you like. Then, if you must have exercise, you can walk home."

"Delightful," Joan agreed.

A fortnight had elapsed since her homecoming from her father's funeral—a fortnight during which it had been increasingly obvious that Warchester was doing his best to keep the two sisters apart. It seemed to Joan sometimes, looking back, that ever since the recognition of Evelyn by Warchester there had arisen a new barrier of reserve between herself and her husband. To her his account of his previous acquaintance with Evelyn was not sufficient to explain the unaccountable agitation that both had shown in that first instant of surprise. And, though she had loyally striven her best to accept it, she could not help the sharp little pain that would stab her now and then when she recalled that meeting in the boudoir at Davenant Hall.

Evelyn, there could be no doubt, was finding her new home dull—the county had not shown any disposition to welcome the new mistress of Davenant Hall with open arms. The fact that she had been on the music-hall stage had leaked out. There could be no doubt, too, that her appearance and style of dress had not attracted such of her neighbours as she had met hitherto.

Joan's acceptance of her sister seemed to make little difference; people shrugged their shoulders and said that Lady Warchester was pleased to be complaisant. The Trewhistles had openly ranged themselves amongst those who declared Miss Davenant to be

impossible, and all Joan's entreaties had not sufficed to get Cynthia
Trewhistle even to call at the Hall.

Evelyn, as was only natural, resented this attitude—she had
by no means as yet realized its extent among the surrounding
families—but she had taken a perverse fancy to Cynthia; it seemed
impossible to make her understand that, while Joan was the
favourite cousin, she herself would always remain in Cynthia's eyes
an intruder, an outsider.

She had driven over to Oldthorpe several times to talk matters
over with her cousins, as she phrased it, and only of late it had begun
to dawn upon her that it could scarcely be merely a coincidence that
Cynthia was never at home. Then her anger was turned upon Joan,
who, she was convinced, was the cause of her rebuff.

Warchester had only encountered his new sister-in-law once
or twice in the most casual fashion since their first meeting and
his interview with her the following morning. She had dined one
evening with them at the Towers, but Septimus Lockyer, the old
vicar and his wife, and Mr. and Mrs. Hurst had also been of the
party, and Warchester had contrived that he saw the very least,
compatible with politeness, that was possible of Evelyn.

Their avoidance was not mutual. That conclusion was forced
upon Joan. It was perfectly plain to Joan that Evelyn was anxious
to see Warchester again, that she had deliberately planned more
than once to obtain a conversation with him, only to find herself
foiled by Warchester's quiet determination. Joan would have been
more than mortal if she had not resented this state of affairs. Her
pride would not let her ask from Warchester an explanation which
he had evidently determined to withhold, and thus the rift between
husband and wife widened.

To-day, however, it seemed to Joan as she took her place beside
Warchester in the car and met his smile that there was a change.
He looked brighter, more like himself than he had done of late;
her spirits rose. If Warchester and Evelyn had met years ago, if
they had been lovers, at any rate that was all past and done with.

It was her day—Joan's—now. Did it not behove her to let the past bury its dead?

Warchester had dispensed with a chauffeur; he drove very slowly down the avenue.

"Shall I drop you at the Hall and come back for you after I have been to the Marsh, and heard what this new man thinks of the operation? Say yes, darling! It is a lovely day for a spin!"

"But that will give me so very short a time with Evelyn," Joan demurred.

"It will give you a nice long time with me," Warchester urged. "You will come, Joan?"

"I don't know," Joan hesitated, looked up into the dark face so near hers and gave way. "Yes, I will come. Yes, Paul, I will come!"

Warchester's head bent lower. After all, though the brief madness of the honeymoon was over, though this strange intangible obstacle had reared itself between them, the thought that she was his held a delicious intoxication. He glanced round; there was no one to see, not a living thing in sight save a stray rabbit scuttling over the soft grass by the side of the drive, a deer standing knee-deep amid the bracken. The great benches drooped their branches, making a green interlacing screen to hide them from sight of the house. He laid his lips on the soft curved ones so near his own.

"Oh, my wife, my darling, you would be true to me, you would believe in me always?"

The lingering kiss, the passionate words gave her a pang of pain; but for Joan all that mattered was that for one brief moment the torturing doubts and fears of the past month were forgotten, and that the lover, the husband of that bewildering love-dream on board the yacht was with her once more.

There was no need for words. As they turned into the high road Warchester's hand still held hers beneath the rug; the sense of his nearness, the warm pressure of his body against hers, brought the colour to her cheeks, the soft light to her eyes. But, delightful, entrancing as the moment of reunion was to both, it came to an end all too soon—the drive to the Hall was but a short one, and it was accomplished in something less than a quarter of an hour. At the gate Joan stopped the car.

"I will get out here and walk up. I would rather, Paul, and when you come back from the Marsh I shall be ready for you."

She sprang out and waved a farewell to him as he waited, watching her slight figure walking up the drive.

Presently he turned to his driving wheel; as he did so, his glances fell upon a stout, reduced woman in black who was looking at him curiously. For an instant he thought she was going to speak to him; then she passed on. Looking back, he saw that she had turned in at the gate.

"I wonder who she is?" he soliloquized as he pursued his way to the Marsh. "Seems to me that I have seen her somewhere, though for the life of me I can't remember where!"

Half-way up the drive Joan heard herself hailed, and Evelyn came hurrying across the grass.

"Here you are! Well, I am glad to see you! I get hipped to death in that great house by myself!"

"It is dull for you," Joan said gently. "Have you no friend you could ask to stay with you, Evie? I think in your place I should engage a companion—some nice girl who would ride and talk with you and be at hand when you wanted some one to talk to in the house."

"And bore me to death!" Evelyn burst into a loud laugh. "No thank you, Joan! A girl of that kind would be just about the finishing touch to this house. It is bad enough now, but with her—"

"Evelyn, do you know if I were you, I would send for Amy—the eldest of our stepmother's children," Joan said gently. "She seemed to me such a nice girl, and, after all, she is our sister. You might get very fond of her, and it would be good for both of you. Come, let us walk across to the fernery and talk it over."

"No, thanks! I am sick of the fernery and all the rest of the place!" Evelyn answered with a grimace. "If you want to walk—why, we will keep in sight of the drive. If a visitor comes, we shall see him. As for me taking one of Mrs. Spencer's children to live with me, no, thank you! I had enough of their mother. But I tell you what I am going to do—I am going to town next week to look up some of my old friends, and I shall stay at one of the swagger hotels and do some shopping—see about a town house, for I have told Mr. Hurst that I must have one. And when I have got it—well," with an expressive gesture, "I don't fancy Davenant Hall will see much of me!"

Joan blamed herself for the throb of relief with which she heard this decision. Nevertheless she felt it her duty to combat it.

"It is all so strange to you here, Evelyn. When you get used to it and have your own interests and your friends you will find it very different."

"I shan't give it the chance!" declared Miss Davenant, twirling her parasol from side to side. "As for Amy—do you know that Mrs. Spencer has written to me wanting me to continue the hundred a year which it seems our grandmother allowed them ever since they gave you up to her?"

"Yes, I know. Mr. Hurst spoke to us about it. What are you going to do? I should like to help the children and Paul is quite willing to do so. But as regards Mrs. Spencer—"

"I told Mr. Hurst to tell her I shouldn't give her a farthing," Miss Davenant stated decisively, "neither her nor her children. So I have done with that. The vicar and his wife have been up twice, Joan, asking for subscriptions—they want a new organ at the church. They have been my only visitors. There is a woman coming now. I suppose it is only some one for the servants. Well, if you want to go across the fernery, I don't mind."

They turned off together.

The woman whom Warchester had seen at the gate was panting up the drive towards them; when they crossed the grass she followed them and quickened her steps. Evelyn glanced behind.

"What a singular looking creature, Joan! What does she want, I wonder? She is coming after us."

Joan turned. Surely there was something familiar about the stout, red-faced woman, who was, so evidently, exerting herself beyond her wont in the endeavour to overtake them. She stopped.

"Why, Evelyn, it is—yes, of course it is! How are you Mrs. Spencer?" as her stepmother came up to them.

"Pretty well, thank you, though very much done up with the heat, my—dear," responded Mrs. Spencer, resolutely combating an inclination to say "my lady," and substituting "my dear" instead.

"But who is this?" staring at Evelyn, who was regarding her with amazement.

"Can't you guess?" asked Joan.

Mrs. Spencer looked critically at Evelyn.

"Surely it can't be—it isn't possible that it is Evie?"

"What do you mean? Why do you speak to this person, Joan? Who is she?" Evelyn questioned rapidly.

Mrs. Spencer's face grew crimson.

"Person indeed, miss! I would have you know—"

"Hush! Hush!" Joan interposed gently. "Miss Davenant does not recognize you naturally. Evelyn, this is Mrs. Spencer, our father's widow."

"So I see!" Miss Davenant returned haughtily. "May I inquire what you want—why you have come here?"

"It is for the sake of my poor children!" Mrs. Spencer burst into tears. "But for their sakes it isn't me that would demean myself."

"If it is what you wrote to me about"—Evelyn stood a little aside disdainfully—"it is no use. I shall not alter my mind, you and your children have no claim on me."

Mrs. Spencer's sobs grew more violent.

"I would not have thought it of you! Your own father's children—and me, that has done my best for you all, not so much as asked into your house—talked to out here as if I was a beggar-woman!"

"Evelyn!" Joan went close to her sister. "'After all, she was our father's wife. I think you ought to let her come into the house to give her a cup of tea. Afterwards I will talk to Paul; I will see what can be done."

"Well, do as you like!" Evelyn said sulkily. "Only remember that I stick to what I have said."

"Come in now, Mrs. Spencer." Joan touched her stepmother's arm. "You shall have some tea and we will talk matters over. I should certainly like to do something for Amy."

"And the best way to do something for Amy will be to help her mother to keep the home together," Mrs. Spencer observed as they all turned towards the house. "I could easily get the licence of the Bell transferred to me, and Gregory he would stay in and help manage, and there would be bread for all of us; but it all means money. And we have had a big family and not been able to lay by. And there has been the expenses of the illness and the funeral. I don't know which road to turn, and that is the truth. If you could see your way to keep on the bit your poor grandma allowed us—"

Her eyes were glancing from Joan to Evelyn; even she could see the difference between the two sisters. Not even her mourning had been able to subdue Evelyn's flamboyant air; her great black hat bore an exaggerated number of feathers that swayed and nodded as she walked; her long skirts trailed on the ground; her sleeves were short and ended in long lace ruffles; heavy gold bracelets clasped her powdered arms; her short, rather red fingers were covered with rings.

"A flaunting madam!" Mrs. Spencer called her to herself as she contrasted her garments with Joan's perfectly cut tailor-made costume.

Evelyn walked on a little ahead; Joan followed with Mrs. Spencer.

"I liked Amy, Mrs. Spencer," she said in her quiet, low tones. "I must talk to my husband about her. If we sent her to school—"

"I don't think so, thank you!" Mrs. Spencer answered defiantly. "I have seen enough of setting girls up, making them think they are above their parents and their home—" She broke off suddenly and looked at Evelyn as they arrived on the terrace.

Miss Davenant stepped into the morning-room and held the curtains aside.

"Come in!" Evelyn said impatiently. "Make haste, Joan, we don't want all the servants gaping at us."

But Joan found her entrance blocked by Mrs. Spencer's rotund figure. The widow had stopped dead in the window-frame, and was apparently examining the broad gold bracelet on Evelyn's left arm.

"Come in! What are you waiting for?" Miss Davenant's patience was soon exhausted.

Mrs. Spencer raised her head slowly; there was a curious look in her eyes, but it seemed to Joan that some of the woman's florid colour had faded, and she noticed that her lips moved.

Joan caught the muttered words.

"Gregory was right! Gregory was right!"

"What do you mean, Mrs. Spencer?" asked Joan.

"Oh, that don't much matter!" Mrs. Spencer said in a loud, truculent voice. "I ha' got a few words to say to you, Miss Davenant. You called me a person just now, I think. Now it is my turn to call you—" She moved forward quickly and her foot caught in the rug.

Miss Davenant's face changed. She put out her hand.

"Mind how you walk!"

At the same moment there was the sound of a motor in the drive. Joan looked round.

"Oh, Evelyn, here is Paul! He wants me to drive to Market Burnham, but he is back from the Marsh much sooner than I expected. However, we did not know that Mrs. Spencer would be here. I will tell him that I cannot go to-day."

Mrs. Spencer went up to Miss Davenant, who had not altered her position.

"Send her away!" she ordered in a hoarse whisper.

Evelyn glanced at Lady Warchester.

"You must go, Joan! I shall be very angry if you do not. I think perhaps, after all, I shall be glad of a chat over old times with Mrs. Spencer!" There was something unnatural in the laugh with which the speech ended.

Joan hesitated.

"Oh, well, if you really don't mind!"

"I don't mind a bit!" Evelyn led her to the window. "Quick; if he sees you he will not come up to the house!"

"I don't quite see why," Joan demurred. But she yielded to the stronger will and allowed herself to be hurried away. "Goodbye, Mrs. Spencer," she called out. "I will write to you about Amy in a day or two."

Mrs. Spencer seemed not to hear her. She was still standing just inside the room, motionless but for the panting breath that heaved her breast, for the restless eyes that followed Evelyn's every movement.

Miss Davenant stood outside on the grass until she had seen Joan join her husband and heard the car down the avenue; then she stepped slowly into the room. Her face was pale.

"Well," she said harshly.

Mrs. Spencer did not answer for a moment. She stood staring at the woman confronting her, a look of vindictive triumph on her red face.

"You were going to take that hundred a year from me, weren't you? Well, it isn't a hundred a year that is going to do for me now, I can tell you!"

Chapter Seventeen

THE OFFICES of Messrs. Hewlett and Cowham, private inquiry agents, were situated in Bruton Lane, one of the dingy streets running parallel with the Strand on the north side. No. 14 was no better than its neighbours, a tall gloomy-looking building let off as offices to different firms, as the names inside the door testified.

Messrs. Hewlett and Cowham occupied the second floor. There was a large office fronting Bruton Street which was used by both partners for the reception of their numerous clientele; doors on either side were labelled Mr. Hewlett and Mr. Cowham respectively, and there was a small room at the back which just held a desk and the high stool on which the solitary clerk to Messrs. Hewlett and Cowham was perched.

Mr. Hewlett was seated in his private room one morning, engaged in the congenial occupation of planning out the day's work for himself and his subordinates, when there was a knock at the door.

"Inspector Hudger of Scotland Yard, sir," the clerk announced.

Hewlett sprang up.

"This is good of you, inspector, you got my note?"

"Or I shouldn't be here." The inspector laughed. "I have brought what you asked me. Don't know that I should have done it for anyone else, but I know the interest you took in the Grove Street case when we were both looking it up, and—well, I made up my mind to stretch a point. You don't mean to say you have found a clue after all this time?"

"I may or I may not," Mr. Hewlett answered enigmatically. "You shall judge for yourself, inspector. What have you brought me?"

The inspector put his hand into his pocket and brought out a small wooden box.

"Just what you told me—the letter that was found in the lining of Wingrove's coat, and the wedding-ring with the other trinkets that were on the chain that was round the girl's neck."

"Just so! One minute before you open it, inspector!" Hewlett put out his hand. "As far as my memory served me, the letter is written on common blue paper of a fancy description, with a little flower sprigged over it in darker blue; and among the trinkets round the victim's neck was the half of a broken-sixpence, which was new when the girl died ten years ago. Am I right?"

Inspector Hudger's keen, clean-shaven face took on an expression of surprise.

"Why, of course you are, Mr. Hewlett! It isn't likely you would make a mistake about that, seeing how we used to talk it over and the theories you used to form on the subject."

Hewlett crossed over to a box in the corner of the room and unlocked it.

"Ay, I was younger in those days! It is a mistake to work on theories, inspector—mostly leads one into a quagmire." He took out the envelope he had received from Lady Warchester and, opening the letter, handed it to the police officer.

Inspector Hudger studied it in silence for a minute; then from his little box he took a half sheet of notepaper and, placing it beside the other, scrutinized them both, his lips pursed, the fingers of his left hand drumming persistently on the table.

Hewlett watched him attentively.

"Well, what do you make of it?"

The inspector looked up at last.

"These two letters were written by the same hand, not a doubt of it, I should say. If you had got the half of the sixpence—"

Mr. Hewlett dived into the recesses of his box once more.

"Here it is! Now, Mr. Hudger," laying the two pieces together, "what do you say to that?" as he showed that they fitted exactly.

The inspector looked at him.

"I should say you are getting close to the solution of the Grove Street Mystery, for I reckon you know where this letter came from. You know who the sister was it was written to?"

Hewlett nodded,

"I know that. And yet, so far from solving the mystery that surrounds the girl who died in Grove Street, I think it is thickening, inspector. You may remember a chat we had when you came in a few weeks back over that Dunsdale affair, when I told you I had been engaged to search for the missing heiress of the Davenant estate—Miss Evelyn Spencer?"

"Yes, I remember." Inspector Hudger was watching the other's face narrowly. "Only I didn't think it was Spencer you called her,

Davenant—that was it—she was to take the name of Davenant as a condition of succeeding to the property. And the younger sister was Lady Warchester, wasn't she? She would come into the property if the other couldn't be found. It is all coming back to me. But you don't mean to say—"

Hewlett looked at him squarely in the face.

"'The letter I have just shown you was the last written to Lady Warchester by her sister Evelyn. Lady Warchester answered it, but received no further communication from Miss Spencer.'"

"And this half of the sixpence was contained in it? I congratulate you, Mr. Hewlett. You have not only found your missing heiress, but you have discovered the identity of the unknown girl who was murdered in Grove Street ten years ago—a question which puzzled us at Scotland Yard, as you know, considerably."

Mr. Hewlett did not speak for a minute or two as he came round to the inspector's side and once more fitted the halves of the sixpence together. The one that the Scotland Yard official had brought with him had a tiny gold ring through the hole and was slung on a thin gold chain in company with a wedding-ring and a small heart of pink topaz. "Then you think the girl who was murdered in Grove Street was—"

"Why, of course it is plain enough!" the inspector interrupted. "This Miss Evelyn Davenant, or Spencer, for whom you have been searching is the girl who was murdered at No. 18 Grove Street."

Hewlett was thoughtfully twisting the end of his moustache. His light eyes looked almost vacant.

"Umph! Yes! But there is one drawback to this theory, my dear Hudger—that at this precise moment Miss Evelyn Davenant is at Davenant Hall, its undoubted mistress and Lady Warchester's affectionate sister."

"What?" Hudger stared at him. "Then what does this mean?"

"That is why I asked you to come here this morning, inspector," Hewlett replied, his manner becoming more genial as he saw the other's amazement. "That is what we must find out. I think when

I spoke to you before about my search for Evelyn Davenant, I told you that I had traced her to a widow's—a Mrs. Winthorpe. With this woman she lodged for some time, being reduced to all sorts of straits. She sang in the chorus of theatres, and when she left Mrs. Winthorpe's she told her she was going to change her name to De Lavelle and go on the music-hall stage. Well, I ascertained that the Sisters De Lavelle had a certain vogue for a year or two at the smaller halls, but that their popularity declined, and that towards the end of 1894 they gave up their partnership and left the stage. That was more than two years before the murder in Grove Street, you will observe. When Lady Warchester showed me this old letter I at once saw the importance of the discovery, for I had had that blue sheet of paper and that weak straggling writing in my mind's eye too often when we were searching for the Grove Street murderer not to feel sure it was the same. Besides, there was the sixpence."

"And yet you tell me that Miss Evelyn Davenant is at the Hall!" the inspector exclaimed. "Well, of all the extraordinary cases—"

"Yes, I fancy there may be a few tangles to unravel before we come to the end of it," Mr. Hewlett assented. "I said that Miss Davenant was at Warchester, but, as a matter of fact, she is in London, staying at the Cawdon—she came up yesterday. Now, Mr. Hudger, you know how the case stands. What do you make of it?"

The inspector looked at the poor little trinkets lying on the table, then glanced at the two letters side by side.

"It seems to me that this is pretty conclusive. The real Evelyn Spencer died in Grove Street. The woman at Davenant Hall is an impostor."

"Umph!"

Hewlett looked out of the window. There was not much in the sombre street to attract him one would have thought, yet he glanced up and down with keen interest. The roar and bustle of the Strand reached him, deadened in a measure by the intervening houses.

Inspector Hudger was not the most patient of mortals, as his subordinates could testify.

"Well," he demanded irritably, "what are you hesitating about, man? There can't be two opinions about that I should say."

There was a far-away expression in Hewlett's eyes.

"You may be right, inspector, but the Grove Street Mystery is not cleared up yet, not by a long way. Ah, here is the witness I was expecting!" in a tone of satisfaction. "Jones," opening the door and beckoning his clerk, "please show Mr. Simpson and the lady with him up as soon as possible."

"Who? What lady?" Inspector Hudger inquired with natural curiosity.

"A lady who has lived at 15 Suffolk Lane, Highgate, for the last fifteen years," Hewlett answered lightly. "I should say that we ought to learn something interesting from her."

Jones opened the door and stood back.

"Mr. Simpson and Mrs. Read, sir."

Mr. Hewlett and the inspector both rose.

"This is very kind, Mrs. Read! I am glad that you were able to come," the former said gratefully as he set a chair for her.

"Thank you, Mr. Hewlett! I am sure anything I can do," Mrs. Read began with a simper, as she seated herself and folded her black gloved hands primly on her lap.

She was a faded looking woman of middle age whose attire and mode of dressing her hair betrayed some hankerings after her vanished youth. Her light hair had manifestly been touched up; it was piled up on the top of her head beneath a toque that had some pretension to present-day fashion, and a few straggling curls were straying over the forehead. She wore a black gown trimmed elaborately, as was the fashion, with jet and fringe; an art necklace was clasped round her throat; art bracelets adorned her wrists. Nevertheless, she retained some traces of former good looks; her features were aquiline, the watery grey eyes were large and had probably once been pretty and appealing. Possibly Mrs. Read had been a beauty in her day, and the consciousness of this fact lent a certain old-fashioned coquetry to her manner now.

"That will do, thank you, Mr. Simpson!" Hewlett nodded to the young man who had accompanied her in—a clean-shaven youth, who had the appearance of a clerk or a shopman.

"Now Mrs. Read, I think Mr. Simpson has told you that we wish to procure some information about a young lady who was staying with you on the 10th of May, 1897?"

"Yes, Mr. Hewlett. Certainly!" Mrs. Read eyed him reflectively for a moment. "It would be Miss De Lavelle, I make no doubt. She was a nice, pleasant-spoken-young lady; she lived with us for the best part of a year, and I call to mind that she left on the 11th of May, 1897, having good cause for remembering the date for private reasons of my own, as you will understand, gentlemen, when I tell you that I was married two days later."

The detective smiled.

"Ah, now we know where we are! That would fix it in your mind, Mrs. Read. How was it that this young lady, Miss De. Lavelle, left you? Was it sudden?"

"No. At least it may have been at the last, but we had been expecting it for some months. She had been looking out for a situation for some time, and at last something turned up—in Florence, I think it was—and of course we knew it would not do to refuse it, though she was terrible upset at having to leave England, but she had her living to get as we knew. And we were glad she should hear of anything."

"I see!" Mr. Hewlett drew out his pocket-book and made a few notes. "Do you remember the circumstances of Miss De Lavelle's leaving?" he asked after a pause. "How she was dressed and what luggage she took with her?"

"Oh, yes, gentlemen!" This time Mrs. Read's glance took in Inspector Hudger also. "I know it was early in the morning when she went. She walked to Highgate Station; from there she was to take the train to King's Cross, and there a friend would meet her and drive with her to Waterloo or Victoria, I forget which. As for, what she was wearing, it was white china silk, for I made the remark that it wasn't the best thing to travel in, and she laughed and said she liked to look nice, and that she should buy herself a serge costume for the voyage either in London or Southampton."

"The luggage?" Mr. Hewlett prompted as she paused.

"Oh, that she sent on in front," Mrs. Read answered at once. "I know she had only a handbag with her, for a young cousin of ours who was staying with us helped to carry her luggage down to the station for her."

"White dress—um!" Mr. Hewlett made several notes in his pocket-book. Inspector Hudger watched Mrs. Read closely. At length Hewlett looked up.

"You had no reason to think that Miss De Lavelle was married, I suppose?"

"Well, since you ask me, gentlemen"—Mrs. Read glanced round—"I suppose I shall do Miss Lavelle no harm by answering. Mr. Simpson told me that there was a lot of money coming to her if she turned out the one you were looking for."

There was silence for a few seconds. Then Mr. Hewlett fixed his monocle more firmly in his left eye.

"We have every reason to believe that Miss De Lavelle will prove to be the heiress to a large fortune," he said briskly. "You must help us all you can, Mrs. Read."

"Well, then, I have had my suspicions," Mrs. Read acknowledged. "I have seen her out with a gentleman and once I saw her with a wedding-ring. She tried to make me believe that it was her mother's but—well, I had my doubts."

"What was this man like—the one you saw Miss De Lavelle with?" Hewlett questioned.

"Well, it was mostly in the dusk, and I wasn't very near them, but I could see he was tall with a dark beard and he wore a sort of big slouch hat pulled down over his brow. Of course they might have been only sweethearts; but the thought came to me that they were married. And I know my mother had the same notion from the little things she said. And she would be more likely to know about it than I should, me being only a girl at the time"—smoothing out the creases in her black skirt with a propitiatory smile.

"So we should imagine," Mr. Hewlett said politely. "Would it be possible for us to see your mother, Mrs. Read?"

"Why, certainly! She is keeping house for a brother of mine at Stoke Newington just now, but when she comes back I know she will be pleased to tell you anything you like. We always liked Miss De Lavelle both of us, though we took it hard that she never sent us a line after she went away."

"Ah!" the detective said absently. "Perhaps it was not her fault, Mrs. Read. Should you know a photograph of Miss De Lavelle, I wonder?" He crossed over to his cupboard once more and took out a long envelope. "Is this she?"

As Mrs. Read took it from him her expression changed, her watery eyes looked frightened and awe-struck.

"Yes, it is Miss De Lavelle," she said hesitatingly. "I should know her anywhere, but she—she—" She glanced up at the detective's face. "Why was she taken like this, when she was asleep? It makes me feel creepy, almost as if she might be dead!"

The detective made no reply.

"Look at her dress," he directed.

Mrs. Read obeyed him.

"Why, I declare she might have been taken in the very gown she went away from our house in!"

"That was what I wanted to know," Hewlett said slowly. "I am much obliged to you for coming this morning, Mrs. Read. It may be that I shall have to trouble you to repeat what you have told me, but I will let you know later on."

Mrs. Read rose slowly. All the simpering smiles had died out of her face now—she looked pale and frightened and looked round the room fearfully.

"I hope—Miss De Lavelle is quite well, gentlemen," she said nervously. "That photograph has frightened me somehow."

Mr. Hewlett glanced at the inspector; he took rapid counsel with himself.

"If Miss De Lavelle is indeed the original of that photograph I am afraid that ill has befallen her, that it did befall her when she left you," he said gravely. "But we are not certain yet; there are several points to be cleared up, and you may rely upon our communicating with you later on. If we can find Miss De Lavelle alive there is good fortune awaiting her."

Mrs. Read was trembling visibly.

"I—I am very glad to hear it, sir. I am sure that the last thing I should wish would be to do Miss De Lavelle harm, for we were always fond of her, me and my mother both."

"I am sure you were." The detective looked at her sympathetically as he moved towards the door. "And now, Mrs. Read, you must allow me to have a cab called for you. Yes, I insist! All this has been too much for you. Mr. Simpson, get a cab for Mrs. Read, will you, and see her to King's Cross?"

He waited until she had gone downstairs; then he turned to the inspector, who was studying the photograph Mrs. Read had laid on the table. It represented a girl in a white dress lying on a couch or a rug—it was difficult to tell which. The features in the photograph were well-defined, and it was easy to see that the girl was young and fair; the eyes were closed, the lips slightly parted. One would have thought at first sight that she was asleep, but as Mrs. Read had said there was something rigid, unnatural about the attitude, about the pose of the hands, the way the head lay. It was not difficult to guess that sleep had passed into its twin sister, death.

Inspector Hudger looked up.

"I am wondering how it was that this was not identified before. The Sisters De Lavelle were on the stage. I should have thought this would have been recognized at once."

For answer, Hewlett took another photograph from its envelope and placed it beside the first.

"I had some little difficulty in getting this. The public is fickle, and photographers have short memories, but at last I unearthed it at a shop in Oxford Street. Looking at it, I think one sees why the other photograph was not recognized."

Hudger looked at it closely. It represented two girls in tights, with the shortest of tulle skirts, the most abbreviated of bodices, with masses of fair hair curled over their foreheads. They were dressed alike in every particular; every curl on the head of one had its counterpart on the head of the other. The two faces were alike too, save that the expressions were dissimilar. The eyes of the one were downcast, her lips were curved in a half smile, the other looked straight out at the world, defiance mingling with the broad smile that showed her strong white teeth. Underneath the photograph was the description, "The Sisters De Lavelle, now performing at the Column."

Hudger laid his finger upon the one with the downcast eyes.

"You don't mean to tell me that this is the girl of the other photograph—the girl who died in Grove Street?"

Hewlett nodded.

"And that"—pointing to the other—"is the Miss Evelyn Davenant who is at present mistress of Davenant Hall." He permitted himself a smile. "Her reign there is likely to be short, I suspect."

"I don't know,'" Hewlett said thoughtfully. "I—it seems to me we want more proof before we take any definite step. You see"— tapping the photograph—"we know now that the girl who died in Grove Street was one of the Sisters De Lavelle. So far the Grove Street murder is one step nearer solution; but the proving that the lady now in possession of the Davenant estates is not Miss Evelyn Spencer is going to be a very different matter. We have only the letter and the sixpence to go upon—and the wrong Sister De Lavelle might have got the half sixpence. We must remember too that Miss Evelyn Davenant is apparently in possession of all the papers necessary to prove her identity. She has been received without question by her sister, and I heard this morning that she has been recognized by her stepmother. My chief hope now lies in Mrs. Winthorpe, but as she has not seen Evelyn Spencer for fifteen years it may be difficult for her to identify the Sister De Lavelle who was Evelyn Spencer and who is now posing as Evelyn Davenant, the mistress of Davenant Hall."

Mr. Hudger produced his cigarette case and handed it to the other.

"Well, at any rate, whether Miss Evelyn Spencer is Miss Evelyn Davenant or not, you have got a good many steps farther in the problem that puzzled us at Scotland Yard for so long—the identity of the victim in the Grove Street murder. I congratulate you, Mr. Hewlett!"

Chapter Eighteen

"I WONDER what Evelyn is doing? I thought I should have heard from her to-day. But the last post is in and she has not written."

"I dare say she is busy," Warchester said indifferently.

He was not particularly fond of the thought of Evelyn at any time. Now that she was for the time being away from the neighbourhood he was thinking only of Joan—who had never looked in his eyes lovelier, more adorable. There was something peculiarly becoming to her tall, slim young figure in an evening gown of richest lustrous velvet, cut square in front to show a glimpse of the white neck, the slender rounded throat; the long sleeves were of pleated chiffon caught here and there across the firm young arms with diamond clasps. It was a sombre gown for so young a woman; on many girls of her age it would have looked out of place, but there was a certain stateliness about Joan's beauty that seemed to demand a rich setting, and the very absence of relief served but to enhance her vivid colouring. Of late she had looked at times pale and distrait, but to-night her vitality was reasserting itself; her cheeks were glowing; her brown eyes as she glanced at Warchester gleamed brightly.

She had been sitting in her favourite room, but as she spoke she rose and stood by the fireplace, one arm resting on the mantelpiece.

"I often feel anxious about Evelyn, Paul," she confessed. "She does not seem to get on with people. I am afraid she will never settle down at the Hall."

Warchester was conscious of a growing hope that she would not.

"Oh, perhaps later on, when she has made friends with her neighbours," he suggested hypocritically.

Joan sighed as she looked down at the glancing flames. August had passed into September; already the evenings were colder and there was a touch of frost in the early morning.

"She has a great deal of good in her really, Paul. You know she said she would not do anything for Mrs. Spencer?"

"Yes. I thought she was perfectly right," Warchester responded slowly.

"Perhaps she was—in a way," Joan said doubtfully, "but it seemed a little hard. However, it appears that her bark was worse than her bite. I had a letter from Amy this morning and she says that Evelyn is doing so much for them; they are staying on at Willersfield, and the younger ones are to be sent away to school."

"Really!" Warchester's tone did not betray much interest. Joan did not pursue the subject. She waited silently, wishing she could bring the conversation round to the point for which she was longing. Fortune was kind to her.

A footman entered the room, a telegram on his silver salver. Joan uttered a sharp exclamation as Warchester took it.

"From Evelyn?"

"No, no! Why should you think of her? This is from Delia Mannering," scanning it eagerly. "Operation entirely successful. Doctors give every hope of complete recovery."

"Oh, I am so glad!" Joan cried with eager congratulation. "You will feel almost as if Basil had been given back to you from the dead, Paul. It is wonderful! Do you think he will remember everything that occurred in the past like other people now?"

"I wonder?" Warchester's face looked gloomy as he gazed into the fire reflectively. "It is impossible to say. The operation is safely over, that is the great thing. For the rest"—he shrugged his shoulders—"of course they would tell Delia there was every hope of recovery. She would not have consented to the operation otherwise."

"I suppose you saw a good deal of your cousin years ago, before his accident?" Joan questioned idly. She was still standing by the mantelpiece.

As she spoke she took up an ivory toy—a Chinese joss-house exquisitely carved; her long fingers toyed with it absently.

"Yes, we were very good friends," Warchester replied. He was not looking at Joan now. He had thrown the telegram into the fire; he watched it burn mechanically.

"He knew Evelyn too, didn't he?" Joan questioned.

"I believe so," curtly.

"Was it in London that you knew her?" Joan persisted, her brown eyes searching his sombre face wistfully. "Sometimes I wonder whether you realize how very little I know of your past, Paul—of the years before I met you. Even Evelyn"—a certain bitterness creeping into her tone—"knows more than I do!"

Warchester took out his cigarette-case.

"May I smoke?" Receiving Joan's gesture of permission, he lighted his cigarette carefully. "There is so little to know, child. I was in the diplomatic service first. Then I got tired of it, found it wasn't in my line, and gave it up to become a wandering stone of sorts."

"Were you in the diplomatic service when you knew Evelyn?" Joan pursued.

Was it fancy or was he trying to evade the mention of her sister's name?

Warchester lay back in his chair and watched the smoke from his cigarette curl upwards.

"No, that was later," he answered at last, "when she was on the stage, and I was a struggling artist trying not very successfully to get my living."

There was a pause. Warchester, puffing away at his cigarette, was apparently absorbed in his own thoughts.

Joan was holding the mantelpiece very tightly now. The colour was receding from her cheeks. He had been an artist! All unbidden, that scene in the studio in Grove Street rose up before her eyes. Warchester tossed the end of his cigarette into the fire—the very gesture of ten years ago.

The ivory toy in her hand cracked.

"An artist?" she repeated aloud.

Something in her tone struck Warchester as strange.

"Well, I wasn't much of an artist, certainly. Most of my productions found their way into the flames eventually, I believe."

"Yes, yes, I know they did!" That deadly nausea she had experienced ten years before was gripping Joan again. She bowed her head. Had she not heard—had not some one told her that if she stooped the faintness would pass?

Warchester looked at her curiously.

"You know? Well—But what is it, Joan? You are ill—faint?" springing to his feet and hurrying to her side.

Joan pushed him away; with a supreme effort she forced the sinking faintness back. Her face was colourless, her great brown eyes, filled with reproach, looked all the bigger by contrast; there were dark shadows beneath the softness of her hair.

"I am—tired," she said slowly. "No, do not touch me, please, Paul! I shall be better alone. I think I will go to my room, please. Will you ring for Treherne?"

"No! I will take you upstairs myself," Warchester contradicted. "Poor child, is your head aching? I ought to have seen that you were overtired before. Lean on me—so!"

But Joan drew herself from him. At all hazards, she must get away, she must think.

"I would rather have Treherne, please!"

Warchester touched the bell in silence. Her rebuff had wounded him deeply; it seemed to him that there had been dislike, almost aversion in the movement by which she had repulsed him. He watched her anxiously as she made her way to the door and crossed the hall. Then as Treherne met her he turned into the smoking-room. It felt hot and stuffy; he flung open the window that led to the terrace, and threw himself down on the divan. He began to be seriously uneasy about Joan again. He had fancied of late that she had been better, but her sudden pallor of to-night, her agitation, were alike unintelligible; coupled with it now, as before too, was that extraordinary distaste for his touch, his very presence even. He drew a deep breath as he took a cigar from a newly-opened box beside him. Certainly the perfect marriage of his dreams was very unlike this reality.

He wondered what Joan was doing, whether her indisposition was passing; it was impossible to settle to anything. Suddenly a sound on the gravelled path outside caught his ear. Some one was walking along softly, gropingly, as if unacquainted with the ground. He started. Surely Joan had not—then he smiled at his own folly as he waited and looked out.

Outside the moon was shining, but by the contrast with the warmth and light of the room the outlook was dark and gloomy. From the terrace it was easy to see inside. Warchester scarcely realized how visible his every movement was as he raised himself.

A dark figure crept into the little circle of light by the window.

"Lord Warchester!"

For the moment he did not recognize the voice. He drew the curtains aside.

"Who is there?"

"I must speak to you!" A woman stepped quickly into the room.

"Evelyn!" Warchester drew back and stared at her as she threw aside the dark motor-veil that enveloped her head and was twisted round her shoulders almost like a disguise.

The woman gave a defiant laugh.

"Yes! You don't seem to have much of a welcome for your sister-in-law!" she said scornfully.

"Why have you come here?" Warchester questioned hoarsely. His dark face was set and stern; a sombre wrath burned in his grey eyes. "What do you want?"

"To see my brother-in-law!" Another laugh accompanied the words.

Looking at his unwelcome visitor, Warchester saw that an astonishing change had taken place in her appearance. The yellow curls were brushed back smoothly and pinned closely to her head; the rouge and pearl powder had been washed from her face; only the eyes—the great, haunting, reckless eyes—remained unchanged.

"What do you want?" Warchester still stood in the shadow of the curtains. He made no attempt to offer any conventional greeting.

His unwelcome visitor came farther into the room and threw her wraps and the bag she was carrying on his writing-table.

"Ah, now we are coming to business! First let me suggest that you draw down the blind. It would be just as well if our little tête-à-tête passed unobserved—just as well for both of us. Next," when with a gesture of distaste he had obeyed her, "as to what I want. Well, my dear brother, it is the usual thing with a woman—money."

"Money? Impossible!" Warchester gazed at her in amazement. "You came into an immense amount of ready money, I know. Mrs. Davenant had not lived up to her income for years. How can you possibly have got through it in this short time?"

"Oh, I haven't got through it! Don't alarm yourself!" She moved over to the divan and flung herself upon it. "You are not very hospitable, my dear Lord Warchester. You don't even ask me to take a cigarette, and yet our tastes used to be very similar in the old time, I remember." She took out her watch and looked at it. "I can spare half an hour. I must have one more smoke with you," helping herself from the open case. "I am sure Joan—"

"I think," Warchester said very coldly, "we will leave my wife's name out of the question, please."

The blue eyes, watching him, narrowed; an odd green light gleamed in them for an instant.

"Yes. Why should we talk of her—you and I—while we have so many interesting memories to discuss together? I shall never forget my surprise when I found that my new brother-in-law, Lord Warchester, was no other than my old friend the artist, Mr—"

Warchester made one step towards her,

"Have I not told you that I will not have that name mentioned? Heavens, don't you realize—have you no thought for my wife—for the sister who has cared for you?"

The curious cat-like eyes were still watching him, as if taking pleasure in the sight of his agitation; the face, haggard and old in its pallor, hardened; the full lips compressed themselves into a straight line.

"Yes, I have thought of her. She has all the things that I have wanted all my life. I should like to see her suffer as I have done—to pull her down, if only one step, from her pedestal!"

"Have you quite finished?" Warchester demanded sternly. "If you have so little gratitude there is the less reason I should bear with you. Say what you have to say as briefly as possible and go!"

Evelyn paused with her cigarette in her hand.

"But, my dear brother-in-law, I have told you what I want—money, money, money! When you have given me what is necessary I assure you I shall not linger, delightful as I find your society."

Warchester moved forward suddenly and gripped her shoulder.

"Enough of this fooling! Tell me what you mean and why you want this money."

Evelyn did not flinch from his grasp; she looked up and laughed mockingly.

"As for what I mean, I thought you might have guessed, my dear Lord Warchester. Ah, you have all been blind! You good people took it so quietly that I was the sister of that milk-and-water piece of perfection upstairs—"

A sudden light was breaking upon Warchester. He looked down at the woman, whose big, restless eyes were in curious contradiction with the lightness of her words; his hand dropped from her shoulder.

"Do you mean that you are not—"

"Ah, you are tumbling to it!" The hard metallic laugh rang out again; she puffed her cigarette smoke in his face insolently. "Your wits were keener in the old days, my friend. Yes, it was a pretty little scheme, but it had one weak point, and of course that ruined me. I might have known it would."

"You are not Evelyn Davenant—you are not Joan's sister?" Warchester squared his broad shoulders as if shaking off some invisible burden. "Good heavens, how could we think you were? And I—I who knew—why could I not see that you were an impostor?"

"Ah! Impostor! If I were you, I would refrain from abuse." The woman pitched her cigarette into the fireplace. "This is an infernally bad brand, Warchester; you did yourself better in the old days. What was I saying? Yes, Impostor is not a nice name, but there is an uglier name still. How if I used it to—"

"You will not!" Warchester said with dangerous quietness. "You will be silent now and for ever!"

"If you pay me enough," the woman said. "Otherwise—"

Warchester's gaze would have cowed most women.

"How much do you want?"

"Ah, now you are coming to business!" she said approvingly. "I should like as much in gold and notes as you can spare, and a cheque for—shall we say a thousand at present?"

Warchester paused, book in hand.

"Upon my word, you are moderate!"

"All that a man hath will he give for his—" she quoted significantly.

He frowned.

"If I help you now, it is once for all—to help you to get away—for the sake of the past, you understand?" he said as he unlocked a drawer and took out his cash-box. "And also because for Joan's sake—"

"Oh, yes, I understand! And for somebody else's sake!" she interrupted fiercely. "Stop that, Warchester! The money, please! I have no time for sermons!"

Warchester took out a shining pile of gold; her eyes watched it greedily.

"How could you be mad enough to come here? To think that such a plot could go undetected?"

"Well, some plots do, you know," she returned. "And I was starving when I saw the advertisement—literally starving. I wonder whether you have any idea what that means? One is not very particular what one does then when one sees a chance of getting something to eat. Ah well, it is the fortune of war! If I had known of your luck I might have come to you instead."

Warchester visibly winced as he tore out a cheque and put a pile of gold in her hand.

"Now go," he ordered, "while I can trust myself, or—"

"Oh, surely you wouldn't!" she echoed with a laugh. "Would it not be a curious coincidence if—Oh, Warchester, this is a shabby cheque! I thought—"

"You will not get any more!" he assured her sternly. "I blame myself—"

"Oh, I shouldn't do that!" she interrupted, rising and drawing her motor-veil round her hat again. "Well, well, you will hear from me later, Warchester. I shouldn't dream of letting an old friend drop out of sight. For to-day—well, I will let this do. Oh, by the way"—pausing outside the window—"I heard in town that your cousin Basil's operation had been a great success!"

"Yes." Warchester's tone seemed to change, to harden.

She paused and looked back before she glided away into the shadows. "I wonder what he will remember?" she questioned mockingly.

Chapter Nineteen

"LUNCHEON is served, my lady, and his lordship is already in the dining-room."

"Is he?" Joan hesitated, put her hand on the door and then walked back again to the window.

Treherne was too thoroughly trained to exhibit surprise, but it was impossible to suppose that in a large household, such as the Towers, the strained relations that had existed at times between Lord and Lady Warchester had passed without comment. On the whole, the elder servants were of opinion that a few tiffs in early married life were to be expected, and that the couple, being fond of each other, were bound to come out all right in the end. Of late it had been evident too that husband and wife were once more on better terms; this morning, however, glancing at the shadows beneath Lady Warchester's eyes, at the dimming of her colouring, having noticed that the key in the door leading into Warchester's dressing-room was turned on the outside, Treherne drew her own conclusions.

"Tell his lordship I have a headache," Joan said, without looking round. "And you might bring me a tray up here, Treherne."

"Yes, my lady."

As the maid was leaving the room Joan recalled her by a sudden exclamation.

"Oh, here is Uncle Septimus! I will go down, Treherne. I must see Mr. Lockyer."

Septimus Lockyer was just drawing up at the front door in his motor-car. Joan ran downstairs quickly and met him in the hall.

"Oh, Uncle Septimus, I am glad to see you! It is lovely that you should have come to-day!"

"Thank you, my dear! That is the prettiest welcome I have had for many a long day," he said as he stooped and kissed her.

Warchester came out of the dining-room with outstretched hands.

"Well, this is luck, Uncle Septimus! Bring him in, Joan. You are just in time for lunch."

The K.C.'s face was grave as he followed them into the room.

"I will sit with you while you have yours. I have already lunched and have come about business—business with both of you."

"Business—with both of us?" Joan looked at her uncle in astonishment. "What, is it about, Uncle Septimus?"

Mr. Lockyer spread out his hands.

"No, no! Lunch first and business afterwards, Joan."

It was not a lively meal and it was with a feeling of relief that they rose when Warchester proposed an adjournment to the smoking-room.

Joan put her arm within her uncle's.

"Come, we must get this tiresome business of yours over. I have ever so many things I want to consult you about."

The sunshine was streaming in through the open windows of the smoking-room; outside on the lawn great clumps of Michaelmas daisies shone white and purple against the soft green.

"You don't mind, do you, Joan?" Septimus Lockyer said as he helped himself to a cigar and stood looking out over the garden for a minute.

When he turned his face was very grave. To Warchester it was evident that he was nerving himself to speak, that he intensely disliked the task that lay before him, and for the first time a pang of something like fear of what they were about to hear darted through the younger man.

"It isn't a pleasant story I have come here to tell you," the lawyer began. "It isn't altogether agreeable to state that one has been made a fool of—that we have all been taken in, perhaps I ought rather to say. Joan, my child, we have all been made the victims of a daring fraud. Your sister, Evelyn—"

"Evelyn!" Joan, who had, taken one of the large easy chairs by the mantelpiece, sprang to her feet. "Is she ill? Do you mean that she wants me?"

"No, no!" Septimus Lockyer put her back quietly in her chair. "'She—is all right. I am going to ask you a strange question, Joan. Do you like her—Evelyn?"

"Like Evelyn?" Joan looked up at him, vaguely perplexed. "Why, she is my sister! Naturally I——But she is my sister—" faltering a little as she met his searching gaze. "I—I would rather not discuss her, even with you, Uncle Septimus."

The lawyer drew a deep breath.

"I think I am answered. And I cannot tell you how glad I am to get that answer, Joan, for—I told you we had all been the victims of a fraud—the woman who has taken us all in, the imposter who has been masquerading as mistress of Davenant Hall, is not your sister Evelyn at all!"

There was a minute's tense silence. Joan stared at him with wide-open, uncomprehending eyes. Warchester was the first to speak. During the long night-watches he had been persuading himself that the pseudo-Evelyn's confession of her impostorship was only a piece of rodomontade.

"Is this true, Uncle Septimus? This woman whom my wife his accepted as her sister is a common adventuress—she is not Evelyn Davenant at all?"

Mr. Lockyer bowed.

"I cannot tell you how I blame thyself that we did not find her out sooner. It is terrible for you, my child!" He took Joan's hand in his. "I am sorry, and yet, do you know, I am glad. She was not a desirable sister for you—she was not a suitable mistress for Davenant. Now in a short time her reign there will be only like a bad dream, if it is not utterly forgotten."

Joan caught her breath sharply; her hand gripped Septimus Lockyer's brown fingers convulsively.

"I don't understand, Uncle Septimus. What is it you are saying? It can't be true that Evelyn—"

"The woman who has called herself your sister, Evelyn, is an impostor!" Septimus Lockyer said firmly. "Pull yourself together, Joan! We have all been taken in, but there is little harm done. She made a clean bolt of it last night with all the ready money and the valuables she could lay her hands on, but the family jewels were in the bank, and you and Paul will not feel the loss of a few hundreds," with a glance at Warchester.

"Certainly not, if we have any say in the matter!" Warchester said quickly. "But you must be a little more explicit, Uncle Septimus. How was this woman able to carry out such an imposture? Where did she get the papers which you and Mr. Hurst gave us to understand were in proper order?"

"Stole 'em, I suppose!" the lawyer said shortly. "It seems she was a great friend of—of the real Evelyn, at one time."

"The real Evelyn?" Joan interrupted him with a cry. "Oh, Uncle Septimus, where's she—my sister, Evelyn? I can't bear to think that I have been trying to give the love that should have been hers to another woman. I ought to have known—surely my own feeling ought to have warned me that she was not my sister! How shall I ask Evelyn to forgive me?" looking up with tear-filled eyes.

"Now, now!" The K.C. patted her shoulder with his disengaged hand. "You—you must not give way, Joan, you really mustn't. As for Evelyn, be sure that if she knows what is going on down here she does not blame you."

"Uncle Septimus!" Joan twisted herself away from him. "I—I don't think you have told us all. You—do you know that you are speaking as if Evelyn were dead?"

Her uncle looked down at her gravely.

"I believe she is, Joan. And that is partly what brought me down here, this afternoon—to tell you how she died."

"Excuse me, but is that necessary?" Warchester asked.

His dark face looked curiously set. His pulses were beating and tingling. So it was true after all, the woman he hated and dreaded was not Joan's sister? That was all he could realize as yet.

"Don't you see that Joan is overwrought—that she has heard enough for one afternoon? Later on if she wants to know the details—"

"I want to hear them now!" Joan brushed his remonstrances aside. "When did my sister die, Uncle Septimus?"

"Years ago, child—more than ten years ago. It isn't a pleasant story, child. You shouldn't hear it if there was a chance of keeping it from you, but in these days when everything gets into the papers—"

"Surely, there can be no question of that!" Warchester said hotly. "If evidence of Evelyn Spencer's death on a certain date is given to the proper authorities, surely that is all that signifies. The imposture here is purely a family matter, for I am sure Joan would not wish any measures taken to punish the woman—"

"No, no! Of course not!" Joan said hurriedly. She pushed back her hair from her brow as she looked at her uncle. "I can't see how you can be sure, Uncle Septimus. How did you find out that she was not my sister?"

Warchester held his breath. What had been the weak point in the scheme the woman had spoken of last night?

"Well, I believe that Hewlett was never satisfied in his own mind that she was the real heiress," the lawyer answered slowly, "though for a long time he was unable to find any flaw in the evidence. I believe it was you, Joan, who gave him the clue when you showed him that last letter of the real Evelyn. It seems he recognized the writing and the paper. And you remember the half of the broken sixpence she sent you—that fitted another half. When Hewlett had ascertained that, of course, the greater part of the battle was over. But we knew that Mrs. Spencer had recognized her stepdaughter, and for a time that baffled us; then Hewlett sent his partner, Cowham, to Willersfield; and what means he took to frighten the truth out of the woman I don't know, but she confessed that she had been bribed. It seems that Evelyn had been burnt on her wrist as a child and there was a scar left. There was no such mark on the wrist of the woman at Davenant, and it appears she paid heavily to persuade Mrs. Spencer to keep silence. Cowham said that apparently the whole family was living on the fat of the land. How the false Evelyn got wind of her deception we can't discover. Hewlett said that Mrs. Spencer might have managed to warn her in some way, for when we went to see her last night we found that she had run away."

He paused. There were other questions that must be asked, he knew, but he would have put off the answering of them to the last possible moment.

Warchester waited. His first sensation of relief was passing. He could not have told why, but he was oppressed by a feeling that all was not told, that the worst was yet to come, though as yet he had perceived no faintest glimmering of the truth.

Joan looked from one to the other with troubled eyes; she too felt a sense of ever-deepening mystery. She was on one side of a dark curtain, as it were, and on the other side lay something, from the relation of which she shrank with dread.

At last she broke the silence:

"Uncle Septimus, you said that Mr. Hewlett recognized Evelyn's writing. How was that possible? He had never seen it even. His very reason for asking for that letter all along was because he wanted to see the writing."

"He had met with it before without knowing that it was Evelyn Spencer's," Mr. Lockyer said gravely. He braced himself up to tell the rest of the story. After all, terrible as it was, Joan had known but little of her sister.

"He—you must be brave, Joan, now;—was at Scotland Yard before he established his private agency. While he was there he was engaged in investigating the circumstances connected with the—er—death of a young woman in Grove Street. It made a great stir at the time; but of course you were only a child—you would not remember it, Well, one of the clues the police had to work upon in that case was a letter, or part of a letter, written, it was supposed, by the girl who died there. Hewlett recognized the writing and the paper on which Evelyn's last letter was written as the same. Moreover, the half sixpence, as I said, fitted one which was on a chain round the neck of the woman who died in Grove Street."

"Uncle Septimus, you can't mean—you are not trying to tell me that the woman who was murdered in Grove Street was my sister, Evelyn?"

Joan's voice was perfectly steady, but every particle of colour had faded from her face; there was a look of horror in her dark eyes. She did not glance at her husband on the other side of the fireplace, but she was conscious through every nerve of her body, that he had made one sharp, incredulous movement, that he now sat with every muscle braced, with head averted, waiting.

"I am afraid there cannot be any doubt of it," Septimus Lockyer went on, thankful that at last the worst of his task was over. "It is a terrible thing, child! I cannot tell you how grieved I am for you. It is very painful for us all."

"It is—very painful!" Joan found herself asserting, with white, stiff lips. She felt a momentary pang of surprise that she was not more horrified, that she could sit there talking calmly to her uncle; but she was conscious only of one thing—that heap of white drapery that had lain on the rug in that upper room in Grove Street had been Evelyn, dead, the living sister for whom the little Polly had just then been longing so intensely. That golden hair had been Evelyn's hair; that buckled shoe had been on Evelyn's foot. And the man who had been putting the pistol in the dead girl's hand, the man who had stolen away, trusting his crime would not be discovered, who had tried to cast the last reproach of suicide on that poor murdered girl, was Warchester, the man Joan had married—the husband she had loved with her whole heart!

Warchester got up and stepped through the open window.

Joan did not look after him; she herself rose slowly, laying one hand on the table at her side. She looked up into her uncle's face.

"Will they hang him, Uncle Septimus?"

"Hang him—who, child?" The lawyer looked momentarily puzzled. "Oh, I see what you mean—the man who caused Evelyn's death! Well, of course they will, if they can find him. But that must necessarily be a matter of difficulty, so long a time having elapsed since her death. Still, there is no doubt this discovery of her identity will give a fresh start to the inquiry. What is it, my man?" as a footman noiselessly entered the room and presented him with a telegram on a salver. "For me? No answer, thank you!" He waited until the man was out of ear-shot; then he held out the form to Joan. "Is it not extraordinary this should come now?"

"'New development in case. Shall be glad to see you as soon as possible, Hewlett,'" she read. "What does it mean, Uncle Septimus?"

Mr. Lockyer walked to the corridor before he answered her.

"Can't say, my child. It may be some clue to the murderer. But I must be off early to see what it is. You have taken this very sensibly. And you mustn't worry yourself over the rest of the details now. I know you may rely on Hewlett to do his best to keep your name out of the papers. Now where is your husband gone? I must speak to him. Good-bye, Joan! I shall be down again in a few days, and then we will have another talk."

He hurried out after Warchester.

Joan stood as he had left her, motionless; catching sight of her reflection in a distant mirror, she gazed at herself as at a stranger. The beautiful features looked pinched and wilted, the face was white as a dead woman's, only the eyes, the great, tragic, accusing eyes, were alive.

An echo of her uncle's voice floated in from the garden; he had found Warchester, evidently.

"Rely upon it, I will keep your name out of it, my dear boy!"

Joan put her hand to her throat.

"Keep his name out of it," she murmured. "Great heavens! Keep his name out of it!"

Chapter Twenty

JOAN waited. The two men went on round the house; she heard their footsteps on the gravel. Probably they were making their way to Septimus Lockyer's motor-car. She had thought in the long watches of the preceding night that she had plumbed the very depth of misery. It seemed to her now, looking back, that by contrast with the present she had then been most happy. She was so stunned by the magnitude of the calamity that had overtaken her that she was for the time being almost incapable of movement. She wanted to get away somewhere where she could be alone, where she could think, but all she could do was to lean against the mantelpiece and wait.

At last she heard her husband returning; his feet dragged heavily. As he stood for a moment in the window, he had the aspect of a man who has had a shock. Joan's gaze rested on his pale, changed face absently, then wandered from him to the old sundial on the lawn, to the tall Michaelmas daisies. Over in the elms a thrush was singing, a bumble-bee tempted out by the sunshine floated lazily into the room, the fragrance of a late rose trained up the wall came in through the window, but Joan neither saw nor heard anything: for the time she was blind and deaf.

Warchester looked at her. He hesitated a moment, bracing his broad shoulders as if for a supreme effort; then he came quickly across the room.

"Joan, my poor child, what can I say to you? I know how this—" His hands were outstretched, but as he met Joan's glance, they dropped to his side. "What is it?" he asked blankly. "What has come between us? Can't you tell me?"

Joan opened her lips; the hand that was clutching at her throat, clenching suddenly, wrenched the lace from the tiny diamond brooch that fastened it.

"I am going to tell you," she said, in a harsh, hoarse voice. "I want you to listen. Ten years ago last May, I was a little child, living in the Grove Street Mews. One day—" She paused and gasped, as if for breath.

Warchester looked at her in amazement. He had thought she was about to tell him the cause of the estrangement between them. What had that old story to do with them how?

"I know, Joan, but don't think of it. Forget it all."

Joan did not seem to hear him; though she was speaking to him, she did not look in his face once.

"I was a little child—such a little neglected child. I ran about the streets, I nursed Baby Tim. Nobody cared much about me—nobody ever did care for me, I used to think, except my sister Evelyn. She did not forget me; she used to send me presents, she used to write to me. Nearly every night I cried myself to sleep over her letters, the only words of love that reached me. My stepmother hated me, I think; she often used to beat me. One day she had been more unkind than usual. She had shaken me for some childish carelessness; she had hit me until my head was aching. I ran away from her to the only place where I knew I should be alone—the loft over the stables."

For the first time, her eyes rested on his dark, haggard face, paler than its wont this afternoon. Surely, surely, now he would guess—he would understand?

But there was no enlightenment in Warchester's eyes—only a great bewilderment, and infinite pity, as he saw the effort with which she spoke.

"Dear, don't harass yourself by trying to tell me anything to-day," he said gently. "I was wrong to ask you. Come, rest on this sofa. Let me make you comfortable among the cushions, and later on, when you are better, you shall tell me just as much as you like."

"No, no!" Joan threw out her hands, as if to thrust his very suggestions aside. "I must tell you—you must hear it all now. I ran into the loft, as I say, but it had always been an ambition of mine to get farther. I had found out a way to climb on the roof of the Grove

Street houses. I managed to get there that afternoon." Her voice broke—trailed off in a sob.

Warchester stood still; not a muscle stirred, and yet in some vague, intangible way Joan knew that at last he was beginning to understand.

"I ran along the roofs," she went on, in the same rough, uneven tones. "It seemed an amusement to me—ah, pitiful heavens, an amusement! —but at last I tired of seeing only the roof and the chimneys. I wanted to look through some of the windows, to find out what the rooms were like. I raised myself up and peeped over a window-ledge. I saw—"

"Yes?" Warchester prompted, in a level voice. His face was unmoved, it looked even a little weary. One would have said that the story to which he was listening bore little interest to him, except that his eyes watched Joan's every movement.

Joan choked back a sob.

"I saw a man moving about, burning photographs, tearing the fly-leaves out of books. There was a white heap on the rug; he bent over it, he straightened it out. I saw that it was a dead woman, with red-gold hair. The man put a pistol in her hand; then a door at my right hand moved, began to open. I made some sort of a sound—I don't know what—and the man looked up. Then I tumbled. I ran back across the roof to the loft."

"You poor little child!" Warchester did not attempt to come any nearer now, but his voice remained unchanged. "And now—now do you think it was your sister; Evelyn?"

Joan's slender fingers clenched themselves nervously.

"I know. I—I told them at home what I had seen, and my father scoffed at me and said I was never to mention it, and I—I was sent for by Mrs. Davenant the next day. The terror of it haunted my childhood, but afterwards I think I nearly forgot it until—"

She paused again, but Warchester did not speak. He waited for her to go on.

"Until the day I fainted." Joan's voice was little more than a hoarse whisper. "I was walking along the terrace, and I came to the smoking-room window, and you were inside. I saw you throw a letter in the fire; then I remembered. I knew—"

"What?" Warchester's question broke across her speech sharp and stern.

"I was sure that you were the man I had seen in Grove Street ten years ago," she answered steadily. "At first I tried to persuade myself that there had been a mistake. It was too horrible! It could not be true! I beat down the voice that told me it was, but all the while, do what I would, I knew. Then the other night, when you told me you had been an artist, when I saw you catch up a paper with the very gesture I remembered—could I doubt then?"

It seemed to Joan that the silence that followed could have been felt.

At last Warchester spoke

"No," he said hoarsely, "no, you could not. I—Perhaps I might persuade you even now that it was all a mistake, Joan. But I will not lie to the woman I love. I was the man you saw, and you—you were the ragged imp of a child who watched me. I cannot realize it—that it should be you, you out of the whole world! That out of the countless hordes of human creatures, we two should meet and marry. Heavens, the irony of it!"

Joan looked at his dark, rugged face, every feature of which was so fatally dear. She shivered; her knees shook.

"And she was my sister! And I never knew till—now. Oh, Paul, why did you kill my sister?" Her voice quivered, her eyes smarted, but the relief of tears was denied them.

Warchester turned sharply from her; standing at the open window, he raised his face to the cool air. What was he to do—what was he to say? The dead girl was Joan's sister. Dared he trust Joan with the truth? At last he went up to Joan.

"You have told me your story," he said heavily. "Now I am going to ask you to listen to mine. But first you must sit down; if you stand up there you will be faint."

He drew forward one of the big, luxurious easy-chairs. Joan's limbs trembled as she obeyed him. He moved over to the fireplace, and took up a position on the rug at the side, one elbow on the high, oak shelf.

"It is not a short story," he said, searching about in his mind for the best words in which to clothe what he had to say, "but I will try to be as brief as I can. My acquaintance with your sister, Evelyn, taking her identity with the woman who died in Grove Street as proved, began when she was singing in the music halls as Marie de Lavelle. I had known her perhaps six months when she left the stage, and for nearly a year I heard no more of her. Then one night a friend of mine, a man named Wingrove"—with a momentary hesitation that did not escape Joan's ears, quickened now by fear—"came to me for help. He told me that he had married Marie De Lavelle privately; and he had told her that for family reasons it would have to be kept secret for a time. At first she had been content, but now she was clamouring for full recognition of her rights, as she called them. There were reasons, urgent reasons why the marriage should not be disclosed just then—to do so would have meant ruin. But he could not make her understand this; and he asked me; as I had known Marie de Lavelle, as I was in a measure the friend of both, to speak to her for him, to persuade her to keep silence. He had a studio in Grove Street and he asked me to come there the following afternoon. He would make an appointment with his wife for four o'clock, and he hoped that I would be able to explain to her how very serious matters would be for my friend if she persisted in speaking out then. I was delayed, and it was perhaps ten minutes past four when I got there. I went straight up to the studio, meeting no one on the way. The door was ajar, I knocked, but, receiving no response, walked in. There I saw—"

He stopped and shaded his face with his hand.

"Go on," Joan ordered huskily. "Evelyn?"

"She was lying there on the rug—dead!" Warchester said in a low voice. "In a moment I saw that all was over. Then I think I must have been mad for the time, Joan. I felt sure that Wingrove had done it; that she had tried him past endurance, and that—I knew he was subject to wild fits of passion—he had shot her in his rage. Then, then—I don't think I have made you understand that I loved Wingrove, that all my life he had been dear to me—the thought came to me that if I put the pistol there, in her hand, people would think she had killed herself. I did not realize that I might be making things worse for Wingrove. I tore his name off his books, I burned some sketches that were signed, photographs that might have given him away. Then just as I finished, I looked up, and saw a pair of dark eyes watching me over the window-sill. I sprang forward, not knowing in the least what I was going to do: The owner of the eyes fell back with a cry, and when I got to the window I saw a small child picking herself up from the roof—a small, grimy-looking child, with ragged brown hair, who went scuttling over the roofs until she was lost to my sight. I turned back, there was nothing else for me to do; a sudden realization of the danger in which I might stand myself if the child told her tale came to me. I stole softly out of the house. The next day, the papers were full of the Grove Street Mystery, but there was no mention of what the child had seen. I told myself that she had not understood it, that she had been too small for it to have any meaning for her. I learned too that my plan to save my friend had been worse than useless; it had but fixed suspicion more surely upon him. That is my story, Joan. What are you going to say to me?"

"What became of Wingrove?" The words seemed to come from Joan's pale lips almost without her own volition.

Warchester did not raise his head; his hand shaded the lower part of his face from view; his eyes were downcast.

"He was never traced, as perhaps you know."

"But what became of him?" Joan persisted in a hoarse whisper. "You—you know, Paul."

"And if I do," Warchester questioned slowly, "what would you have me do, Joan? I—I could not bring your sister back."

"No!" Joan said painfully. "Before it was different, but now—now that you know that she was Evelyn—you will help to punish her murderer?"

"Joan!" Warchester came swiftly across the room and caught her hands in his. "Let him alone, child! The tracking down and punishment of criminals is no part of our duty, thank Heaven! All that matters between you and me now is that you understand that it was no murderer you saw at work that afternoon, but only a half-frenzied man who was doing his best for his friend. You do believe me, child? You will forgive me?"

But Joan wrenched her hands away. Her sleepless nights, the long, wearing anxiety, culminating in the shock of this afternoon, had strained her already overtaxed nerves almost to breaking point. She was in no mood to judge fairly. Over and above this too, beyond the wildness and improbability of Warchester's story, neither his manner nor his accent had been such as to carry conviction. There had been a hesitancy, a weighing of his words before he spoke. Joan felt a crushing certainty that, though he had offered her a plausible explanation, he was keeping something from her.

"Oh, I don't know," she cried wildly, "I don't know what to believe! I —I will forgive you when the police have found Wingrove. When I know the real name of my sister's murderer I will forgive you perhaps!"

Chapter Twenty-One

"WHY, HEWLETT, this is kind!" Septimus Lockyer stepped out of his motor at the door of his bachelor chambers in St. James's Street. "I was coming up to you as soon as I had had a bath and a change. But now we can have our talk here instead. Come in!"

Hewlett obeyed him.

"Thank you, sir! But I wonder whether you would mind your man helping me up with a box I have in the taxi outside? It is awkward carrying it alone, and I want to be careful with it."

"Why, of course! Can't he manage it altogether?" Mr. Lockyer asked in surprise.

"I think not, thank you, sir. I would rather see to it myself."

Mr. Lockyer looked at, him with some curiosity as he reappeared bearing one end of what looked like a common, tin trunk carefully strapped and in addition tied with packing-cord and sealed with big, red blobs of sealing wax. Blake, Mr. Lockyer's servant, carried the other end, visible disgust on his stolid features.

"May we bring it into your room, sir?" Hewitt questioned. "I want to keep an eye on it."

"Certainly, by all means," Septimus Lockyer acquiesced. He had learned in his profession not to be surprised at anything, but he could not help speculating as to the contents of the mysterious tin-box.

Hewlett had it carefully deposited on the hearthrug; then he stood up.

"Now I think we shall get on, sir."

"What is it?" Mr. Lockyer asked, wonderingly. "But no—wait a minute, Hewlett! I have had a long ride, and the air is keen this afternoon. I must have a drink first. What will you take? There are wines over there. I shall have coffee and a glass of cognac myself."

"I think I will do the same, thank you, sir!" The detective waited while the manservant brought in a coffee-service with a steaming silver jug and a couple of covered dishes. As soon as Blake had finally retired, Septimus Lockyer took a sandwich and looked at his companion.

"Well, Hewlett, I gathered from your telegram it was something urgent."

"I hope you will think it of importance to warrant that telegram, sir. At any rate, we could not take the responsibility of opening it without one of her family being present, and of course we could not trouble Lady Warchester. That sir, belonged to Miss Evelyn Spencer; it has remained unopened ever since it left her possession. We are hoping that in it may possibly be found some clue to her murderer."

Septimus Lockyer was startled for once out of his usual calm.

"How in the world did you get hold of it, Hewlett?"

The detective permitted himself a smile of self-satisfaction,

"You may remember that I told you of Mrs. Read's visit, sir— the woman with whom Miss Spencer had lodged at Highgate? Well," as Mr. Lockyer nodded, "she and her mother lived together. The daughter managed the lodgers, but I found in the course of conversation that she had been married two days after Miss Spencer left, and, as you and I know, Mr. Lockyer, there is nothing for muddling a woman's wits like a wedding, I thought I had better look the mother up. She was nursing a son who was ill at Stoke Newington, but I made a special journey, and found myself well rewarded for my pains. Mrs. Thompson—that was the mother's name—told me what had apparently escaped her daughter's memory, if she had ever paid any attention to it, that Miss Spencer had asked them to take charge of a box until she was in a position to send for it, and, as of course they never heard from her, it was still in their attic. I had some little difficulty in inducing her to part with it, but when she heard who I was, and that there was only too much reason to fear her former lodger had met with foul play, she gave way. I placed these seals on it before I brought it away, and you can see that they are still unbroken."

He knelt down and carefully cut the cord, preserving the seals intact.

"I got a bunch of keys at a locksmith's as I came up. He assured me that one of them would be sure to fit; he said it was quite a common lock."

"That was well thought of," Septimus Lockyer assented. "You have found what ought to be a most valuable clue, Hewlett. Surely we shall discover some hint at least of Wingrove's identity."

"I hope so." The detective was fitting one key after the other to the lock. At last one turned; he threw the lid open. "Now, sir!"

Both men bent forward, then, as if by common consent, halted. There was something pitifully commonplace about the neat little garments that met their gaze, about the smell of camphor with which their nostrils were assailed.

Septimus Lockyer's eyes softened. For the first time this dead, unknown niece of his seemed to have in his eyes a separate identity of her own; she was not only Joan's sister to him now—she was a girl of his own blood, who had lived and loved, who had been shamefully deceived and foully murdered. His brow darkened.

His hesitation over, Hewlett was already lifting out the contents of the box with quick, dexterous hands. At last he came upon a cardboard box at the bottom, and, opening it, uttered an exclamation of satisfaction.

"Ah, this was what I was hoping for!" he said as he picked out a quantity of old papers. "Now, sir, we must be careful!"

Septimus Lockyer did not speak. He took up a few of the first that came to hand; some of them were merely printed comments on the performances of the Sisters De Lavelle cut out and pasted on clean sheets of paper. Evidently the dead girl had been proud of her successes. There was a letter, written in big, childish, writing, signed "Your loving little sister, Polly"; a couple of strongly scented effusions merely ending with initials "C. De L." which made the lawyer draw in his lips; last of all, a photograph representing a young girl, evidently Evelyn Spencer, sitting on a sofa with a young man, not a very attractive-looking young man as far as could be judged, heavy of jaw, with dark eyes set closely together, and ears that showed a tendency to occupy more than their share of the canvas. He was wearing a nondescript suit and a bowler hat. Underneath it was the inscription, "Evie, from her own Jim."

"Now what in the world does this mean?" inquired the lawyer, gazing at it. "This is not Wingrove."

Hewlett glanced up quickly from his papers.

"What is it, sir? Oh, that!" as the lawyer displayed his find. "No, that is not Wingrove, certainly. It does not answer in any particular to his description. It isn't a man of his class, either. We will put that by itself, please. It is evident that Miss Spencer had two lovers—this fellow and the dark man with whom Mrs. Read saw her, who may or may not have been Wingrove. It is possible we shall find that jealousy was at the bottom of the crime. Here are a couple of letters in a man's writing—'185 Jermyn Street.' Ah, I should say this would be Wingrove!" He turned rapidly to the signature.

"Well?" Septimus Lockyer said impatiently as the detective paused suddenly. "What is it, man? Are they Wingrove's?"

"No—yes—I mean they are not." Hewlett cast a swift look at the lawyer; his monocle dropped from his eye unheeded. "This is very curious, sir. Both these letters are signed—"

Septimus Lockyer stated at him.

"What? Bless my life, man, don't beat about the bush! What are they signed?"

"Why—it is merely a coincidence but I wasn't prepared—" The detective stumbled; then, warned by Septimus Lockyer's expression, he finished hurriedly, "It is signed, yours devotedly, Paul Wilton."

"Wilton!" A silence fell upon both men. Septimus Lockyer held out his hand for the letter and read it over, his bushy eyebrows drawn closely together.

The detective watched him closely for a while; then he took up the second letter and opened it. His face changed as he read it; his usual calm expression gave place to one of keen interest.

At last Septimus Lockyer looked up.

"I don't know that we ought to be so much surprised at this, Hewlett," tapping the sheet of paper. "Lord Warchester told us that he knew the Sisters De Lavelle, or at least the one that has been at Davenant Hall. No doubt he was acquainted with both; in fact I should imagine the one presupposes the other. And we know as men of the world that young men of unstable principles often write to young ladies of the ballet in exaggerated terms. However, it is quite possible that Lord Warchester may be able to give us some information that may put us on Wingrove's track. I shall make a point of ascertaining that at the earliest opportunity."

"Yes, sir." The detective's gaze wandered uneasily round the room, rested for in instant on the exquisite Greuze that hung on the opposite wall, and then was turned to the window. A troop of soldiers went clattering by on their way to Buckingham Palace. He looked at them mechanically, at anything rather than at the K.C.'s face. "I think you must read this, sir."

Septimus Lockyer took it from him quietly. A glance at Hewlett had prepared him for bad news, but in spite of his self-control, a sharp exclamation broke from him as he read. This was merely a note; it was addressed like the other, from 185 Jermyn Street, to "Miss Marie De Lavelle, 12 Basingstoke Road, Great Yarmouth." The letter ran:

"My dear Queenie,

I shall be with you, all being well, by the first train on Saturday, and if your tenor is not recovered, and your manager shares your flattering opinion of my voice, I shall be pleased to help you out of your dilemma. But, as you suggest, my name must not appear. I will take instead one I have used on occasion in Paris, and when you make me known to your company, you must introduce me, please, as "Mr. Wingrove." Till then au revoir, my dear Queenie! Give my compliments to Cécile, and believe me, yours as ever,

Paul Wilton."

Septimus Lockyer caught his breath sharply as he finished, and sat gazing at the paper. Warchester! It was unthinkable! And yet there were the written words.

"Warchester must explain this," he said at last. His voice had a weary, depressed intonation which was quite unlike the great K.C.'s clear, ringing tones. "But of course it is out of the question that he can be Wingrove. He may have been casting about for a name to use on the stage, and he may have heard of that—Wingrove may have been a friend of his even. But the other—the other is impossible!"

"Yes, sir!" The detective's tone was distinctly noncommittal. In his eyes the letter could bear but one interpretation.

Mr. Lockyer got up and began to pace the room.

"It is a miserable thing that he should be brought into the affair," he exclaimed, "and that she should be Joan's sister—poor thing, poor thing!"

A vague speculation as to which sister the expression would be more applicable came into the detective's mind. He knelt down on the rug again and examined the other contents of the trunk. There was nothing else, so far as he could see, that had any bearing on the case, and he neatly restored the things in their former order. Then he stood up.

"I think that is all, sir. About that letter—"

The K.C.'s head was bent; his hands were clasped behind his back under his coat-tails. He had the air of a man trying to solve a knotty problem. He looked up abstractedly as Hewlett spoke.

"Ah, the letter! You can leave it with me. I must think matters out by myself. We have not solved the Grove Street Mystery yet. About that other man—the one in the photograph? What about him?"

Hewlett was locking up the box now, leaving out only the photograph and the two letters.

"I will look him up, sir. But I shouldn't say he had anything to do with the murder. I imagine he dates further back. You see, he addresses her as 'Evie,' her own name, which she evidently discarded when she went on the stage. Now Paul Wilton—I don't know whether you noticed, sir"—dropping his voice—"speaks to her as Queenie. And the letter found in—er—Mr. Wingrove's coat was signed 'Ever Your Own Queenie.' It was evidently the name by which Miss Evelyn Spencer was known to—some people," after an imperceptible pause.

Mr. Lockyer resumed his walk; it was obvious that he was greatly disturbed.

"I had forgotten that, Hewlett," turning suddenly as the detective was about to move quietly towards the door.

"What do you make of this? Speak out, man!"

"Well, I have not had time to form any theory yet, sir. I can only see that Paul Wilton must have known Miss Evelyn Spencer very well, and that at one time, at any rate, he had some thought of taking the name of Wingrove. Whether he did so or not we shall have to ascertain. I can't help thinking it is a great pity Lord Warchester was not quite open with us before this was found."

"It is a pity," Septimus Lockyer assented gravely. "But still," with a determined attempt at cheerfulness, "'he has not had much time. I only told him this afternoon that Evelyn Spencer was the Grove Street victim, and naturally his first thought was for his wife."

"I meant with regard to the name Wingrove. It was widely enough advertised at the time," the detective reminded him. "And he speaks of having used it in Paris."

"So he does, so he does!" Mr. Lockyer assented. "Well, we must wait until we hear his explanation, Hewlett. And now what are you going to do? What is your next move?"

The detective hesitated.

I was going to see what I could make out from the caretaker, at 18 Grove Street," he said doubtfully. "But now I am not sure. I must think it over, sir."

Chapter Twenty-Two

MR. HEWLETT the detective, picked his way cautiously over the cobbled streets of Willersfield, wincing now and then as a stone made itself felt through his thin, town-made boots.

"That will be the Bell, I suppose," he soliloquized, as, following his directions, he turned down the street to his right.

The Bell it proved to be, as the sign testified; apparently the licence had not been transferred to the widow—the board still bore the name of John Spencer. Mr. Hewlett looked at it for a moment;

then he stepped inside the passage and put his head in at the bar. A stout, red-faced woman sat at the other side, knitting.

Rightly concluding her to be Mrs. Spencer, Hewlett advanced.

"Good morning, ma'am! I'll take a glass of your ale, if you please. It's a hot morning."

"It is, sir," answered the woman in a dejected tone. Mr. Hewlett fancied she had been crying. He looked at her sympathetically as she drew the ale.

"You'll do me the favour of having a drop of something yourself, ma'am, I hope. You've had trouble here of late I know; and you look as if it had told upon you if I may say so."

Mrs. Spencer drew out a handkerchief and applied it to her eyes.

"Yes, it is nothing but trouble I have had of late, sir! I might have made shift to bear it perhaps if I had had a little human sympathy and kindness shown me, but when your own flesh and blood turns against you—"

"Ah, that is bad!" Mr. Hewlett took a draught of his beer and screwed his monocle in firmly. "Now you will have that drop of brandy, ma'am; it will brace you up."

"You are very good sir." Mrs. Spencer did not need much pressing. "If everybody had your feeling heart—"

The detective sat down and chatted affably about the weather while she drank her brandy and water.

"Is there any room where you could give me the pleasure of a few minutes' private conversation, Mrs. Spencer? There is a little matter I must consult you about."

Mrs. Spencer looked surprised and flattered. Hewlett was a personable-looking man from her point of view. The thought crossed her mind that he might have heard she had been left comfortably off, and visions of a rose-coloured future, in which he bore no inconsiderable part flitted across her mind. Calling her daughter to look after the bar, she led the way into the parlour, and, pulling one of the horsehair chairs forward with a shy smile, invited the detective to be seated.

Mr. Hewlett accepted her offer with a word of thanks and deposited his hat on the mahogany centre table.

"It is a little matter of business that I have come about, Mrs. Spencer. You had two stepdaughters, I believe?"

Mrs. Spencer's delightful visions began to fade; she cast a sharp look at Hewlett from behind her handkerchief.

"Yes, I have," she assented, unconsciously altering the tense. "A pair of ungrateful hussies! If it is about them you want to talk, sir, you have wasted your time calling here. It is little enough I can say for either of them. And I have made it a rule when I can't say good of folk, I won't say bad!"

"And a very good rule too, Mrs. Spencer, a very good rule," the detective assented, "If I ask you to make an exception in my favour, be sure it is not without reason, as you will see if you will just look at this card. That is my name, ma'am."

Mrs. Spencer took the card somewhat gingerly.

"Mr. Thomas Hewlett from Messrs. Hewlett and Cowham, Detective Agents."

She uttered a slight scream, and flung it from her on the floor.

"If I had known! Another of them detectives! And me thinking you were that pleasant and friendly—"

"So I am, ma'am, so I am," Mr. Hewlett assured her. "It is only that I want a bit of help, and you are the only one that can give it me. It may be that something I have to tell you will give you a bit of a shock too, and it is well that you should hear it from me instead of reading it in the papers, where I expect it will all be to-morrow."

Mrs. Spencer was too much agitated to take in the meaning of his words.

"If it is about that woman at Davenant Hall, I have made up my mind I won't say another word. That Mr. Cowham—your master he is, I suppose—he pretty near frightened the wits out of me the other day."

Mr. Hewlett smiled slightly at the reference to his master.

"Ah, he is inclined to be a bit rough, is Mr. Cowham!" he said diplomatically. "As for the lady at Davenant Hall, I should not think of alluding to her again; I should put her out of my mind if I were you, ma'am. We all make mistakes sometimes. My business with you is about a very different matter. You may remember an affair that took place in Grove Street at the time that you were living in the mews behind. It made a great stir at the time. 'The Grove Street Mystery,' they called it. A young lady was found dead in a studio at No. 18."

Mrs. Spencer was now alert.

"Of course I do," dropping her handkerchief in her excitement. "I often think of it now. Quite a girl she was, and the police could not make out anything about where she come from."

Mr. Hewlett coughed.

"They could not," he said pointedly, "but I think some light has been cast upon the matter at last. You never had any idea who the young lady was, I suppose, Mrs. Spencer?"

The woman stared at him.

"Me, sir? How should I? I never heard a word about her except what was in the papers for everybody to read!" Her surprise at the question was evidently genuine.

The detective leaned forward.

"Mrs. Spencer, I am afraid there is no doubt, there can be no doubt"—she spoke impressively—"that the poor young girl who met her death under such mysterious circumstances was your elder stepdaughter, Evelyn."

"What? It—it can't be!" Mrs. Spencer's heavy cheeks turned a mottled purple; her knees shook. "I don't believe it! Who would have killed Evie?"

"Ah, that is, another question!" Mr. Hewlett drew nearer confidentially. "And that is where I want your help, Mrs. Spencer. As I say, it has been proved beyond question that it was Miss Evelyn Spencer who was murdered in the studio in Grove Street. Now there are two or three questions I must ask you. First, there is a photograph." He felt in his pocket.

"It wasn't Evie," Mrs. Spencer said hoarsely. "No" —with a sudden gleam of recollection—"of course it could not have been Evie! Little Polly would have known her sister."

The detective was drawing the photograph of Evelyn and the unknown man from its envelope. He stopped.

"Who is Polly?" he asked sharply; the name was new to his recollection of the case. "And what did she know, what did she see?"

"Why, I had given her a whipping for idling about and letting her brother, Tim—that is my youngest boy, sir—get into mischief, and she ran away from me and must needs get scrambling about on the roof that very afternoon, and from what she said I believe she saw the whole thing done. It wasn't my fault the police were not told of it, 'twas her father's. He would not have her frightened, and he said she had fancied everything about it, but I knew better. She kept me awake all that night crying out that she had seen a dead woman in white, and a dark man with a gun."

"I must see this Polly." The detective made, a rapid note in his pocket-book. "Her evidence may be most important. It is a serious matter that it was not brought to the notice of the police at the time. Is it possible for me to see her this morning?"

"No, sir, it isn't! Leastways, not here, and whether she will see you at all I don't know, for she has become very grand, has Polly, married a lord if you please, and as good as told me she washed her hands of me—at least he did!" Mrs. Spencer's face was resuming its normal colour now. "But of course, if that girl she saw killed was Evie, it stands to reason that Polly would have known her—her own sister, and the two so devoted to one another."

Light was breaking in upon the detective now.

"You don't mean that it was Lady Warchester?"

Mrs. Spencer nodded.

Mr. Hewlett sat staring meditatively through the open door at the rows of pewter cups and mugs in the bar. He was thinking that, taking it all round, the Grove Street Mystery held as many astounding developments as any ordinary five cases put together. Mrs. Spencer had opined that it would have been impossible for the child not to have recognized her own sister; the detective's thoughts went further.

After a pause, devoted apparently to cogitating over the injustice of her lot compared with that of Lady Warchester, Mrs. Spencer spoke again:

"You spoke of a photograph, sir. If it is one of poor Evie, I should be glad to see it. There was a portrait of the young lady that was murdered in the papers, I know, but neither her father nor me recognized it, if her it were, which I haven't given in yet."

Mr. Hewlett woke up from his abstraction.

"I am afraid there is no doubt of it, Mrs. Spencer. Lady Warchester had not seen her sister for five years before the latter's death. If she did witness anything of the nature of what you describe, she evidently could not identify her. But you have given me something to go upon. Now with regard to this photograph"— laying it on the table beside her—"I want to find out who the man is. Can you help me?"

Mrs. Spencer bent forward curiously; then she gave a short laugh.

"Why, of course! I wonder where they had it took! There is no mistaking him. It is Jim Gregory."

"Gregory?" repeated the detective questioningly. "Was he engaged to Miss Spencer?"

Mrs. Spencer laughed again.

"No, bless you! There was a bit of sweethearting between them maybe, and I believe he went to see her once or twice after she left us. If her father had ever heard of it he would have given her what for; he was angry enough when he found that she had worked Gregory a tobacco-pouch."

"Tobacco-pouch!" repeated Hewlett.

"Yes, she worked one for him! Girls are that silly!" Mrs. Spencer went on. "And her father gave her a good talking to for it. Jim

Gregory came here with us you know, sir. If so be as I can keep on the Bell, he will stay on and manage like."

"Will he?" The detective's voice sounded absent. He gazed vacantly into the bar, where Amy had now taken her mother's place. His mind was lost in a maze of bewilderment and conjecture. He was thinking of the soiled tobacco-pouch found by the dead girl's body. Gregory had been Evelyn Spencer's first sweetheart—there could be little doubt of that, but even though the acquaintance had been kept up longer Hewlett was unable to connect him with the unhappy girl's death. Yet Grove Street was very near the Mews, and, as he knew, jealousy was the mainspring of half the tragedies he attempted to trace.

In any case, one thread of the tangled web which fate had woven round the death of Evelyn Spencer was thus placed in his hands, and he was resolved to follow it up.

"Would it be possible for me to speak to Gregory this morning, ma'am?" he inquired.

"Oh, yes!" Mrs. Spender answered cordially enough. "I expect he is somewhere about. Amy"—raising her voice—"send Tim down the yard and tell Jim he is wanted, will you? I haven't been pleased with Jim of late," she went on. "After that Mr. Cowham of yours had been here the other day I was that upset, just when I thought my troubles were over to have them all reaped up again, that I gave way a bit, and let out what he had said and what I had told him. Jim Gregory he was in and out of the bar and heard it all, and he went away and wrote a letter without saying a word and took it to the post himself. Tim walked up with him, and he saw it addressed to Miss Evelyn Davenant."

Mr. Hewlett looked puzzled for a minute, then his face cleared.

"Ah, he thought it was the real Evelyn at Davenant Hall, I expect! You tell me he was a friend of hers."

"Oh, no, he didn't!" Mrs. Spencer contradicted belligerently. "'Twas him as first put it into my head that it wasn't the real Evie at Davenant Hall. When Polly came over here to her father's funeral she told us Evie were at the Hall, and I never doubted it was Evie. Why should I? I should have given Polly credit for sense enough to know her own sister. Jim Gregory it was as first set me thinking. 'Evie is never there,' he says. ''Tis somebody pretending to be her, belike; but it isn't never Evie.' The fool I was to listen to him! But you see, sir, he knowed, and he must take it upon him to warn that nasty madam. And she gets off scot-free, while me, as had nothing to do with her going to Davenant, never knew a word about it till afterwards, gets all the blame, and has police officers coming to question me." She relapsed into noisy sobs once more. "I shan't forgive Jim Gregory in a hurry, that I shan't."

At this juncture, the sound of heavy steps along the passage was heard. Mrs. Spencer looked up.

"Ah, here he is to speak for himself, sir! Jim"— raising her voice—"here is this gentleman, a detective, wants to speak to you about Evie. He has got a photograph."

Hewlett got up and advanced to the half-open door. He would scarcely have identified the original of the photograph taken fifteen years earlier but for Mrs. Spencer's assistance; time and hard living had altered Jim Gregory considerably. But the heavy jaw was there, and the closely-set eyes were regarding the detective with suspicion; then the man touched his forehead.

Hewlett held out the photograph.

"Perhaps you can tell me where this was taken?"

Gregory's expression changed as he looked; he drew, a deep breath of relief, it seemed to Hewlett.

"Oh, that! 'Twas taken years ago, soon after Evie left home, at a little place off the Mile End Road. I forget the name. Yes, there it is, on the back of the card —'William Wile, 10 Merton Street, off Mile End Road.'"

"Yes, there it is," assented the detective, who had already paid a visit to Mr. Wile's establishment without any satisfactory result. "When did you last see Miss Evelyn Spencer, Mr. Gregory?"

Gregory hesitated a moment; he passed his hand through his long hair.

"It would, maybe, be six months after she left home. She was at the Melpomene then."

"Oh!" The detective nursed his chin in his hand reflectively.

"Jim!" Mrs. Spencer broke in. She had controlled herself with difficulty all this time. "And what do you think this gentleman has been telling me, Jim? That that young lady that was killed in Grove Street when the master was at Sir Robert Brunton's was our Evie!"

Gregory's face suddenly grew older, greyer.

"'Tain't possible!" he said roughly. "Why, that young lady's photo was in all the papers! Do you think some of us wouldn't ha' recognized it?"

"Ah, but it was a newspaper photograph!" The detective spoke slightingly. "Taken after death too! I don't think there can be any doubt of her identity, Mr. Gregory. I wonder now what made you so sure that the real Evelyn Spencer was not at Davenant Hall?"

Gregory cast a quick glance from his small eyes at Mrs. Spencer, who was still emitting a convulsive sob occasionally.

"When we heard she wouldn't come to her father's funeral I began to have my suspicions, sir; she always thought a deal of her father, did Evie."

"Still, as she had not written him for fifteen years I don't see anything very astonishing in her not coming to the funeral," the detective said. "You must have had more than that to go on, Mr. Gregory."

Gregory twirled his cap about between his big, red hands.

"I didn't think as what Polly—her ladyship told us about her sister sounded like Evie," he answered slowly. "That is how I come to pass the remark to the missis as I didn't believe it really was Evie at all. But of course I wasn't thinking she would let it go any further, least of all that she would go down to Davenant Hall."

"That is enough, Jim Gregory!" Mrs. Spencer interrupted him sharply. "You can let my doings alone, if you please. Mr. Hewlett wants to know why you wrote to that hussy so as to let her get off before the police come."

"What are you talking about?" asked Gregory roughly. "You told me it was Evie, and I believed you, like a fool! When the policeman come here making inquiries it did seem to me as somebody ought to tell her, me taking it as it was Evie, as I had been told, sir"—addressing himself to the detective—"for I didn't hear what the missis told the police."

"If you can't keep my name out of it, Jim Gregory—"

In Mrs. Spencer's wrath she threatened to become apoplectic.

"You shouldn't ha' poked your nose into it, then!" Gregory growled.

"Well, well, it is a matter that interests all of us," the detective interposed pacifically. "It won't be easy for any person who knew Miss Evelyn Spencer to keep out of it, I am afraid. And you must have been a particular friend of hers, to judge by the photo, Mr. Gregory."

The man looked down sheepishly.

"I was good enough for her till she got in with grander folk," he muttered sulkily. "Then she give me the go-by quick enough. Is there anything more you want to ask me, sir, because I have my horses to see to?"

"Can you tell me the name of the man Miss Spencer married?" Hewlett asked.

Gregory shook his head.

"I know nothing of Evie after she left the Melpomene. There was a lot of young fellows always after her, but I don't know as I can remember one of them. I never knew she was married."

Mr. Hewlett smiled politely.

"Then I don't think I need trouble you further to-day, Mr. Gregory. I should not say no to a cup of tea if you were to offer me one before I started, ma'am," turning to Mrs. Spencer.

That good lady looked much gratified.

"I'm sure I shall be honoured, sir! Tell Amy to put the kettle on as you go out, Jim!"

Chapter Twenty-Three

"Grove Street Mystery. It is rumoured that with the identification of the victim of this long-past tragedy some startling developments have taken place. Some valuable clues are in the hands of the police, and it is confidently expected that a sensational arrest will be made in the course of the next few days."

"What does it mean, Cynthia?" Joan laid the newspaper on the table and gazed anxiously at her cousin.

Mrs. Trewhistle frowned as she scanned the foregoing paragraph.

"Mean? Nothing!" she exclaimed scornfully. "If you worry yourself over every silly report that appears in the papers you will be in your grave before long."

Joan caught her breath.

"If Evelyn were your sister, Cynthia—"

"If I had never spoken to her since I was five years old, and she had been dead over ten years I should not worry about her," Mrs. Trewhistle interrupted philosophically. "I can't help it, Joan; it does seem to me that you are exciting yourself unnecessarily. After all, it does not rest with you to track the murderer down. If your sister left home, and wandered round the world getting herself mixed up with all sorts of undesirable companions, one of whom finished by shooting her, the responsibility does not rest with you. Now you promised to come with me. I must go to my milliner's; she is doing me the sweetest little toque—all shades of lilac and natural foliage, with a jet aigrette on one side to show I am still in mourning."

Joan was twisting her hands together nervously; two red spots burned hotly on her cheeks.

"I don't think I can come to-day, Cynthia. I must see Uncle Septimus. You don't mind, do you, dear?"

"Oh, no, of course I don't! It is a delight to go alone!" retorted Mrs. Trewhistle with fine irony. "I—I never liked Granny at her best!" with sudden fire. "I always thought her an old beast, but I never imagined that even she would bring this upon us!"

Joan stared at her cousin in surprise.

"Granny—bring this upon us! What do you mean, Cynthia?"

"Why, if she had behaved like a Christian and left her money to you instead of making that idiotic will," Cynthia explained, "we should never have known about Evelyn; we should have avoided all this worry; and she would have been just as well off, poor thing!"

Joan made no reply; she crossed to the window and looked out over the Square garden. The two had come up to London the previous day ostensibly for a week's shopping. In reality, since her fancied recognition of Warchester had become a certainty, Joan had found life at the Towers unendurable. It was unbearable for her to live in daily, hourly contact with Warchester, to know that between them lay that terrible barrier of doubt and suspicion, to meet the look in Warchester's eyes, and remember that it was he who had placed the pistol in her murdered sister's hand. Nor had there been signs wanting that the strain of the situation was telling upon Warchester also; he was distinctly thinner; his dark face had a worn, haggard look. It had been impossible, of course, with the uncertainty hanging over them as to what turn the police investigations might take next, to hold their projected house-party for the autumn shooting. Fortunately, the invitations had not been issued, and Joan caught eagerly at Cynthia's suggestion that they two should go up to town together to see about winter gowns. Warchester had made no objection; nay, Joan fancied that the very notion was a relief to him. He had contented himself with insisting that the two should make his town house their headquarters instead of staying at an hotel.

Joan, however, was finding now that even London failed to afford any distraction from that terrible anxiety that was worrying her. Constantly wondering what was going on at the Towers in her absence, she could not spend her days as Cynthia did, in driving from one shop to another.

This morning she had constrained herself to accompany her cousin, but now that luncheon was over, with all her fears revived by that paragraph in the midday papers, she felt that another such round would be an impossibility. At all hazards she must see Septimus Lockyer, she must ascertain how the inquiries were progressing.

So, despite Cynthia's air of ill-usage, she insisted on seeing that lady off to her milliner alone in the motor, while she directed the man to call a taxi for herself.

Luckily, Septimus Lockyer was at home and disengaged. His face was unusually grave as he rose to greet his niece.

"You are the very person I was thinking of, Joan! I was just wondering whether I should be likely to find you at home if I called. So Warchester is coming up to-night?"

"Warchester!" Joan faltered as she took the chair he drew up for her. "No, he is too busy with the improvements to leave just now. I do not expect to stay more than a few days."

For answer her uncle showed her a telegram he had just received.

"Can you make it convenient to give me an hour any time this evening—Warchester."

"I have telegraphed to him to dine with me at eight," the K.C. went on. "So I expect he is on his way now. And what can I do for you, child?"

"Oh—I—nothing!" with a guilty flush. "Cynthia has some shopping to do, and I—I wanted to know how you were, Uncle Septimus, that was all."

"That was very sweet of you." Unseen by her, the K.C. permitted himself a faint, incredulous smile. "You don't ask why I wanted to see you, child."

"N—o." Joan felt herself begin to tremble. "It—was it about the paper?"

"Paper—what paper?" Septimus Lockyer stared at her.

Joan threw back her furs.

"I saw just now that they have an important clue—that an arrest may be expected in a day or two," she faltered.

Her uncle frowned.

"Now that public interest has been aroused by learning that the victim of the Grove Street Mystery has been identified as Miss Marie De Lavelle, a former music-hall artist, they will put that sort of thing in every day for a week," he said sceptically. "No, what I wanted to say was this—Hewlett has been talking to your stepmother. Why didn't you tell me the other day that you saw something of this murder, Joan?"

Joan sat suddenly motionless, her eyes fixed in a horrified stare upon her uncle. "What do you mean?"

Septimus Lockyer's keen gaze was upon her.

"I think you know, Joan. Your stepmother says that you were scrambling about upon the roofs, and that you saw something through the window of No. 18. Be quite frank, please, child, for that is the only thing now."

"Uncle Septimus!" Joan's exclamation was almost inaudible; she felt unnerved. Strangely enough, this contingency had never occurred to her. The night of terrors which had followed upon her expedition along the Grove Street roofs, and in which she had been unable to keep from her stepmother the fearful sight she had witnessed had almost faded from her memory. She recalled it now, all the more vividly perhaps for that past forgetfulness. How much had she told? she asked herself helplessly. How much had Mrs. Spencer remembered and repeated?

She glanced up desperately into Septimus Lockyer's face.

"How—how can I remember? It is so long ago."

"Don't you remember?" the lawyer asked pointedly.

Joan shivered; warm though the room was, she had grown suddenly cold. She drew her furs around her again. How much did Septimus Lockyer know?

"I—I was very little, Uncle Septimus—only ten years old. It is impossible that I can recall things clearly after all this time."

Septimus Lockyer's gaze did not alter. With his vast experience of cross-examination he gathered almost by instinct when a witness was hostile, when there was something being kept back, something that it was material he should elicit.

"Will you just tell me all that you can remember?" he said very quietly.

It could not be that he was seeking her testimony to inculpate the man she loved.

Mechanically she fastened her sables round her neck.

"I had been longing to get on the roof—that was the first time I had been able to manage it," she said, in an expressionless, unemotional voice which, as Septimus Lockyer well knew, was very different from her usual clear, ringing tones, "but I think I was disappointed. It was not so amusing as I had imagined, playing there by myself. At last I came to a window—it may have been No. 18—I do not know. My head was just level with the window-ledge, and I peeped in. A woman lay dead on the hearth-rug; a man was stooping over her, placing a pistol in her hand."

"Yes?" Septimus Lockyer prompted as she paused, his eyes still watching her keenly.

Joan caught her breath.

"I was frightened, terrified—and there was a door at the right hand; it was opening slowly, I thought there was some one on the other side. I cried out—I fell back. Someone would shoot me too, I thought, as I picked myself up and ran back along the roof to the Mews. Then—then I told my stepmother about it, as you know. The next day Mr. Hurst came to fetch me to Davenant Hall, and after that, though for a long time I used to lie awake, too frightened to sleep when I thought of the dead woman I had seen, it gradually faded from my memory until—until I heard someone speak of the Grove Street Murder. I could not help thinking that it must have been the woman who was murdered that I had seen. But it was so long before, it did not seem to me it was any use my speaking then. I never dreamt that it was Evelyn—how could I, when I had a letter from her that very morning? Yet since—since you have told me I have thought that the hair was the same colour. But oh, Uncle Septimus, isn't there some mistake?" her voice breaking suddenly in a quiver. "It couldn't have been my own sister I saw lying there!"

The K.C. gave her arm a kindly pat.

"Don't blame yourself for that, my child. You could not be expected to recognize her after five years. Besides, you did not see the face, I gather. What was the man like?" he asked quickly.

Joan was taken off her guard.

"Oh—he—I—I don't know, Uncle Septimus! I only had a glance at him, you see!"

"It was not Gregory, I suppose, your father's stableman?"

The question was so unlike anything Joan had expected that for a second she could only stare at her questioner in stupefaction.

"No, no, of course it was not!" she said at last. "What could make you think of such a thing, Uncle Septimus?"

"You are sure it was not Gregory?"

Septimus Lockyer drew a notebook from his pocket and consulted it for a moment. Then there came one of those quiet thrusts of his that had made him one of the most dreaded cross-examiners at the Bar.

"Have you ever seen this man—the one who put this pistol in the dead girl's hand—since?"

But with a woman's quick wit Joan had decided upon her plan of action now. She would not, by an unguarded answer, place in jeopardy the liberty, perhaps the life, of the man she loved. She was not looking up; one hand was gently touching the great bunch of Parma violets tucked in front of her coat.

"No," she said quietly. "No, I have not seen him, Uncle Septimus. I should scarcely be likely to, should I? And I could scarcely recognize him now if I did. He—I do not think there was anything remarkable about him in any way."

Her grand-uncle's keen eyes took in every detail—the fair face, a little pale perhaps, but otherwise unmoved, the slender hands that did not tremble as she readjusted her flowers. To him, as a student of human nature in all its phases, there was something suspicious in her very calm, in the absence of all excitement.

The door at the other end of the room opened, and the manservant looked in.

"Mr. Hewlett, sir, would be glad if you could speak to him for a minute. I was to say that his business is important. I have shown him into the study."

"Quite right, Blake! Tell Mr. Hewlett that I will be with him in a minute."

As the man withdrew Septimus Lockyer looked across at his niece.

"And that is all, Joan? You cannot help us further? Remember perfect frankness is always the best course, child."

"Of course it is," Joan assented. She stood up and glanced out of the window. "Ah, my cab is there, I see! I must not keep you from your visitor, Uncle Septimus. I only wish I had known my evidence would have been of any importance earlier. But, you see, my father forbade me to mention what I had seen, and when you told me the other day what had really taken place I was too utterly horrified even to remember the past. Then when I did recall it it seemed too indefinite to be of any use. However, you will let me know if anything turns up?"

"Certainly!" Septimus Lockyer assented. "I want to help you, you know, Joan."

Lady Warchester moved to the door.

"You have always been very kind to me, Uncle Septimus; I wonder what made you ask me about Gregory?"

"We have to think of everybody in a case like this," Mr. Lockyer replied evasively. "Do you remember whether Gregory was in the loft when you got on the roof, Joan?"

"No, he would have stopped me if he had been there!" Joan's laugh sounded forced. "But Gregory would not have hurt Evie, Uncle Septimus; he was always devoted to her."

"I see."

The K.C.'s face was very thoughtful as he escorted his niece down to her cab. He handed her in and waited until the cab had turned into Piccadilly, then he went back into his flat.

The study door was half open. Hewlett sat on a chair near the door; he rose as Mr. Lockyer entered.

"Good afternoon, sir! I took the liberty of calling, for I felt I should like to consult you at once. I have just been calling at Scotland Yard, and while I was there some news came."

"Scotland Yard! Ah!" Septimus Lockyer's face did not alter, but in some way the detective divined that he was prepared for what was coming. "What was it, Hewlett?"

Hewlett fidgeted with some papers he held in his hand.

"You know that they have been making inquiries from registrars and others with a view to discovering whether Miss Evelyn Spencer was married, and to whom?" he said at last.

Mr. Lockyer nodded.

"I know. A very sensible proceeding too."

"Well, sir, the entry of the marriage has been discovered in the register of the church of St. Gudule in the little town of Larnac in Guernsey. A special messenger arrived with a copy while I was with Inspector Hudger just now."

"Yes?" Septimus Lockyer questioned quietly. "What was the husband's name, Hewlett?"

The detective looked away from him and studied a paper in his hand with apparent interest.

"Wilton, sir!"

Septimus Lockyer made no rejoinder for a minute; he went over to his spirit-stand and, pouring out two tiny glasses of green Chartreuse, drank one.

"Let me see it," he said then, holding out his hand.

Without a word Hewlett handed it to him. It was an ordinary copy of a certificate of a marriage solemnized on January 16th, 1895, between Evelyn Cecil Mary, daughter of John Spencer and Mary Evelyn, his wife, and—

Septimus Lockyer rubbed his eyes and stared at the bridegroom's name again. His expression lightened.

"Why, Hewlett, Hewlett, don't you realize that this is not Lord Warchester? It is his cousin Basil! What a fright you gave me, man! Don't you see that this is Herbert Basil Paul Stavordale Wilton, eldest son of Herbert Basil Wilton, clerk in Holy Orders, and Margaret Stavordale Wilton, his wife! This—this alters everything!"

"What?" Hewlett stared at him, for once astonished out of his stolid calm. "You don't mean that this is the cousin that owns the Marsh, sir—the one that has been having the operation?"

"The very same," Septimus Lockyer assented. "This explains a good deal."

The detective pulled his fair moustache and looked blank. To his mind, instead of clearing up matters this complicated them very considerably.

"Then was it this one or Lord Warchester that wrote the letters we found in the trunk, sir? They were signed Paul Wilton. But it seems this one was christened Paul too."

"Quite natural that he should be," Septimus Lockyer assented. "Old Warchester, the grandfather of both of them, was Paul. But the clergyman's son was always called Basil. As for the letters"—his face clouding as he remembered that terrible sentence, "You must introduce me as Mr. Wingrove"—"I don't know. The writing was like his lordship's. We shall have to think it over again, Hewlett—we shall have to think it over again."

Chapter Twenty-Four

THE TRAIN from Worcester steamed into Paddington Station.

Jim Gregory stepped out, looking clumsy and ungainly in the ill-fitting black suit that had been made for the funeral of the landlord of the Bell. He held a handbag, which he shifted from one arm to the other uneasily. After looking about him for a minute or two to collect his bearings, he started off briskly; turning to the right and walking quickly up Praed Street for some little distance until he neared Edgware Road. A short, thick-set man with an unkempt brown beard, who had left Willersfield by the same train as Gregory, and, like him, had changed into the express at Worcester, walked up Praed Street on the opposite side, loitered along, stopping now and then to look in the shop windows, never overtaking, but keeping close in sight Gregory's ungainly figure.

Gregory stopped in a side street before a little shop bearing the inscription, "George Dickinson, General Dealer." A few jars of sweetmeats, a quantity of slate pencils, a large tray of miscellaneous goods occupied the window, and a slatternly young woman with a baby in her arms stood at the door.

She looked at Gregory for a moment in amazement; the man with the brown beard, contriving to drop something as he passed, caught her words distinctly.

"Why, Jim, it is ever you? Who would have thought of seeing you?"

"Ay, it is me sure enough, Eliza!" Gregory answered in his gruff tones. "You will have to give me a bed for a night or two. Oh, I am going to pay you, though you are my sister!" jingling the money in his trouser pockets. "How is George?

The man with the brown beard heard no more. He strolled on in the same leisurely way until he reached the end of the street, where he stopped to speak to a ragged-looking urchin who had been hanging about at his heels ever since he left Paddington; then, quickening his steps, he hailed a passing taxi-cab and gave the driver the address of Messrs Hewlett and Cowham's offices.

Half an hour afterwards, when Gregory came out of the shop, there was more than one group of ragged children playing in the street. He did not so much as glance at them—certainly he did not observe that one of the biggest boys quietly detached himself from the rest and, keeping well behind him, followed him as he crossed over Praed Street and Oxford and Cambridge Terrace and straight on through Devonport Street to Hinton Square and thence to Grove Street. There Gregory seemed for a while disposed to linger. He walked up and down, gazing at the houses, glanced down the Mews, stood for a second or two at the top; then, as if he had come to a sudden determination, he walked sharply up to No. 18 and rang the bell.

Gregory's follower seated himself now by the railings close at hand and began to lace up his old boots.

Mrs. Perks appeared in the doorway, looking much as she had done when interviewed by Joan. At sight of Gregory, she stared, started; her face turned chalky-white; she came forward quickly.

"What do you want here, Jim Gregory? I ha' told you—"

"I want a word with you, Maria Perks, first, and then I want my rights!" Gregory said heavily. "I mean to have 'em too. You won't do me out of 'em this time, neither you nor nobody else, so I tell you!"

Mrs. Perks began to shake all over.

"I don't know what you mean by your rights, Jim Gregory, I have had naught to do with you—"

Gregory took a step forward.

"Don't you know what I mean by my rights neither?" he asked truculently. "Well, maybe you don't. That is neither here nor there. What you have got to do is to pass the word to them that does. Do you hear?"

Mrs. Perks emitted a slight scream. Seen thus at close quarters, there was something particularly unattractive about Mr. Gregory. His small eyes were bloodshot; he was not a believer in overmuch shaving, opining that twice a week was enough for any man; as a consequence his chin and lower part of his face presented a chronically rough blue appearance; a couple of his front teeth were missing, and his linen would have been much improved by a visit to the wash-tub.

"I wish I were dead, I do!" the woman cried, throwing her apron over her face.

"That won't do you any good, Maria Perks!" Gregory returned, with a malevolent laugh. "I'll come into your parlour and have a talk with you. Then if you don't see reason maybe others will—"

"You would never go for to speak now?" Mrs. Perks sobbed.

Gregory's answer was to take her contemptuously by the shoulder and walk her back to her room.

It was a lengthy interview; the watcher outside got tired of waiting. Once he went to the end of the street and spoke a few words to a gentleman who had passed by and tossed him a copper as he went on his way. Meanwhile it was easy to see that it was perfectly simple for any number of people to enter No. 18 without attracting attention, provided they had the means of obtaining access to the different flats. People came in and out, appearing for the most part to prefer making their own inquiries upstairs to interrogating Mrs. Perks on the ground floor.

At last a tall, well-dressed young man with a keen, clean-shaven face appeared and rang the bell. The boy in the road looked after him with interest.

"Ah, he is a cute one, he is!" the boy said to himself.

Mrs. Perks appeared in the doorway with a flurried expression.

"I hear you have some furnished rooms to let," the stranger observed in a pleasant, musical voice. "I should like to look over them, if you please."

"Certainly, sir!" Mrs. Perks hesitated a moment, "They are not one of our best sets, sir. They are up at the top of the house."

"Now it is very nice of you to mention that"—the man smiled at her pleasantly—"but as a matter of fact, it will be rather a convenience to me than otherwise. I have a young brother living with me, and I always think the air at the top is purer, and we are both young enough not to mind a few extra steps."

Mrs. Perks stepped back and took a key from a rail over the dresser; then she looked at Gregory. The newcomer was near enough to catch her words.

"I shall be back just now. You will be careful, Jim!"

"Ay, if I get what I want, I will be careful enough!" Gregory promised roughly.

Mrs. Perks panted a little as she walked up the stairs. The stranger looked round curiously.

"So all these rooms are taken, Mrs. Perks? Ah, well, it shows you make everybody comfortable! And a nice, quiet house. Mr. Godson told me I should find it so, and that is most necessary for me, for I have a good deal of writing to do wherever I am. Do all the tradespeople have to use these stairs, or have you a lift somewhere in the back premises?"

"Not a lift, sir," Mrs. Perks smiled mirthlessly, her respect for the would-be lodger greatly increased by his mention of Mr. Godson, the trustee in charge of the Grove Street property. "There is a back staircase here"—opening a door at her left—"it comes out just by my room, and it is handy sometimes for coals or such-like, but most folk use the front. These are the rooms, sir. There are three."

"And very pleasant they look!" the man said as he glanced into the big room in the centre and the smaller one on each side in turn. They were plainly but comfortably furnished. "And the rent is three guineas a week, Mr. Godson told me. I think I shall close with them on the spot. Now, Mrs. Perks," turning to her confidentially, "tell me, would it not be possible for me to move in this afternoon? That is my name"—handing her a card on which she read, "Mr. Edward Wallace, 32 Buckingham Street, Strand"—"and I am anxious to get away from my present quarters as early as possible. They are dark, they are noisy, they are damp from the river; in fact, they are everything that is objectionable."

Mrs. Perks looked rather staggered.

"To-day! Well, that don't leave much time for anything; but, there, I always keep the rooms clean!"

"I am sure you do!" Mr. Wallace slipped something in her hand. "You will do for us then, Mrs. Perks, and give an eye to my brother sometimes. He is studying for an exam, so he is a good deal at home just now."

"I shall do my best, sir," Mrs. Perks promised, much gratified.

"And that will be very good, I know," Mr. Wallace concluded. "Oh, it isn't flattery, Mrs. Perks! I may be from the country but I know what it is when I see it. You are not a Londoner yourself, I think, Mrs. Perks?"

Mrs. Perks wiped her eyes with the corner of her apron.

"No, sir, I come from Leicestershire, and many is the time I have wished myself back in Saxelby when the noise and bustle of London gets on my nerves."

"We all of us do," Mr. Wallace said sympathetically. "But we have our living to get. Well, I shall bring my brother in a couple of hours' time and as much luggage as we can manage. The rest may be sent after us. Good-bye, for the present, Mrs. Perks!"

He ran lightly down the stairs. Mrs. Perks followed more slowly, thinking that he would certainly prove an acquisition. Gregory was standing' up in her room when she entered.

"Well, Maria Perks, be you going to do what I asked you?"

"Haven't I told you I can't?" Mrs. Perks returned irritably. "You won't get bread out of a stone, Jim Gregory!"

"No! But maybe I shall get words from them that don't mean to speak," Gregory returned significantly. "You have had your chance, Maria Perks."

"What do you mean, Jim Gregory?" Mrs. Perks gasped.

Gregory drew out a fold of shining sequin gauze from beneath a heap of coarse, black stuff.

"Be this yours—or hers?" he asked, with an evil grin.

Mrs. Perks fell back against the door with a cry.

"Save us, Jim Gregory! Where did you get this?"

*

Mr. Wallace arrived before the stipulated two hours had elapsed. He arrived with a couple of portmanteaux and a boy in an Eton suit, with a broad white collar, who bore, to a close observer, a strong likeness to the unwashed youth who had taken so strong an interest in Gregory's movements outside.

Mrs. Perks accompanied them to their rooms, and Mr. Edward Wallace expressed himself as delighted with everything. His brother, he explained, was older than he looked, being nearly sixteen; he had been compelled to leave school owing to an illness and was now studying for the Civil Service exam.

"He is terribly mischievous, Mrs. Perks," he complained. "But if he annoys you in any way, let me know, and I will soon put an end to it."

"Oh, he won't do that, sir!" Mrs. Perks assured him confidently. "Young gentlemen will be young gentlemen, and I shan't mind that!" as she backed out of the room.

As soon as Mr. Wallace heard her footsteps to the end of the flight of stairs he closed the door.

"You know what you have to do, Archer?" His tone and manner had altered singularly.

The boy looked up.

"Yes, I think so, sir."

"You are to remain at the window until you get the signal from below," Mr, Wallace pursued. "Then you will steal as softly as possible down the back stairs and hear all you can of what is going on in Mrs. Perks's room. Hear and remember, you understand, Archer. If Mrs. Perks should catch you—well, you are hiding to give her a fright. You are a very mischievous boy, you know, Archer!"

Chapter Twenty-Five

"You!" Lady Warchester looked up in cold surprise as her husband entered the room and closed the door behind him.

"Yes, it is I!" Warchester answered, advancing.

Joan was seated before her writing-table. She wore a high gown of black cashmere, with no relief but a white frilling at neck and sleeves. She wore no jewellery save her broad wedding-ring; her hair was taken plainly back from her forehead and twisted in a thick burnished coil low down on her neck. Her great brown eyes as she raised them to Warchester's held only mingled shrinking and fear.

Her husband stood before her tall, and broad-shouldered; his clean-cut features set in lines of stern melancholy, but as he returned her gaze there was neither guilt nor anger in his eyes, only a great sadness.

"Joan," he said softly—"is this state of things to last? Can you not trust me?"

A momentary wave of longing swept over Joan.

"How can I—how can I?" she muttered brokenly. "When I saw with my own eyes—"

Warchester outstretched his hands. "Won't you accept my word, Joan? Won't you believe that, foolish, culpably foolish, though my conduct may have been, there is at least no darker stain of guilt upon me?"

For a second or two Joan hesitated. With a great rush of gladness Warchester thought that his battle was won, that she was his, then the softening in her face passed, the fear came back to her eyes, her lips grew rigid.

"I can't! I can't!" She rose to her feet and faced him defiantly.

"You are killing yourself by inches, Joan," Warchester said unsteadily. "Dear, don't you realize what it means to me to see you growing daily thinner, to know that you give yourself no rest by night or day, and to think that it is my fault, that I—Have pity, Joan, have pity!"

But Joan's regard to principle was not yet moved.

"And yet you deliberately prefer to see my suffering to giving up the name of your friend, the man whom you are shielding!" she answered firmly. "When you bring to justice my sister's murderer, when you prove to me that you had no part or lot in her death, then—then we will talk of peace!"

Warchester drew back quickly; he squared his broad shoulders; a dull flush dyed his forehead.

"I thought once that you would have trusted my word," he said in a low, pained voice. "But since proof is needed, I—I will do my best to give it to you. For the rest we must leave it to time, I shall not plead again for what should be mine by right—my wife's love and trust!"

He turned sharply on his heel and walked out of the room.

Left alone Joan stood for a moment motionless; then her throat caught in a harsh, tearless sob. With an exclamation of despair, she flung herself prone upon the couch. Now that Warchester had gone from her in anger, the recollection of his constant unvarying kindness, of the love that had encompassed her and shielded her, would obtrude itself. What sort of a return was this that she was making him? A longing to rush after him, to bid him lay his arms round her, to tell him that only their love counted, that the rest did not matter, swept over her. Then she thought of that other girl who had loved and trusted, the dear elder sister of her childhood, done to death in that studio in Grove Street; and with a moan she buried her head deeper in the velvet cushions.

Warchester, meanwhile, went straight out of the house. They were still staying in Grosvenor Square, or rather Joan and Cynthia Trewhistle were. Warchester himself, after coming up for his interview with Septimus Lockyer the previous week, had returned to the Towers. His visit of to-day was prompted mainly by an inability to keep away from Joan; a desire to ascertain how Hewlett's investigations were progressing more fully than was possible at Warchester had also its share in the matter; and last, but not least, a wish to see his cousin, Basil, whose progress since the operation had been all that could be desired, and who was now, as Mrs. Mannering informed him, asking to see him every day.

He bent his steps towards his cousin's house in Curzon Street. As he walked he would scarcely have been human if some feeling of bitterness towards Joan had not surged in his heart. He had counted so surely on the girl's faith in him. He had failed to allow sufficiently for the shock her recognition of him had proved.

His face was very grave as he knocked at his cousin's door.

Mr. Basil was better, the butler informed him, and Mrs. Mannering was at home and desired to be told at once if Lord Warchester called.

She came to him directly.

"Thank Heaven you have come, Paul! Basil has been asking for you all the morning. He is working himself up into a fever. If we had not had your letter saying you would be in town to-day and would call I should have wired to you. The doctors say he is to be kept perfectly quiet, but at the same time his mind must be set at rest, and he is most anxious to ask you some question. You will try to keep him calm, won't you, Paul?"

Warchester promised gravely as he followed her upstairs. He had always been fond of his cousins, Paul and Delia. In their earlier days before her marriage, Mrs. Mannering had been almost like a sister to him. She was a petite, sparkling brunette, with a pretty, vivacious manner, which neither her long residence in India nor her anxiety about her brother had noticeably diminished.

She opened the door into a big front room.

"Here is Paul, Basil! Now if I leave you two alone for a chat, you must both promise me to be good and not allow yourselves to be excited."

Basil was sitting in an easy chair near the fireplace, propped up by pillows; his tall frame looked long and gaunt as he tried to raise himself. His face was white and drawn, the hand he held out to his cousin was pathetically thin and shaky, but his blue eyes held the light of reason once more, his look was full of anxious questioning.

"Paul, old fellow—at last I thank heaven!" Warchester was no less moved. He had never really believed in the power of any operation to restore his cousin's mind to the clearness which it possessed before his accident. It seemed to him that a miracle had been performed.

After that first exclamation, however, Basil said no more, but waited with ill-concealed impatience until Mrs. Mannering settled them both to her liking, and, after placing a medicine bottle and glass on the table and bidding Warchester administer a dose if Basil should get exhausted, left them alone, promising them half an hour's conversation. Then as the door closed, he raised himself eagerly.

"Paul, what of Queenie? What of my wife?" Warchester looked at him in consternation. Was it possible that the return of memory was only partial? What was he to answer in face of Mrs. Mannering's warning as to the result of excitement? Before he had made up his mind as to how it would be possible to delay matters, to prevaricate, Basil started forward and gripped his hand in a tight, feverish clasp.

"It is not true that she is—dead? Paul, I asked for the papers this morning; the doctors let me have them, they said they would help to occupy my mind. Occupy my mind!" He laughed aloud—a hollow, mirthless sound. "I saw something about the murder of 'Miss Marie De Lavelle' in Grove Street. The murder of 'Miss Marie De Lavelle'! Merciful Heaven! I think my brain has been on fire since. What does it mean, Paul?" His grasp tightened in its feverish intensity. "I know it isn't true! It is a mistake! But speak, man, tell me—"

Warchester deliberated a moment.

"Don't you remember?" he said at last.

Basil's eyes were fixed upon him, as though they would wring the truth from his lips.

"How should I remember? Heavens, Paul, don't you realize that for these ten years I have been an animal, a log?"

"Yes but—" Warchester paused and looked across. It seemed to him that if Basil inquired he was bound to learn the truth, and he knew that now his cousin's suspicions were aroused he would not rest. It was better that he should gather some idea of what had happened from him than from a stranger. Then Heaven help him if he remembered!

"Yes, but don't you recollect what happened before your accident, Basil?"

"My accident!" Basil repeated. "Why of course I do! I was coming to Grove Street to meet you and Queenie when I saw that great dray bearing down upon me. Then it is all confusion. I remember no more until I woke up here."

"You are thinking now of the day before your accident, Basil," Warchester corrected quietly. "I was to see Queenie at the studio on the 11th of May. Your accident was on the 12th. I remember Delia writing to me in Paris and telling me how terribly ill you were, and that you had been knocked down by a dray on the afternoon of the 12th."

"Delia made a mistake then," Basil said shortly. "Heavens, I have heard enough of the date of my accident since I have recovered, and no mistake! I was hurrying away from the Edens' wedding to meet you and Queenie. But that does not matter now. The one thing that does is that Queenie—my wife—" He covered his face with his hands. "That for ten years I have been a useless log, and she—my poor girl!—when I think what she must have suffered—"

"She has not suffered, Basil," Warchester interrupted. "Don't you understand that for these ten years she has been at rest?" Warned by the change in his cousin's face, he sprang forward and, pouring out a measure of the stimulant, held it to his lips.

Basil took it unwillingly, but it brought a tinge of colour to his white cheeks, and after a minute or two he was able to speak.

"Tell me all," he whispered faintly. "This paper spoke of Grove Street, but it is not possible—"

Warchester saw that matters had reached such a pitch that suspense would be worse than the truth.

"Queenie met her death in your studio in Grove Street on the afternoon of May 11th, 1897."

"My poor Queenie!" moaned Basil. "But who—"

Paul watched him closely from beneath his drooping eyelids. Soon—soon he would, he must remember, and then—he shivered as he answered:

"That has never been discovered. We can't do her any good now, Basil."

"No," Basil said very quietly, though his eyes were glittering feverishly, "we can't do her any good. But we can punish her murderer. Do you imagine that I, her husband, shall rest, shall leave one stone unturned until she is avenged? Tell me everything now, Paul. How was it done?"

In Warchester's breast a slight, faint hope was beginning to dawn. Not yet would he allow himself to dwell on it, but he watched his cousin closely.

"She was shot with your pistol in the studio in Grove Street!"

"What!" Basil's face was full of incredulous horror. "Then she was followed! She was dogged by—"

Warchester's hope was growing now. Was it possible that all these years he had been under a terrible delusion, that the horror that had haunted his manhood was a chimera? A spectre of his imagination? He drew a deep breath, he straightened his back with the involuntary gesture of a man who throws off a burden.

"Basil, does that mean that she had some reason—that you think—"

Basil rested his arms on the table on his right and laid his head on them.

"She had only one enemy in the world, my poor Queenie!" he said brokenly. "There was only one person who had reason to hate her. And that—that was my fault. But it can't be—I can't see clearly now. I must think!"

Warchester laid his hand on his shoulder.

"Basil, try to tell me—"

"Well, the time is up, and how are we getting on?" a gay voice questioned behind them.

Unperceived, Mrs. Mannering had opened the door. The nurse, a pleasant, capable-looking woman, stood behind her.

Delia's tone changed.

"Oh, nurse," she said helplessly, "what is it? Has it been too much for him?"

"That will soon be all right." The nurse's practised eyes did not betray any of the dismay she felt at the condition in which she found her patient. "But I think perhaps if his lordship went down now, Mrs. Mannering—"

"Of course, of course," Warchester agreed hastily.

But though he left the room, he could not bring himself to leave the house. He waited in the library until Delia came to him.

"Nurse says she does not think there is any real harm done," she assured him. "It is only that it is the first time he has seen anyone, and he is weak."

"Ah, yes, he is weak!" Warchester acquiesced abstractedly. He could not tear his thoughts for a single instant from the one overwhelming discovery of this afternoon, a discovery which, every moment he told himself, must turn out to be merely a will-o'-the-wisp—a creation of his own fancy.

"Delia," he said quickly, "could you tell me the date of Basil's accident?"

Mrs. Mannering looked a little surprised at the question.

"Certainly! It was on the 11th of May, 1897."

"The 11th?" Paul repeated. "Delia, are you quite certain? You said in your letter telling me of the accident that Basil had been knocked down by a motor just outside your house on the afternoon of May the 12th."

"Oh, no, it was the 11th." Mrs. Mannering said positively. "I couldn't make a mistake about it, because it was Cecily Eden's wedding, and I was bridesmaid. Basil had been there too, but he had an appointment, and had to leave early. There was a smash-up, and Basil's head was frightfully hurt. For weeks we thought he couldn't live. They fetched us away from the wedding—mother and me—and I got a great ugly stain on the front of my bridesmaid's gown. Ugh! Don't talk of it, Paul!"

Chapter Twenty-Six

MR. HEWLETT was walking along Albany Street, St. John's Wood. His face was grave and absorbed. The various complications that faced him at every turn in connection with the Grove Street Mystery were puzzling him not a little. At the time the murder took place, when he was on the Scotland Yard staff, it had interested him enormously. Now that he had returned to it afresh, every faculty stimulated by the new and extraordinary developments which had taken place, it threatened to obsess him altogether. Nor was his absorption lessened by the fact that, though up to a certain point his investigations had proved unusually successful, he was as far as ever apparently from solving the enigma. He had found it by no means uncommon to feel sure of a criminal's identity himself and yet lack the means to bring it home. But the Grove Street murder differed from others in this respect—he felt quite unable to make up his mind as to whose had been the hand that fired the fatal shot. To himself he seemed to be wandering in a maze; fresh clues appeared on every side, only for him to find on following any of them that he was brought up short by a blank wall.

He had gone up to Barnsbury with but scant hope of obtaining any useful information. By chance he had learned that for some three months while they were engaged at the Melpomene, Marie De Lavelle had been very intimate with a certain Rose Merivale, who was now considered a star in the music-hall world, and was living in a maisonnette in St. John's Wood. There was a possibility that she might be able to give some helpful information, and he had written to ask for an interview.

Miss Rose Merivale had replied by fixing this afternoon. Mr. Hewlett took out her profusely-scented, highly-glazed epistle and glanced at it.

"Blandford Road. Ah, here we are"—as he took a turn to the right—"and this will be No. 6!"

He knocked at the door, and was admitted by a maidservant, who told him her mistress would be down directly. Hewlett glanced about him. The numerous small tables, the whatnots and brackets, the mantelshelf, all were bestrewn with photographs, many of them signed with names familiar to him as those of music-hall celebrities. There were quantities of flowers, many of them already faded, in innumerable little vases, and there were chairs and couches piled with cushions.

The rose-coloured blinds were drawn half-way down, producing a half light, no doubt considered by Miss Merivale as becoming; an odour of stale tobacco clung about the room, producing a combination with the smell of the faded flowers that was anything but agreeable.

The detective looked longingly at the closed windows as he heard the click-clack of high-heeled shoes on the tessellated flooring of the hall.

Miss Rose Merivale entered the room—a tall, finely-proportioned, largely-developed woman, with a profusion of auburn hair and a large amount of rouge and powder on her ample cheeks.

"How do you do, Mr. Detective?" she began, with jocund familiarity. "You wanted to see me about poor Marie De Lavelle, you said in your letter. We were great chums once, though I lost sight of her when she left the stage, but I was never so shocked in my life as when I saw this horrible affair in the papers. I hope you will hang the beast that did it!"

"We shall do our best if we can catch him, madam," the detective responded grimly. "It is on that very account that I have ventured to trouble you to-day."

Miss Merivale had thrown herself down on the sofa in a remarkably free-and-easy attitude, motioning Hewlett to the nearest easy-chair. She opened her violet eyes now to their fullest extent.

"But goodness me, Mr. Detective, what good can I be to you? Why, I hadn't seen her for more than eighteen months before it happened, so I don't see that I—"

"I know you don't, Miss Merivale!" Hewlett leaned forward and spoke impressively. "But when a tragedy such as this occurs, the seed of it, so to speak, generally lies far back in the life of the deceased. If you would tell me anything you could of Miss De Lavelle it is quite possible that a chance word of yours might put me on the right track."

"I wish I might!" Miss Merivale said heartily. She took a cigarette and lighted it thoughtfully, then tossed the case over to Hewlett. "Help yourself, please! What I knew about Marie De Lavelle didn't amount to much really. We were pretty chummy for a time when we were doing our turns at the same hall—should have been more so, I dare say, if she hadn't taken up with Cécile. I couldn't stand her at any price, and so I told Marie. That was the reason of the first coolings between us. I wonder what has become of her, by the way? Cécile, she would be the one to tell you anything there was to tell."

"I should very much like to have an interview with Miss Cécile," said the detective, with perfect truth. Septimus Lockyer and his co-trustee, Sir Edward Fisher; had agreed, that for the sake of the family name, it was inadvisable that the search for the pseudo-Evelyn should be too vigorously prosecuted and the details of her imposture made public; but Hewlett had come to see of late that it was possible she could have given them valuable information that might have led to the apprehension of the murderer, and a close search was now being instituted with a view to discovering her whereabouts. So far it had been without success. She had taken a considerable amount of money with her, and Hewlett was beginning to think that by its means she had placed herself beyond the reach of pursuit. "I suppose Miss Marie De Lavelle had several lovers," he hazarded at last.

Miss Merivale smoked her cigarette reflectively.

"Well, she had—and she hadn't. You see, she was a dear, and she was pretty too, but she hadn't much go about her; and after a while the boys used to get tired of her and seek other society that was a little more lively."

Hewlett looked disappointed.

"Then she had no special lover?"

Miss Merivale shook her head.

"Not as long as I knew her. I saw in the papers she was supposed to be married, but I have no notion who it could be. Not but what the De Lavelle girls always had plenty of men to take them about, but it always seemed to me that Cécile was the attraction: she had plenty of *diablerie*—or whatever you call it. The Demon and the Saint, you know. That was what the boys used to call them. It was one of the Wiltons that gave them that name first, I believe, but it stuck, Marie was the Saint."

"Of course," the detective assented mechanically. This was almost better luck than he had hoped for—the introduction of the Wiltons' name—but it behoved him to walk warily now. He hesitated a moment. "They—the De Lavelles—were very intimate with the Wiltons, were they not?"

"Oh, I shouldn't say that!" Miss Merivale responded carelessly. "Basil Wilton was mad on Cécile for a bit, but I think his cousin, Paul, only came to look after him; to see he didn't get into mischief. Well, in a way Paul got friendly with Marie—Queenie as we used to call her then—but there never was any love-making between them, bless you! Paul is Lord Warchester now, you know. I wonder whether he remembers, and what he thinks about this affair when he sees it in the papers."

So did Mr. Hewlett wonder, but there was little to be gained by speculation in that quarter.

"I thought it was Marie that Mr. Basil Wilton admired?"

Miss Merivale shook her head.

"No, it was Cécile. Basil Wilton was just crazy about Cécile for a while, and then there was Caliban," with a laugh.

Mr. Hewlett pricked up his ears,

"Caliban?"

Miss Merivale laid her head back on the pillows with an air of luxurious abandonment.

"Ah, he was a great lout of a fellow that was a sweetheart of Marie's before she came on the stage! How she ever stood him I can't think. But she would have had a tremendous bother to get rid of him when she found her bearings and saw what other men were if he hadn't been like the rest and fallen in love with Cécile. Let me think now, what was his name?"

She wrinkled up her artificially-darkened eyebrows.

"Gregory—that was it of course—Jim Gregory."

Gregory! The detective drew a long breath. Was there ever a case like this? he asked himself despairingly. It seemed that Miss Rose Merivale was about to prove another blank wall.

"Yes, Jim Gregory!" Miss Merivale repeated, blowing a thin blue cloud of smoke into the air. "I remember once I asked Queenie—we used to call her Queenie sometimes because of her funny little airs, you know—why she didn't shake him off, why on earth she ever let him know what she was doing. And she told me that he gave her news of her little sister, who was left under her stepmother's care at home. Queenie herself had run away, and she was afraid the child might be treated so badly that she too might not be able to stand it. Gregory had promised to keep a watch and let her know."

"Ah, yes, he could do that!" Mr. Hewlett said slowly. "I have heard they were sweethearts once, Gregory and Miss De Lavelle—he has told us as much."

Miss Merivale looked a little surprised.

"Oh, has he? But that was all over before I knew Queenie. Then he was head over ears in love with Cécile—used to follow her about and glower at her all over the place."

Hewlett laughed a little, though his eyes had a far away expression. "And what did Miss Cécile think of him?"

"Not much, as you can guess, if you have seen Gregory," Miss Merivale responded. "She used to throw him a word now and then as you might a bone to a dog. I have told her many a time she ought to be careful, for I have seen a look in his eyes sometimes when she has been teasing him as if he would like to make an end of her there and then. If it had been she that was murdered I should have said, 'Look up Jim Gregory'; but as it is poor Queenie I don't know what to think."

Mr. Hewlett did not know what to think either; various wild theories and suspicions chased one another in a nebulous state, through his brain.

"I suppose the Sisters De Lavelle were not sufficiently alike to be mistaken for each other?" he hazarded at last.

"Off the stage, do you mean?" Miss Merivale questioned. "Bless your life, no! Their faces were the same shape, but Cécile's fair hair was a transformation, if you know what that means, Mr. Detective— her hair was brown. And the rest of the likeness was mostly make-up. Cécile was stouter and bigger in every way, but she used to dress up to Marie very well."

"I was thinking," the detective said slowly, "I was wondering whether it was in any way possible that Marie was murdered by mistake for Cécile by some jealous lover."

"No, indeed it wasn't!" Miss Merivale said emphatically. "You may take my word for that. No, discovery doesn't lie that way, Mr. Detective, I can assure you. And now"—she looked at the tiny jewelled watch pinned in front of her gown—"you said a few minutes' conversation, and I believe you have had half an hour. I have to go to a rehearsal directly. If there is anything else I can tell you—"

200 | THE WITNESS ON THE ROOF

Hewlett rose. He was still looking puzzled; his monocle hung by its cord.

"I am much obliged to you for sparing me so much of your time, Miss Merivale," he said politely. "There is nothing else that I can think of this afternoon, but if anything should occur later—"

"You will come again—that is understood," Miss Merivale finished. "And I wish you good luck, Mr. Detective. I would give a good deal myself to see poor Queenie's murderer punished, I would indeed."

Mr. Hewlett shook hands and went out. As he walked slowly back to Swiss Cottage he was thinking harder than he had ever thought about a case before. It seemed to him that never had he been engaged on one that seemed at once so absorbing and so provoking. It reminded him of a game he had played as a child, where an object is hidden, and when the searcher is near it he is told that he is "warm." Mr Detective Hewlett continually had the feeling that he was quite near the solution of his problem, that he was "warm" in fact, only to find the next minute that he was as far as ever from it.

As the bus tore on its way down Finchley Road he pondered once more the facts, as he knew them. For the past month, ever since the discovery that it was Basil Wilton that Evelyn Spencer had married, he had been strongly of the opinion that her death must be laid at the door of one of these three men—either one of the two cousins Lord Warchester and Basil Wilton, or James Gregory. To some extent of late he had been compelled to exonerate Basil Wilton. Inquiries had shown that his accident had occurred at least half an hour before the time at which the doctor's testimony proved that Evelyn Spencer met her death, and his long illness fully accounted for Wingrove's silence, which had appeared at first to be so suspicious.

At the same time, Mr. Hewlett was not inclined to be entirely satisfied; there might be a mistake in the time at either end, he told himself—and an alibi is always the most unsatisfactory of defences.

He, at least, might have had some sort of motive—the desire to rid himself of a wife of whom possibly he was tired, and who was obviously desirous of a recognition which would offend his mother and endanger his inheritance.

In the case of Lord Warchester, as of Jim Gregory, there was apparently no reason which could in any way account for the murder. To Lord Warchester, in spite of the letter dated two years back, Evelyn Spencer had been, as far as could be ascertained at the time of her death, merely his cousin's wife; to Jim Gregory she had been merely the sweetheart of his younger days, long since forgotten in a newer passion.

Yet Mrs. Spencer had identified, in the most positive fashion, the pouch found beside the body as the one the dead girl had worked for Gregory. If her evidence was to be trusted, his presence in the room at the time of or immediately prior to her death might be taken as proved.

Think of it as he would, Mr. Hewlett could arrive at no satisfactory conclusion. That the guilt lay with one of those three he felt convinced. The question was—which? And this question his interview with Miss Merivale had not, so far as he could see, in the least answered.

He got off the bus at Charing Cross and, turning up Bedford Street, made his way down Maiden Lane to his offices. At the door he almost collided with some one coming out.

"Why, Hewlett, the very man I was looking for!" Septimus Lockyer exclaimed, "But I have not a moment to spare now. Walk back with me as far as the post office."

"Any news, sir?" asked Hewlett as he complied.

Septimus Lockyer looked at him.

"The best time to call on Mr. Edward Wallace is between five and six, Hewlett."

"So we have found, sir. But the door fits like wax: it isn't possible to hear much."

"It was not," Septimus Lockyer said significantly, "but Mr. Wallace's young brother has a taste for carpentering; he has eased the door at the bottom so much, Mrs. Perks says. But there—boys will be boys, and there's no harm done!"—with a mimicry of Mrs. Perks' manner that made the detective smile.

"Have you any engagement for to-night, Hewlett?" Mr. Lockyer went on, with a sudden change of tone.

"No, sir, nothing I can't put off if there is work to be done," the detective said hopefully.

"I want you to come to a music-hall with me."

"A music-hall, sir?" Hewlett stared. "I don't understand!"

"Down Islington way," Septimus Lockyer went on. "Not a swagger sort of place at all, Hewlett. We need not put on our evening clothes, and I know that moustache of yours comes off on occasion. Suppose you leave it at home to-night."

"Of course, sir!" Hewlett looked more mystified than ever

They made their way into the orchestra stalls. Hewlett glanced around the house; it appeared to be fairly full. A much painted lady was on the stage singing one of the usual inane songs, which received but faint applause. Hewlett saw that Mr. Lockyer was not looking at the stage, that he was half turned round, as if to get a better view of the occupants of the gallery.

Instinctively the detective's eyes followed. To his surprise he saw Gregory leaning forward, his gaze fixed on the stage.

A voice began to sing in the flies, words commonplace enough in themselves, yet given with an accent that seemed to lend a certain coarse suggestiveness; then a woman bounded upon the stage and began to dance. She was veiled from head to foot in shining golden tissue—even her face was covered, save for two holes through which her eyes gleamed oddly.

As she floated across the stage, rising and sinking in a motion that was at once graceful and bewildering, one caught glimpses through the glittering tissue of white rounded limbs, of waves of dark hair, but the face—the face remained veiled always.

From chance remarks he had overheard as they were entering the hall, Hewlett had learned that the veiled dancer had appeared for the first time only a month ago, that she had caught on at once, and that so for no one, not even the manager, had seen her unveiled. Consequently, curiosity and speculation as to her identity were rife.

Septimus Lockyer looked at him.

"I told you you would recognize an old acquaintance."

"I have." Hewlett indicated Gregory with a jerk of his head.

"Two old acquaintances I should have said," the k.c. corrected. "Look at the veiled dancer, Hewlett. Graceful figure, isn't she? A bit big perhaps, but—" He shrugged his shoulders.

Hewlett looked at her again, but there was nothing familiar about the lissom figure enveloped now in golden clouds.

"Carry your mind back to the Towers," Septimus Lockyer whispered, "to the day Lady Warchester gave us her half of the broken sixpence. Do you remember meeting some one in the drive?"

"Why, of course!" A sudden flash of recognition gleamed in Hewlett's face. "You mean Miss—"

"Precisely!" The k.c. nodded. "Take another look, Hewlett."

But the veiled dancer's turn was coming to an end; a tremendous clapping from the audience testified to the satisfaction she had given. Gregory got up from his place and hurriedly made his way to the exit. Septimus Lockyer glanced at Hewlett.

"Seen enough? The veiled dancer only does one turn a night."

Still puzzled, Hewlett assented, and they both left the hall. Neither of them spoke until they were once more in a cab: then the k.c. looked at his companion.

"Well?"

"If that is Miss Cécile De Lavelle," Hewlett said sturdily, "I am of opinion that she ought to be interrogated at once with regard to her life while she was dancing as one of the Sisters De Lavelle. It is possible that she might be able to give us most valuable information that might lead to the discovery of the Grove Street murderer, and we might manage to frighten it out of her by threatening to prosecute her for imposture."

A curious smile curved Septimus Lockyer's lips.

"We might," he assented, "but I don't think we will try that plan just yet, Hewlett. I have a plan of my own. You must help me with that, and then very soon, probably within the week, you shall have your interview with Miss Cécile De Lavelle—the pseudo-Evelyn Davenant."

Chapter Twenty-Seven

MR. EDWARD Wallace sat in his room, waiting quietly. Presently there was a knock at the door—three distinct taps. Mr. Wallace got up lazily and opened it.

Mr. Hewlett, the detective, stepped inside.

"Any news, Simpson?" Mr. Hewlett had not resumed his moustache to-day, and its absence made a considerable difference to his appearance.

"Our man is here, sir," answered Simpson, alias Mr. Edward Wallace, "and we think Archer's plan with the door will answer all right; he has managed to shave a bit off the wainscoting too. He is there now; I am expecting him up every minute. In the meantime, sir—" He went over to the cupboard and, bringing out a pair of black list slippers, handed them to Hewlett, who took off his boots at once.

He had just put on the slippers in their stead when the boy, Archer, came softly into the room.

"He is there, sir, and Mrs. Perks and somebody else. I can't see plain through the crack, but I think it is a woman." Hewlett stood up.

"You wait here, Simpson."

He crept softly down the back stairs and found himself in a sort of square hall into which the back door opened. That was locked and bolted, as Mr. Hewlett soon ascertained; of the other two doors, one led into Mrs. Perks's sitting-room, the other into the large pantry and kitchens. There was no one about; Mrs. Perks did all the work that was needed with the help of a charwoman. A streak of light beneath the parlour door testified to Archer's handiwork. Hewlett caught the sound of voices within—a low, deep, guttural growl easily to be recognized as Gregory's, and Mrs. Perks's tearful accents mingled with a louder, more defiant voice.

"You won't play me false twice!" Gregory was speaking. "You understand! I have made the appointment and you will have to keep it or you will take the consequences this time."

"I don't know but what I'd just as soon take the consequences!"

As Detective Hewlett, with his ear close to the keyhole, caught the answer he started violently. Surely he was not mistaken—it was the voice he had heard in the avenue at the Towers, the voice of the veiled dancer of last night, of the one-time mistress of Davenant Hall.

Gregory laughed harshly.

"Suppose you try them! The worst of it is you won't be able to tell us how you like them!"

"Oh, Jim, Jim, don't!" The low, wailing cry was Mrs. Perks's. "I—I am sure I don't know how to sleep o' nights when I remember!"

"It takes a good deal to keep some folk awake!" was Mr. Gregory's unsympathetic rejoinder. "I dare say though, if Cissie there isn't punctual to time to-morrow that you won't need an alarm for a week or two!"

A low hoarse sob broke from Mrs. Perks.

"You—you are a brute, Jim Gregory!"

"If I am, it is the fault of the folk that made me so!" the man returned in a stubborn voice. "It's no use you trying on that game with me, Maria Perks. I've been done out of my rights once, this time I'm going to make sure. It has got to be the one thing or the other."

"Don't put yourself out, Jim!" The loud, hard voice of Evelyn Spencer's impersonator was a little subdued now, the detective fancied. "If I make a promise, I keep it."

"No, you don't—not always!" Gregory rejoined uncompromisingly. "But you are a-going to this time, my girl, so you needn't make any mistake! And if my Lord Tomnoddy, or whatever his name is, sends his flowers and his presents to the veiled dancer again—why, he will have to reckon with me, that is all!"

There was a pause; then the dancer laughed unsteadily. "What a fool you are, Jim! Why, if Lord Sandford chooses to give me diamonds, do you suppose I am going to refuse them? But as for anything else, haven't I promised you—"

"Ay, and I'll see you keep it!" Evidently Gregory was not going to be smoothed down. "'Tain't going to be Basil Wilton over again, anyhow!"

"You beast!" There was a sound as of a heavy missile being flung across the room. "You keep a civil tongue in your head, Jim Gregory, or I don't go a step to the Harrow Road to-morrow, do as you will!"

"Oh, yes you will, Cissie!" Gregory's voice had dropped to a kind of rough pleading. "It—it isn't altogether my fault if I cut up a bit rough sometimes. It drives me mad when I see you looking and smiling at other fellows! If—if I was sure of you it would be different. I should be that gentle and loving!"

"Ugh! I dare say you would, but I haven't any use for that sort of thing." The dancer's tone was very scornful. "I'll do what I said, but remember I won't have any of your nonsense!"

"It will come, though, Cissie, it will come," Gregory urged. It was quite evident to the listener that the man was unwontedly moved, that the dancer was correspondingly calm. Mrs. Perks continued to sob weakly. "I have waited for years and years," the man went on. "I ha' known my time must come at last, and come it has. But I'm not going to be done out of it by any lordlings!" with a sudden accession of fury. "When I saw him waiting at the stage door the other night I could ha' stuck a knife into him with a will!"

"More fool you!" the woman responded with a laugh, yet Hewlett fancied there was a touch of real anxiety in her voice. "You would not have mended your cause by that, I can tell you!"

"Nor hurt it!" Gregory finished stolidly. "You are a-going to give me my way because you have got to, my girl! I don't make no mistake about that, no more need you! Ten o'clock to-morrow morning, and see as you don't keep me waiting!"

"That is enough!" There was a stir as if the dancer had kicked back her chair in a rage. "I shan't stand much more of this, Jim Gregory, so I tell you! I have promised you. Best for you to be off while I'm in the same mind!"

"Ah—ah, I am going!" Gregory apparently bestirred himself. "Well, so long till to-morrow morning, Cissie! So long, Mrs. Perks."

Hewlett held his breath, fearing that Mr. Gregory might elect to go out the back way, but in a moment he heard him open the other door and knew that that danger was passed.

The two women were left alone; there was a silence broken only by the sound of Mrs. Perks's sobbing. At last the other spoke:

"I have brought my pigs to a pretty market! Stop that crying, Maria, or I shall do you a mischief! It aggravates me!"

"I can't bear to think of it, Cissie! That Jim Gregory frightens me. Suppose he don't keep his word after all!"

"Oh, he will do that for his own sake," the dancer returned. "He hasn't the wit to see—"

"What?" Mrs. Perks questioned breathlessly,

"That a few mumbled words can't tie a woman down for ever," the other finished. "I must be off now; Maria. I have got an early turn to-night. Shall you be there to-morrow?"

"No, no! I couldn't bear it!" Mrs. Perks said huskily.

"All right, then! I shall see you later on. Good-bye! I am going to walk to Southwick Crescent and see if I can pick up a taxi." There was another silence; the door into the hall opened again, then the dancer stepped back. "Don't cry, old girl! I haven't been much of a sister to you. You have no need to fret about me." Then the door closed softly and Mrs. Perks was alone.

Hewlett stole silently up the stairs and back to Mr. Edward Wallace's room at the top of the house.

Hewlett looked at him.

"I can't make much of this, Simpson. Gregory has got some sort of hold over this woman, but what it is I don't just see."

Simpson hesitated.

"I know he has some sort of a hold, sir—I made out as much the other day—and it might be over her pretending to be Miss Spencer. I dare say Gregory has heard we are making inquiries about her, and of course he does not know that we can lay our hands on her at any minute."

"That may have something to do with it," Hewlett assented thoughtfully. "Curious she should turn out to be Mrs. Perks's sister! Well, the next thing for me to do is to go round to Mr. Lockyer and tell him what we have heard. It may be useful, or it may not. I shall have to go over it a bit before I make up my mind."

As Mr. Hewlett went downstairs he noticed that the door of Mrs. Perks's sitting-room stood ajar; he even caught the sound of a low sob.

"Now does she know anything, or does she not?" he soliloquized. "The husband was all right, but I don't feel so sure of her. And yet—well, it is a puzzle altogether!"

In Edgware Road he took a cab to St. James's Street. Septimus Lockyer was at home and expecting him.

"Any news, Hewlett?" the K.C. asked as he drew a sheet of blotting-paper over a note he had just written. Hewlett looked a little depressed.

"I have overheard an interview between Miss Cécile De Lavelle and Gregory and Mrs. Perks, sir; but I'm not sure that it sheds much light upon matters. Here are my notes, if you can make them out."

Septimus Lockyer held out his hand for the book and studied it in silence for a minute, his brows drawn together, his fingers tapping rhythmically on the table. At last he looked up.

"I think this is just what we wanted, Hewlett."

"Is it, sir?" The detective looked thoroughly at sea.

Septimus Lockyer nodded.

"Yes, you have done good work over this case, Hewlett. But for you I doubt whether the Grove Street Mystery would ever have been elucidated. I shall see that your share of it is heard of in the proper quarter. If I have been more fortunate than you in tracking down the real criminal at the end it is merely because the luck has been with me. All the real hard work—the tracing of Evelyn's Spencer's identity— was done by you. Now for what time did Mr. Gregory make this appointment? Ten o'clock in Harrow Road. Humph! May I trouble you to pass me that directory, Hewlett?"

The detective did as he was asked. His mind was in a more chaotic state than ever. He was unable to see what possible bearing upon the Grove Street Mystery the conversation he had overheard was likely to have. It seemed to him that it might refer to something very different.

Septimus Lockyer lifted the blotting-paper, took out the note he had written, tore it in two, and tossed it into the fire. Then he went over to the telephone and carried on a colloquy of which Hewlett could only catch stray sentences.

Coming back, he took a fresh sheet of paper, and, seeming for the moment to forget the detective, scribbled a hasty note. Presently, however, he threw it across.

"Read that, Hewlett."

The detective took it blankly, and read:

"Dear Inspector Hudger,

You will be glad to hear that Mr. Hewlett and myself have succeeded in discovering the secret of Grove Street. I shall be delighted if you will call upon me about nine o'clock this evening. Will you have your men in readiness to make the arrest—say at the corner of Gray's Inn Road—at ten o'clock to-morrow morning? A subsequent arrest will have to be made later in the day.

I am yours faithfully,

Septimus Lockyer."

"Well?" the K.C. interrogated as the detective looked up.

"I am beginning to understand what you mean, sir," Mr. Hewlett said slowly, "but I don't quite see now—"

Chapter Twenty-Eight

MR. LOCKYER rang the bell and despatched his letter; then he crossed over to one of the big easy-chairs near the fire and motioned the detective to the other.

"Draw it up, Hewlett, and help yourself to a cigar; you will find them at your elbow. It may be as well to get our explanation over before Hudger arrives. Well, in the first place"—putting the tips of his fingers together and gazing over them reflectively into the fire— "it is largely a matter of deductions. From the first I was positively certain that neither Basil Wilton nor his cousin, Lord Warchester, had anything to do with the murder; I knew them both, and felt sure of them in spite of everything. And things did look pretty black for one or the other at one time—I'm not blaming you for thinking as you did, Hewlett. There remained Gregory. Of him I was doubtful, but I could conceive no adequate motive; and Lady Warchester's testimony showed that he, at any rate, had nothing to do with the placing of the pistol in the dead girl's hand. Yet his manner was unconvincing, so also was Mrs. Perks's; I felt sure that both of them knew more than they would say. Then one day an illumination came to me. Mrs. Read had spoken of a handbag that Evelyn Spencer had carried when she left her house on the morning of her death. Now there was nothing of the kind found in the studio, though it was possible she had left it at a cloak-room. Anyhow, the idea was worth considering. I paid Mrs. Read a visit. She remembered perfectly well that Miss Spencer told her she was putting a few valuables in the bag that she didn't dare to trust to the boxes she was forwarding. Mrs. Read remembered being shown the ruby cross, which Miss Spencer said had belonged to her mother, that very morning of the 11th of May—the day Evelyn Spencer met her death—as well as a quantity of papers which the girl put in the pocket of the bag with the case containing the cross. Now I had seen that cross, and knew that it had come down to my niece, Mary Davenant, Evelyn's mother, from her grandmother. I had seen it on the neck of the false Evelyn at Warchester, and I knew that it was among the proofs of her identity offered by her to Mr. Hurst. Ah, that simplifies matters, does it not?" as the detective with a sharp exclamation sat upright in his chair.

"It does, indeed!" Hewlett agreed emphatically. "The dolts we were not to think of that!"

"Well, it was a point that I fancied needed clearing up," Mr. Lockyer went on. "Then—and here I had Lord Warchester's help, which was not at the service of the police—I learned that at one time Cécile De Lavelle was the friend of Basil Wilton, and that he had deserted her for Marie—Evelyn Spencer. There I found my motive, inadequate possibly, but still more obvious, it seemed to me, than in the case of any of the three who have been suspected by the police. Then, when I could not help noticing that the false Evelyn had apparently no fear of the real Evelyn turning up, I argued that the probabilities were that she knew of the other's death."

"I believe you are right, sir," said Mr. Hewlett. "I think you are, but beyond the ruby cross, which she might have become possessed of in some other way, this is not evidence."

Septimus Lockyer nodded.

"Quite right, Hewlett! Trust you for seeing the weak points in a story! You supplied me with two important clues—one when you told me that Mrs. Perks came from Saxelby, in Leicestershire, and that her maiden name was Shirley. I went down there and found that there had been two sisters Shirley; one—the elder—was undoubtedly Mrs. Perks, the other I could not help recognizing as my quondam niece, Miss Cécile De Lavelle. After that I had an interview with Basil Wilton, who told me that Cécile De Lavelle had been furious when he transferred his affections to Evelyn. She had vowed vengeance on them both; it was partly that fact that made

Evelyn consent to her marriage with Basil being kept secret. For some time Basil and his wife travelled, using the name of Wingrove. Wingrove was the name that his cousin Paul had occasionally used in Paris when exhibiting. It was a family name, and the two associations combined to recall it to Basil's memory when he wanted a pseudonym. When he was summoned to England on account of his mother's illness, for a time they lived together; then a quarrel ensued and Evelyn refused to live with her husband until he acknowledged their marriage. As a result she took rooms in Highgate, and he went back to live at home, later on renting the studio in Grove Street in the name of Wingrove, in the hope that she might return to him there."

"I see, sir," the detective said slowly: "We were hoping to get valuable information from Mr. Basil Wilton, but we were given to understand that at present his condition would not admit of an interview."

"Ah, there you were handicapped!" Septimus Lockyer said gravely. "Now I am a privileged person. As I say, luck has been with me; nevertheless all the hard work has been done by you."

Hewlett felt in no mood to be soothed by the great lawyer's praise. Later on no doubt it would recur to his memory pleasantly; at present he could only remember how very near he had been to the solution of the secret of Grove Street and yet how very far from the right path his suspicions had wandered.

"You said I had unconsciously given you two clues, sir," he observed at last. "One that Mrs. Perks was a native of Saxelby. Would you mind telling me the other?"

"The other?" Septimus Lockyer repeated carelessly. "Oh, that was with regard to Gregory! I could not make him out for a long time. From the first I felt sure that if he did not commit the murder himself he knew who did. I inclined to the latter opinion, but the problem that presented itself to me was why had he kept silence? When you told me of his love for Cécile De Lavelle, of which you heard from Miss Merivale, I began to see my way. The interview at which you assisted to-night has removed my last doubts; Gregory is using his guilty knowledge to force Cécile De Lavelle into a marriage with him. I have just telephoned to the registrar, and he tells me the names have been hung up for the last three weeks at the office, and the marriage is to take place to-morrow morning. Doubtless had he known of her whereabouts all this time he would have brought forth his weapon sooner. Now he has had his way; in return for his promise of secrecy she has promised to marry him at the registry office in Harrow Road at ten o'clock to-morrow. Why do you look so grave, Hewlett? Don't you agree with my theory?"

The detective hesitated.

"Yes, sir, I do as far as it goes. The worst of it is that it is a theory—that so far we seem to have but little evidence to prove it. We might justify an arrest, but I am afraid we could not obtain a conviction without more proof."

Septimus Lockyer nodded thoughtfully.

"Quite right, Hewlett! You mean that we must have definite evidence to offer with regard to Cécile De Lavelle's being actually on the spot at the time the murder took place."

"That is what I mean, sir," the detective assented. "And proof that Gregory was in a position to know anything with regard to the murder."

The K.C. did not answer for a minute.

"Gregory himself will supply the necessary evidence to-morrow," he said at last, without raising his head.

"Gregory?" The detective looked at him. "I don't understand—"

Septimus Lockyer gave a curious little laugh.

"I have been thinking out my scheme since you came in; I don't think it will miscarry. When Gregory finds that his bride does not appear to-morrow morning, when he discovers, as he imagines, that he has been made a fool of—for you must remember it is evident that Cécile had eluded him once already—when he is arrested as an accessory, I fancy we shall find him ready to tell us all he knows."

"And she—I suppose you will arrest her before? But then will she not send to him—let him know somehow?" questioned Hewlett, looking puzzled.

Mr. Lockyer puffed at his cigar.

"I think my plan will provide for all that. A taxi sent by Gregory will arrive at the veiled dancer's rooms in Islington at nine-o'clock to-morrow morning; it will take her by a circuitous route to the corner of Gray's Inn Road, where it will stop at a signal from two police officers, who will then enter and make the arrest, driving their prisoner safe to Scotland Yard. In the meantime Gregory will be kicking his heels outside the register office in Harrow Road, and —you know the vengeance he vowed if the girl played him false again—he will be ready to turn King's evidence when he is arrested. Oh, I don't think our case will present any extraordinary difficulties now! What do you say?"

Hewlett's face cleared as if by magic.

"Say? What can I say, sir, except that it is a grand scheme? I believe you will carry it through all right."

"I believe we shall," Septimus Lockyer assented. "The watching of Gregory shall be your part, Hewlett. See that he is looked after until he is safely in the hands of the police. And tell Mr. Edward Wallace to keep an eye on Mrs. Perks—we shall want her too. I think that is all."

Hewlett took the hint and rose.

"I will put things in train now, sir."

"Perhaps it would be as well." The great K.C. held out his hand. "It has been a tough bit of work, but I think we have managed it very well together—you and I."

"You are very good, sir!"

Nevertheless, the chagrin on the man's face was patent to Septimus Lockyer's keen eyes. Hewlett walked slowly along Piccadilly towards Charing Cross. He had a modest couple of bachelor rooms in Buckingham Street. It was expensive, perhaps, but it was on the spot for his work. Cowham, who was a married man, lived out at Streatham and grew flowers and vegetables in his spare time. The senior partner had always been of the opinion that it would not do for both of them to cultivate the domesticities. He had never been better pleased with his proximity to the scene of his labours than on this particular night; it was sufficiently near for Inspector Hudger, after his interview with Septimus Lockyer, to come in and talk over the plans for the next day—sufficiently near for Hewlett himself to go to his office and get out his notes of the Grove Street Murder and go over them for the hundredth time. How was it that he had missed such a very obvious solution? he asked himself despairingly over and over again. It seemed to him now, looking back, that from the very moment he found out that Evelyn Spencer had been murdered his attention ought to have been directed to her impersonator. Now that he knew how it had occurred, Wingrove's flight was so easily explainable that he was inclined to underrate the suspicion to which it had given rise.

The long hours of that night seemed endless. He was up betimes; his share of the business was to watch Gregory. Well, he would at least do that thoroughly.

Gregory was still staying with his sister, Mrs. Dickinson, in the little side street off Praed Street. At half-past nine he emerged in a new and particularly ill-fitting suit of clothes, with a flower in his buttonhole. Hewlett, keeping himself well out of sight, followed at a respectful distance. As he expected, Gregory made straight for Harrow Road. The register office stood some distance down. Gregory did not hurry himself; he sauntered slowly along, glancing now and then at the passing cabs, as though expecting that one of them might contain his bride. It wanted five minutes to the hour when he finally reached the office and went inside. Presently he reappeared and stood on the step, gazing up and down the road. A church clock close at hand struck ten; he still waited.

Mr. Hewlett turned into a restaurant which commanded a view of the office, and ordered a cup of coffee, taking care to secure a seat in the window. He was long-sighted enough to note how lowering

Gregory's face looked as the time went on, how he kicked his feet savagely against the doorpost, regardless of the registrar's paint. Presently another customer came into the coffee-shop, a man who had been lounging at a street corner higher up. He handed Hewlett a paper from Inspector Hudger—Cécile De Lavelle, alias Shirley, had been arrested, and was now safely lodged in prison.

So far Septimus Lockyer's plan had prospered, but, as the detective well knew, the most ticklish part of the work remained to be accomplished.

A boy came slowly sauntering down the street—a boy who might have been Mr. Edward Wallace's younger brother save that he wore the uniform of a messenger. Mr. Hewlett left his coffee and boldly crossed the road just as the boy accosted Gregory.

"Mr. James Gregory?" the messenger said airily.

Gregory looked at him.

"That is my name; what do you want?"

"Lady said you was to be told she was prevented from coming," the messenger said glibly. "Went away in a taxi early this morning, she did. You ought to have had the message sooner, afore you started, but Mrs. Jones, the landlady, it was her busy day, she says, and she couldn't send round at once. She hopes you will excuse it."

"Excuse it!" Gregory exclaimed. "I—I'll be level with her for this, the lying hussy! I'll let her fine lord see what sort of a woman he has gone off with!"

The moment for action had arrived. Hewlett stopped to read a notice. As Gregory swung himself off the steps two men in plain clothes came towards him. As if by magic a couple of policemen appeared on either hand. Inspector Hudger touched Gregory's arm.

"James Gregory, I arrest you as an accessory after the fact in connection with the murder of Evelyn Spencer on the 11th of May. And I must warn you that anything you say will be taken down in writing and used in evidence against you."

"What!"

It was evident that Gregory's first instinct was towards flight. He thrust out his bullet head and tried to shake himself free. But he had not reckoned with the strength of the Inspector's grasp or with the men that in a trice surrounded him. Before he had in the least realized his position the handcuffs were securely on his wrists and be was being marched off to the police-station. Then his big frame seemed to collapse, his face turned a curious bloated purple.

"This—this is her doing, the hussy!" he said between his teeth. "I'll be level with her yet! I promised her I would. Just you take me to the proper folks, and I will make a clean breast of it!"

Chapter Twenty-Nine

"HAVE YOU seen the papers this morning, Joan?"

Lord Warchester's tone was abrupt, almost curt.

Joan was standing in the hall, warming her hands at the fire and waiting for Cynthia. At the sound of her husband's voice she started violently, the tell-tale colour flooded her cheeks. She did not turn for a while. Warchester looked at her. No one would have guessed the mad passion of longing that seized him as he gazed at his wife's dainty averted cheek, the hot revolt against the fate that had been his for the last three months.

At last Joan turned.

"No," she said slowly—"no, not this morning. Why?" Her face was very pale now; the shadow of a terrible dread lay in her brown eyes.

Warchester averted his gaze.

"Cécile De Lavelle was arrested last night for the murder of your sister, Evelyn."

"Ah!" Joan put up one ungloved hand to the lace at her throat; her eyes were fixed on Warchester, haunting, accusing. "Is that why you have come up this morning?"

"I came up last night," 'Warchester corrected. "Your Uncle Lockyer wired to me. He thought no good purpose could be served by telling you last night, but to-day you were bound to know. It is most probable—nay, almost certain—that you will be called as a witness."

"What!" Joan exclaimed. "What am I to do?" she cried wildly. "What can I do? How can I stand aside and let them accuse her when I know?"

Warchester made no answer. His face was very white; his grey eyes were dark with pain. She stepped swiftly across to him and laid her little hot hand on his wrist.

"What must we do, Paul? You—you must go away —right away where no one can ever find you. Then, when you are quite safe, I can tell—I must tell! You will, Paul!" a ring of agonized pleading in her voice. "You must! And you must be quick, lest they should find out!"

Very deliberately Warchester shook her hand from his arm. He bent his cold gaze upon her.

"So this is how you think of me! This is how you regard my word! You believe that I would allow a woman to be accused in my place!"

With a gesture of intolerable wrath he swung away from her. Joan moved forward quickly, her hands clasped.

"Paul! Paul!"

But already he had passed into the vestibule. She heard him speak to the butler; then the door closed.

At the same moment, Cynthia came downstairs.

"Joan, what do you think I have just heard? That wretched woman who pretended to be Evelyn has been arrested for murdering her—your sister, Evelyn, I mean! Of course they only call her Marie De Lavelle. Isn't it terrible? To think that we even knew the wretch! I am glad of one thing—I never was as civil as you wanted me to be! Now Reggie will see I was right!"

"How did you hear?" Joan asked faintly.

"Celestine told me," Cynthia replied as she buttoned her gloves. "Now I do hope you are not going to worry yourself about the creature, Joan"—as the change in her cousin's face struck her—"she is a bad lot."

"She had nothing to do with Evelyn's death," Joan returned as she rang the bell. "Bring me a newspaper, please, John" to the footman. "Any of them—it doesn't matter which."

Cynthia opened her blue eyes.

"Now, Joan, how can you possibly tell?"

Joan made no answer. She seized eagerly upon the paper the man brought her and turned it over with trembling fingers. She had not far to look. The Grove Street murder had attracted a considerable amount of public attention lately; it was accorded a paragraph on the front sheet.

GROVE STREET MYSTERY. Miss Cécile De Lavelle, otherwise Shirley, was arrested by Inspector Hudger yesterday morning and charged with the wilful murder of Marie De Lavelle, otherwise Evelyn Spencer, on the 11th of May, 1897. Later in the day the accused was brought before the magistrate and formally charged. Merely evidence of arrest was taken, and she was remanded until this morning at ten o'clock. James Gregory, stableman, was charged with being an accessory after the fact. It will be fresh in the recollection of the public that the ill-fated victim of the tragedy had been on the music-hall stage as one of the Sisters De Lavelle; it is her companion and so-called sister who has now been arrested by the police. It appears that for the last month she has been performing at the Alexandra, Islington, under the mysterious cognomen of "The Veiled Dancer." A touch of romance has been added to the circumstances by a rumour that the Veiled Dancer was on her way to her wedding when arrested.

Joan read it with avidity; she laid the paper on the table.

"Cynthia, I am going to hear the case."

"What!" Mrs. Trewhistle stared at her in deep disgust. "How can you, Joan? You arranged to be at Céline's to have your gowns fitted this morning."

"They will have to wait!" It was evident that Joan was in no mood to trouble about her dresses now. "It is no use, Cynthia, I must go—I must hear!"

"But you can't!" Cynthia said blankly. "I don't believe women ever do go to those places alone. And you don't even know where it is. It only says 'Before the magistrate.' Now I am sure I haven't the least idea—"

"The chauffeur will find that out," Joan returned obstinately. "It is no use, Cynthia, I must go! Uncle Septimus is sure to be there—he will look after me."

"Well, if you go, I suppose I must," Cynthia said unwillingly. "And to think that I had been looking forward to a delightful morning's shopping! This is another result of that idiotic will of Granny's!"

Joan made no reply; she waited with tragic eyes until the car appeared at the door.

The chauffeur fully justified her confidence. He found his way without difficulty to the dingy city court where Cécile De Lavelle was again brought up on a charge of murder.

It was fairly early, but the case was already proceeding when they arrived, and a great crowd round the entrance testified to public interest in the charge. Joan and Cynthia left their car and with difficulty made their way to the door. A message to Septimus Lockyer brought him out, radiant with the success of his investigations, but inclined to be angry with Joan for coming before she was summoned.

"You might have known that you would get a subpoena!" he grumbled. "But there—in such things women never have any sense!"

In spite of his vexation, however, he successfully piloted them to seats near his own, where it was possible to see and hear everything. Cécile De Lavelle was in the dock alone. All her mannerisms, her recklessness had deserted her now—she looked shrunken, smaller, Joan fancied. She was seated with her head down, a long shiver shaking her every now and then.

In the witness-box opposite Basil Wilton was giving evidence.

Joan stared and rubbed her eyes when she recognized this fact. She had missed the earlier sensation that had stirred the court when he had stated that he was the Wingrove for whom such long and unavailing search had been made, but a few whispered words from her uncle enlightened her and she bent forward eagerly. Basil, however, had little to relate that bore upon the actual tragedy. He looked wan and haggard as he described how he had asked his wife to be at his studio at four o'clock on that afternoon of the 11th of May, and identified the torn portion of the letter produced by the police as part of her reply. Questioned as to his reason for making the appointment, he stated that it was in order that his cousin, upon whose judgement his wife was wont to place reliance, might explain to her the reasons that rendered it imperative that their marriage should remain a secret for a while. He added that it had, of course, been his intention to present himself, but that his accident had taken place that very afternoon and had thus accounted for his supposed mysterious absence.

Counsel for the prisoner put no questions to this witness, who left the box amidst a sympathetic murmur from the court. Then there was a pause of expectation as Viscount Warchester was called.

Joan started; regardless of the spectators, she craned forward. It could not be that Paul was here—that they were going to question him! She caught her breath in an agony as she saw him making his way through the crowd. He did not look towards his wife; apparently he did not see the appealing eyes, the pallid, anguished face. Having taken the oath, he waited quietly for his examination to begin. Harvey Wilberforce, a man well known to Warchester by name as one of the greatest criminal lawyers of the day as well as a great friend of Septimus Lockyer's, was for the Crown. He was a tall, spare man, with a luxuriant crop of red hair and a particularly bland, benevolent smile. He rose now, hitching up his gown over his left arm.

"Can you carry your memory back to the afternoon of the 11th of May, 1897, Lord Warchester? Will you tell us whether you kept the appointment which Mr. Wilton has told us he made, with your consent, to meet his wife in the studio at Grove Street on that afternoon?"

Warchester bowed gravely.

"I did."

Mr. Harvey Wilberforce smiled ingratiatingly.

"Will you please tell us precisely what took place?"

Warchester waited a moment as if to collect his thoughts.

"'I was a few minutes late," he said very quietly. "The appointment was made for four; it was perhaps ten minutes or a quarter past when I arrived at my cousin's rooms. I went up without meeting anyone, and found, to my surprise, that the door of the flat was ajar. As no one answered my knock, I pushed it open and entered. There, to my horror, I saw on the floor the body of my cousin's wife. I knew at once as I bent over her that she was dead—had been dead for some minutes. I saw on the floor near the door my cousin's pistol, one of a pair I myself had given him having the initial W upon them in silver. Then, I—I—" He paused and faltered for a moment.

"Yes?" Harvey Wilberforce prompted quietly. "What did you do next, Lord Warchester?"

Warchester braced himself for the telling of his tale with a manifest effort.

"My first instinct was, of course, to call for assistance, to send for the police. I was already turning to the door for this purpose when I stumbled over the pistol I have mentioned. Then—then I think I must have lost my head. I knew that of late Mrs. Basil Wilton had been demanding the public recognition of her marriage, that she had quarrelled with my cousin, and I thought—I feared that in a fit of passion he—in short, he must have used the pistol! I—I—"

He paused and glanced involuntarily across at his cousin. Basil's eyes met his, and his smile flashed sympathy and comprehension.

Warchester seemed to gather strength visibly.

"The only thing for me to do, I thought, was to try to avert suspicion from him. I placed the pistol in the dead girl's hand. I tore and burned up any photographs or letters I saw about that might prove that Wingrove was in reality Basil Wilton. The cane found in the corner of the room was mine."

He stopped.

"That night I went away to Paris first, afterwards to Southern Nigeria. Until my cousin's memory was restored the other day I had no idea that his accident had occurred before and not after his wife's death. That is all, I think."

"Thank you, Lord Warchester!" Harvey Wilberforce said blandly, and sat down.

Counsel for the defence arose.

"Though I am reserving my cross-examination of the witnesses until I have had an opportunity of conferring with my client, I wish to ask Lord Warchester two questions—first, whether the idea that the murdered woman had committed suicide entered his mind at first."

"No." Warchester replied, without hesitation.

"Why not?"

"I did not for one moment think that Mrs. Basil Wilton was a person likely to take her own life," Warchester replied slowly.

"You did not think Mrs. Basil Wilton a person likely to take her own life?" repeated counsel, Mr. Roy Denman. "But is it not an established fact that people who commit suicide are usually the last persons one would have expected to do so?"

Warchester paused.

"It may be so—I do not know."

"You do not know. Very well!" Mr. Roy Denman commented. "But now I must ask you, Lord Warchester—you were aware that there were two rooms communicating with your cousin's studio?"

"Yes, I knew that."

"Had you any idea that any person whatever was concealed in either of those rooms?"

"Not in the least!" This time Warchester's answer was prompt. "I am quite clear that when I entered there was no one in either, as my first impulse was to look round to see if I could find any traces of my cousin."

"And you heard nothing to lead you to think that anyone came in afterwards?"

"Nothing at all."

"You neither heard nor saw anything at all to make you imagine an unseen witness was lurking in either of these rooms?"

"No."

"That is what I wanted to ascertain. Thank you, Lord Warchester," and Mr. Roy Denman sat down.

There was a pause in the proceedings. Counsel engaged conferred with the solicitors. Cécile De Lavelle still sat silent, motionless; not once had she looked round the court. Her head had bent lower and lower while Basil Wilton was giving his evidence; more than once the wardresses on either hand had stooped as if to assure themselves that she was not fainting.

The prosecuting counsel leaned towards an official of the court.

"Call James Gregory!"

"James Gregory!" A stir rang through the crowded court. It was a confirmation of the rumour, which had been gaining ground in the last hour, that James Gregory had turned informer. All heads turned to the side door, through which two warders presently conducted Gregory, The unhappy prisoner in the dock looked up once; then, with a gesture of utter despair, she cowered down in her chair lower than ever.

Gregory was not an attractive-looking person as he stood in the box. He was unshaven; the ill-fitting black coat and grey trousers that had been destined for his wedding looked creased and dusty. His small ferret eyes were strained and bloodshot; they wandered uneasily round the court from the hostile countenances of the crowd behind to the magistrate sitting impassive on the bench, then rested for a few seconds on the bent head of the woman in the dock.

He gave his name and age and occupation in an inaudible growl in response to the counsel's questions. Then, while Mr. Harvey Wilberforce momentarily consulted his notes, Gregory hunched up his shoulders and protruded his lower jaw. Seen thus, there was something particularly repellent in his expression. More than one of those present felt a touch of sympathy for the unfortunate prisoner.

"In May, 1897, you were in the employ of Sir Robert Brunton as a stableman, I believe?" Mr. Harvey Wilberforce went on, his dulcet tones in curious contrast with the witness's gruff, surly voice.

Gregory nodded.

"That is right."

"Sir Robert Brunton was in town for the season of 1897, I think, residing in Hinton Square, while you, in accordance with your duties, were lodged in the mews behind Grove Street?

Again Gregory nodded.

"Yes, sir."

"Can you carry your mind back to May 11th, 1897?"

This time there was a noticeable hesitation before Gregory answered.

"Yes, Sir."

Harvey Wilberforce's tone altered.

"Please give us your account of what took place in your own words," he said curtly.

Gregory looked round the court again as though seeking inspiration.

"I was having a pipe at the end of the Mews," he said slowly, "when I see Cissie Shirley—De Lavelle, as she liked to call herself— come round the corner from Hinton Square and go into No. 18. I knew Mrs. Perks, the caretaker there, was her sister, and, as I was anxious to see Cissie, as soon as I had had a wash and a change I slipped round and went in after her. She was sitting talking to her sister, the door of the room open a little way, for it was a hot afternoon."

"Please explain to the court the exact position in which you yourself stood to the prisoner," said Mr. Harvey Wilberforce.

Gregory fidgeted from one foot to the other.

"I was a fool, I suppose—I was in love with her. I had been in love with her ever since I used to go and see Evelyn Spencer—her as was called Marie De Lavelle—when she was play-acting with Cissie."

He paused.

"You were in love with the prisoner," said Mr. Harvey Wilberforce, "and therefore, when you saw her going into No. 18, Grove Street, you thought it was a favourable opportunity for an interview, I understand. Go on please, Mr. Gregory."

"I—I went in," Gregory stammered. "Cissie, she wasn't ill-pleased to see me, for it seems she had lost sight of Evelyn—Marie De Lavelle—and was anxious to see her again. I had been sitting with them—Mrs. Perks and Cissie—for the best part of an hour maybe, when who should I see come into the hall and go up the stairs but the very girl we were talking about—Marie herself? She was all in white and carried a black handbag. 'Why, there she is!' I cried out, too surprised like to remember that maybe it would have been better for me not to ha' spoke. Cissie jumped up, but Mrs. Perks was before her. 'Why, that is a lady as comes here sometimes to see Mr. Wingrove!' she says. 'Wingrove!" I said, and laughed. 'I see him the other day. I don't know why he should call himself Wingrove; it is Mr. Basil Wilton.'"

"How did you know that?" Mr. Harvey Wilberforce questioned.

Mr. Gregory moistened his dry lips.

"I knowed Mr. Basil Wilton well enough by sight. He used to be always about with the De Lavelles when they were singing at the halls. 'Twas Cissie that was his fancy then, but after a while he cooled off with her and took up Marie. That was the cause of the De Lavelle girls parting. Cissie was that jealous over Basil Wilton that Marie wouldn't stand it!"

"You knew this, and yet you told the prisoner that Wingrove was really Basil Wilton, and that Miss Evelyn Spencer—or Marie

De Lavelle, as she called herself professionally—had gone up to his rooms. That was scarcely judicious," Mr. Harvey Wilberforce commented. "Go on, Mr. Gregory. Tell us what happened next."

"Next!" James Gregory repeated vaguely, looking at the rail his hands were clasping as if to gather inspiration from that. "Well, Cissie, she jumped up as if she was shot!" he proceeded. "Basil Wilton!" she cries out, and she runs off upstairs as hard as she could go. Maria Perks and me, we waited a bit; then the thought came to me it would be as well to go and see what they were doing. We went upstairs the back way. The door of the flat was shut, but we listened, and soon we found they were quarrelling. I heard what Evelyn Spencer was saying. 'I am his wife,' she says, very cold and proudlike, 'and you—you were never anything to him but—' Before she could finish there was the sound of a shot, and then silence. We beat at the door, me and Maria Perks, when we come to ourselves as it were, and Cissie opened it. 'Oh, it is you!' says she. 'I've done for her!' There was Evie, lying on the hearth-rug—dead, and the pistol on the ground by the door where Cissie had throwed it."

There was a hushed silence in the court, which was broken only by what sounded like a cry of relief coming from the place where Joan was seated.

"Go on, Mr. Gregory," said Mr. Harvey Wilberforce.

"We went over and looked at Evie, but there was nothing to be done for her," Gregory went on. "'They will hang me,' she says, 'but she won't never be able to call herself Basil Wilton's wife again!' Mrs. Perks she cried and wept, but presently we persuaded Cissie to come downstairs again to the sitting-room. Cissie caught up the handbag—it was open. Evie had been taking out some paper to show she was speaking the truth about being Basil Wilton's wife, and we took it down, along of us. Then, when we had been downstairs a bit, it comes to us that perhaps, after all, Evie mightn't be dead, and I found I'd left my tobacco pouch upstairs so I went back. When I got near Mr. Wilton's rooms I heard somebody moving about. The door was shut, but I'd got Mrs. Perks's pass key, and I opened the door and got into the bedroom. The door into the studio wasn't quite closed. I pushed it a little further open; then I see a man—Mr. Paul Wilton he was then—moving about, burning photos and things, and last of all putting a pistol in Evie's hand. "I couldn't make out what he was doing it for, but it wasn't no business of mine. I went downstairs, again and told them what I'd seen; and we began to think what we could do to get Cissie away. She was pretty frightened then, and she promised to marry me if I could keep a still tongue about what had happened. I helped her, like a fool, and when she was safe, or thought she was, she wouldn't marry me. Wouldn't even let me know where she was!"

Gregory stopped and wiped the perspiration from his brow.

"That is all, sir."

"One minute, Mr. Gregory!" Mr. Harvey Wilberforce looked at his notes. "'Can you identify the man you saw putting the pistol in the dead girl's hand?"

Gregory looked round the court.

"There he is," he said, pointing to Lord Warchester, "though he wore a beard in those days."

Mr. Wilberforce nodded.

"How long had you known that Mrs. Perks and the woman you knew as Cécile De Lavelle were sisters?"

Gregory considered.

"It would maybe be a matter of six weeks. I met Cissie coming out one day, and she told me."

"Did Miss Evelyn Spencer know of the relationship?"

"I should say not." Gregory passed one hand over his face reflectively. "She would never have let Mr. Wilton come there if she had known, for they were fearful jealous of one another, them two De Lavelle girls."

"I see! That is all for to-day, Mr. Gregory."

Mr. Harvey Wilberforce resumed his seat, and Mr. Roy Denman rose.

"I do not propose to cross-question this witness, your worship, as by my advice my client is reserving her defence. It is impossible for us to go into this evidence on such short notice, so utterly unprepared was my client for the nature of the charge the witness was about to make." He sat down.

"Call Maria Perks!" ordered Mr. Harvey Wilberforce; and once again every head in the court was turned towards the witness-box as Mrs. Perks, in her best Sunday bonnet, a fearsome erection covered with bugles and black hearse-like feathers, was marshalled into the box.

The widow was shaking and trembling with fright.

Her evidence, was in the main merely a recapitulation of Gregory's. It was evident that she was a most unwilling witness; the answers to his questions seemed to be dragged out of her by Mr. Harvey Wilberforce. Nevertheless, it was impossible to withhold a meed of sympathy from the woman when the spectators remembered that the poor cowering creature in the dock against whom those same answers were telling so terribly was the sister of the weeping witness.

Septimus Lockyer glanced at Warchester.

"This is very painful," he whispered. "Those two"—with a jerk of his head towards Joan and Mrs. Trewhistle—"ought not to stay!"

Warchester shrugged his shoulders.

"I should have said it was a most unsuitable place for them to come to at all, but I can do nothing."

Septimus Lockyer made his way towards his nieces.

"It will be over directly—adjourned till Friday. You had better come with me now. There is such a crowd that it may be difficult later."

They rose at once, and with some difficulty Mr. Lockyer made a way for them to the side door.

"Well," said Mrs. Trewhistle. "I did not expect it to be nice; but I did not think it would be so bad as this!" She turned on hearing footsteps on the stone corridor. Warchester had left the court behind them. She stopped. "Oh, Paul!"

The other two went on; Joan did not heed her cousin's exclamation. She looked up at her uncle, her eyes piteously dilated.

"Did she murder my sister, Uncle Septimus? Did she—that woman—murder my sister Evie?"

Septimus Lockyer looked down at the white face from which the enshrouding veil was thrown back. As he marked the traces of tension and of strain his heart grew very pitiful; he guessed something of the ordeal through which the girl had passed.

"I think there can be no possible doubt of that, Joan," he answered gravely.

Joan put out her hand and caught at his arm; her limbs felt strangely dull and heavy. By contrast the solid, stone, walls of the passage seemed to be whirling round in the air.

"She—she murdered Evelyn!" she gasped. "And, you know, Uncle Septimus—you know, I thought it was Paul!"

Chapter Thirty

LADY Warchester's knees trembled as she got out of the motor and went into the house. She glanced up timidly at her husband, whose face was stern and melancholy. Septimus Lockyer had parted from them at the door of the police-court, and Warchester had escorted his wife and her cousin, Mrs. Trewhistle, home. Both husband and wife had been glad of Cynthia's presence; it was a relief not to be alone in the car.

When inside, Joan allowed Mrs. Trewhistle to go upstairs alone. She herself lingered on the great bearskin before the hall fire and waited for her husband.

"Paul," she said, a new timidity in her voice, "Paul," with a little catch in her throat, "Paul, can you ever forgive me?"

He made no motion to take the hand she half held out.

"Certainly!" he returned with disconcerting promptness. "There is nothing to forgive, as a matter of fact. I have no doubt with your beliefs the majority of wives would have acted precisely as you did."

The arresting coldness of his tone seemed to freeze the blood in Joan's heart; for the moment she was incapable of speech. Only her eyes—her large, flaunting eyes—as they fixed themselves on his, sought vainly to express the anguish and the shame that were struggling to find voice within her.

But Warchester would not meet them, would not read their mute appeal.

"Will you excuse me?" he said politely. "There are letters that must be answered."

Joan bent her head silently as she turned towards the stairs. The burning words of love and sorrow that were in her heart remained unspoken, frozen by Warchester's tone and look. She made her way to her room too worn and spent to do more than submit in silence to her maid's ministrations. When at last she had been arrayed in a comfortable tea-gown, and her shining hair had been loosely brushed back as in the old days Warchester had best loved to see it, she lay down on her couch before the fire, feeling too utterly stunned, too weary almost to think. They had had no luncheon, and Treherne brought her a tray of *pâté de foie* sandwiches and a glass of champagne, but Joan turned from them almost with disgust.

She was staring into the fire with wide-open, miserable eyes when Cynthia entered the room with her usual air of bustle. She glanced at the tray.

"Good gracious, my dear Joan, do you mean to say you have had no lunch? Those *pâté de foie* sandwiches are excellent. Try one!" She picked one up and bit it with an air of relish. "So Warchester is going off by the boat train to Dublin to-night."

"No!" Joan sat up among the cushions. "I didn't know. I mean—" catching Cynthia's look of surprise. "No doubt he told me, but I have been so busy lately, I have forgotten."

"He is going to see that man who is organizing an expedition to find the North Pole or the South Pole, I forget which. Warchester said that if this wretched girl's trial came off in time he thought he should join him," Cynthia went on, helping herself to another sandwich. "I shouldn't let him, Joan. I am sure if Reggie wanted to find the North Pole—what is it, Treherne?" as the maid tapped at the door.

"A young person from Madame Céline's, ma'am, about your gown!"

"What a fool I am—I forgot all about it!" exclaimed Cynthia. I will come back in a minute, Joan." She darted away.

Left alone, Joan sit motionless for a minute or two.

Could it be that she had finally estranged Warchester's love? she was asking herself. As she gazed into the fire with hot, aching eyes it seemed to her that she saw her past conduct in its true light. She recalled Warchester's kindness to her when her father died, his unfailing patience under the false Evelyn's presence at the Towers, their mutual love in the early days of their marriage. A little trust, a little faith—that was all he had asked from her, and in the hours of his need she had failed him. Tears welled up in her eyes and rolled down her cheeks.

At last she sprang up. What was it Cynthia had said? Warchester was going to Ireland by the boat train that night. It was possible that she might yet see him—that she might implore his forgiveness once more. With the hope that this thought inspired she went downstairs and across to the study as quickly as her trembling limbs would allow.

"Come in!" Warchester called out in response to her tap.

He looked up in surprise as she entered. He was sitting at his writing-table with his papers spread about in front of him. Before he had time to rise Joan crossed swiftly to him and laid her hands on his shoulders.

"Won't you forgive me, Paul?"

"There is no question of forgiveness, Joan, you could not help yourself."

"But Cynthia told me you are going away!" Joan's lips trembled childishly.

"You asked me to go away only this morning."

"Ah, but you knew that was only because I thought—" Joan caught her breath. "I was so frightened, Paul. And, besides, afterwards I should have come to you." Warchester's face softened suddenly.

"You would have come to me?"

"Why, of course! That was what I meant. I—I couldn't have stayed away, Paul!"

Warchester caught the soft hands that were still resting on his shoulders and pressed them in his.

"Why wouldn't you trust me, Joan?"

"I—I was blind," Joan said, her lips quivering. "But I loved you, Paul, always. You won't leave me now?"

"I don't think I shall." Warchester pointed to the paper in front of him. "I am writing to tell Gormanton it will not be possible for me to join him. As for leaving by the boat-train to-night, what would Cynthia say if I took you with me just for a three days' honeymoon, eh, sweet-heart?"

Joan sat down on the arm of his chair, and his right arm slipped round her waist.

"I don't know what Cynthia would say," she remarked demurely, "I know what I should."

Warchester's eyes held their old fond smile as he looked up.

"What would you say, sweetheart?"

"I—I want to come," she whispered childishly, clinging to him. "Take me, Paul!"

He caught her in his arms and drew her head to his shoulder.

"You love me a little still, Joan, in spite of all."

"I loved you always!" She yielded herself to his embrace with a sigh of content. "I was mad then—I am sane now, that is all, Paul.

Tell me again that you forgive—that in time you will love me again—just the same!"

Warchester pressed her to him and kissed her sweet lips.

"Not the same," he murmured passionately, "but better and better, more and more, my wife!"

That dreadful time of estrangement and suspicion seems like a dream to Joan Warchester now. She is happier than she ever dreamed of being in the old days—happier even than in her first married bliss. For there are children now at the Towers, a white-frocked mite of nearly two, with his mother's lovely colouring, and his father's brave grey eyes, whom the outside world knows as the Honourable John Wilton, but who to his mother and father is simply Sonnie. Nor is Sonnie alone in his nursery; there is a creature, still in long frocks, who is Basil Wilton's namesake and godchild, and who will succeed some day to the broad lands of the Davenants.

Warchester Hall is let now to Septimus Lockyer, who has settled down to a green old age in the country. He has retired from his profession, and astonished everybody by marrying an old sweetheart from whom he was separated by circumstances in his youth.

Sometimes in the twilight Joan's thoughts will wander pityingly to her sister—Basil Wilton's wife; to the mother whose mad marriage ruined her life, later on dwelling a moment on the fate of the woman whom for a few short weeks Joan had tried to give a sister's love.

The result of Cécile De Lavelle's trial had been a foregone conclusion from the first. There was no getting away from the evidence, and the jury had returned a verdict of guilty, with a recommendation to mercy. The story told by Gregory and Mrs. Perks showed no evidence of pre-meditation. The public took the matter up and signed numerous petitions, and the sentence of death passed upon her at her trial was commuted to penal servitude for life.

Mrs. Spencer is happy too, now—not in the Bell at Willersfield, but in a comfortable house of her own, provided by Joan. Amy is engaged to a curate, for whom Lord Warchester is expected to find a living, and all the rest of Joan's half-brothers and sisters are doing well. Lady Warchester has no reason to be ashamed of them. Altogether it seems to Joan that after her troubled childhood and girlhood, her life has fallen truly in pleasant places. She is secure in her husband's love; her children are the joy of her home as well as the delight of three houses—the Lockyers', the Trewhistles', and the Marsh, for Basil Wilton, contrary to prophecy, has not married again.

THE END

Lightning Source UK Ltd.
Milton Keynes UK
UKHW021854110122
396967UK00009B/2260